To Kelley, for being the first reader
and for her persistent and caring support.

MID-CENTURY
MELEE

TONY V. GEORGE

Printed in the United States of America

First Printing, 2025

6 7 8 9 0

ISBN 979-8-9992262-0-4

Family tree and information about *Mid-Century Melee* available at end of book and at www.tonyvgeorge.com

LGR Publishing

P.O. Box 4072

Palm Springs, CA 92264

1

Asshole

HANK ENTERED THE COURTYARD of the coffeeshop and scanned a patchwork of patrons seated at white plastic tables bathed in the sunlight. His search of the morning gatherers ended when a familiar voice came out of the crowd.

"Hank! Does this mean I know a celebrity or at least someone related to one?" Thomas yelled from a nearby table.

"What are you talking about?" Hank replied, as he grabbed a chair.

"It's happening in a couple hours! Your grandfather is getting a star on the Palm Springs Walk of Fame for being a big deal, right? Are you going to be a speaker? What are ya wearing to the unveiling? Will we see ya later at the party?"

Hank scrunched his face as he looked to Reese and Kate for help defending against the morning interrogation.

Although Thomas was four years Hank's junior, his enthusiasm fit a tween-ager winning concert tickets and not a man of twenty-four years. Hank found no support from the other two at the table and opted not to respond. He wondered why he didn't get invited to the family event. Instead, he heard the news from these three individuals, the ones to whom he had revealed secrets. Secrets he hadn't previously admitted to himself. They weren't friends, but what do you call the people from AA meetings who still want to spend their free time with you?

"There's a party after the star reveal at your grandpa's swank mansion. Reese and I snagged cater-waiter jobs there. It's next-level lit so we need a glow-up to work there. I'm stoked to see your place," Thomas said.

"It's . . . not my place."

"You know what I mean, where you grew up. Right?"

"It's not where I—"

"Let's not fill the morning with Hank's biography," Reese said as he dropped his homemade tea concoction into some hot water.

Hank checked his phone. He didn't see any missed text or email invitations. A vibration announced a new message from Thomas, showing screenshots of the catering schedule and event details. Hank did a quick read and forwarded the images to his mother with the message, *Did you know about this?* The aroma and first sips of coffee roused him enough to realize there would be no additional information about the event to discover at the coffeeshop. He stood and told the group he needed to get ready to attend his grandfather's recognition, the event with no invitation.

Getting no response from his mother, he sent a text to his sister while walking home. His pace increased to a jog, either to escape the morning questions or actually go to the event. He wasn't sure which. A third option was to retreat to his apartment bedroom, close the shades, and stay in bed grasping a pillow or two. The message to his mother showed as received and read. Hank figured a lack of response from the overly attentive phone user meant she didn't get invited and didn't want to talk.

His phone buzzed with another message from Thomas containing a selfie with Reese and animated words flashing *C U soon*. Hank's relaxing morning with *friends* turned into a full-out run home while considering his current inventory of clean clothes. Then, a block from home, his phone rang and brought him to a complete stop.

"That asshole!"

"Which asshole?" Hank asked his sister, Willow.

"Your brother, Spencer. The biggest effing *asshole* in our lives. Did you forget?"

"Just checking in case someone else had taken the title. What's this star thing?"

"Aren't you on the group chat? Asshole! Sorry, Hank. I never looked and thought you were part of it. I think everyone's going. He kept sending so many instructions that I stopped reading them. He seriously didn't tell you?"

"No."

"That's our brother. Asshole! Listen. Get yourself downtown and then we're going to a party at Dad and Granddad's place. So. Help. Me. If Spencer gives you shit, tell him you're my plus-one."

"Well, that's gross, and are you sure I'm invited?"

"Okay, not as my plus-one but as my brother. Or should I call you *half brother*, like Spencer does?"

Hank remained silent.

"This is for *our* grandfather," Willow said. "You're *his* grandson. We have the same father. The party afterward is at their house, not Spencer's. Granddad expects you no matter what Spencer thinks. Get your ass there!"

Hank arrived home, drenched from running in the desert heat. The need for a shower and sunscreen got added to the growing mental checklist. Inside his apartment, the urge to get ready decreased with each glance to his bedroom and the beckoning bed. Still no response from his mother. Hank replaced thoughts of cocooning with taking a shower and getting dressed. After a final look in the mirror, he grabbed his bike and headed to the inevitable verbal sparring match with his half brother, the asshole, in front of an audience of his entire family minus his mother.

2

Walk of Fame

HANK RODE DOWN THE MAIN STREET of Palm Springs past an array of tourist-filled restaurants, gift shops, art galleries and interior design stores. The sidewalks in front of the businesses displayed embedded marble stones containing names of celebrities and contributors to the community. Hank followed the trail of stars until he reached the makeshift sidewalk event where he spotting a photographer behind a tripod. An assistant attempted to direct his relatives. The goal to arrange the family around their grandfather had all but been abandoned as the patriarch sat fidgeting in his wheelchair. Hank dismounted his bike and began a personal assessment of the situation. *Willow invited me. This is my blood, my family, or at least half family. He is definitely my grandfather. That is my father up there. I belong here even if my sort-of brother didn't invite me or my mother.* He locked his bike and approached the guest of honor.

"Hey, Mr. Star Power, congratulations!"

"Hank! I've been asking where you were hiding. How's my grandson?"

"Pretty proud of my grandpa. All's well."

"Excellent, now move into that menagerie of my offspring so we can get this recognition going."

Hank kissed his grandfather on the top of his head and circled round to the back of the group where he found Willow. She hugged Hank and pointed him forward to comply with previously received instructions. The assistant pointed to her clipboard while talking to the photographer. Hank tried to guess what they were saying as they motioned to him. He'd been spotted. The photographer decided an extra person could be edited out of the proofs more easily than adding one. The assistant scribbled on the clipboard and her face said everything. *Unknown attendee. Next to granddaughter. Green shirt. Possible extra grandson?* The assistant rejoined the group for final touches and used a towel to dab the sweat off the honoree's forehead. Robert's face would not be shiny for the unveiling of his star. The family settled into place with jostling to stay under a small canopy and out of the burning sun. Spencer, a.k.a. *the asshole*, and the person responsible for orchestrating the event, instructed his children on how to pull away a cloth to reveal the personalized granite star embedded in the sidewalk.

"There's Mr. Company President," Willow whispered to Hank. "Holding a staff meeting with people who will listen to him." She pointed to Spencer and his children.

"What's supposed to be happening here?"

"Hank, I don't know why you weren't part of this. Hold on, let me grab my phone." Willow reached into her purse. "You dodged days of drama not having to read all these damned messages. Shit! You aren't on here, and neither is Tiffany."

"I can guess why I'm not included, and we know Spencer hates my mom even more."

"He's an asshole, that's why, and I guess I'm one too for not checking, but look at all these messages. Here's one reminding us to portray ourselves in our best image, for the company of which he's president."

Hank grabbed the phone. "He actually reminded you he's the president in a text? Asshole!"

"Give me my phone." Willow grabbed it and started scrolling to show the best-of messages. "Here's one where he says not to approach any attending celebrities."

They both looked up and scanned the gathering of local friends and community leaders. No A-List celebrities were in sight.

"What's that message?"

"This one's great," Willow continued, "He gave talking points in case the press approaches us. We're supposed to reinforce that he's the third-generation leader of the company and stress the names: Granddad Robert and him being the grandson, Robert Spencer."

"Except no one calls him Robert or Robert Spencer. He's the one who demanded that we use his middle name."

They looked up again to see Spencer had moved from his children to check in with the media. He began instructing the newspaper reporter, a photographer, and the TV camera operators with unsolicited directions. Willow and Hank filled the time by pantomiming taking tequila shots each time they heard Spencer say he was in charge or president. At the top of the hour, the mayor arrived. His aide caught Spencer's eye and tapped his wrist on an imaginary watch. Hank and Willow's antics evolved into laughing so loudly that their brother's pasted-on smile eroded when they drew his attention. His eyes grew dark upon seeing Hank. Spencer started heading their way as the mayor cleared his throat at the microphone. The presentation had started, leaving Spencer to fall into place behind his grandfather. There was no time for him to get Hank out of the picture.

The mayor, a longtime friend of the elder Robert, started by greeting the attendees. He looked down at his notes as he described his friend's accomplishments after moving from New York City to California.

" . . . with a dream of being in the movie industry, Robert began in acting before finding bigger opportunities on the technical side. There he focused on voice modulating equipment, which he first sold to improve the clarity and emotional pitch of recorded voices in movies and then continued with the uses in the television and music industries. All this work became Asuproz, a leading company in the entertainment industry, now led by his son, William."

Spencer tried to interrupt the mayor regarding the recent

transition of leadership from his father to him, but the mayor kept speaking over Spencer's objections.

"I should use his enhancements to the laugh track technology at council meetings." The mayor paused, looked up to silence, and continued.

"He turned his success into giving. Ongoing donations have supported our International Film Festival, local library, and to the remarkable non-profit addiction recovery center his daughter runs. It is based right here in our Palm Springs." For this pause, the mayor got his anticipated applause as he looked up again with a sense of accomplishment. "This organization produces jobs for our desert community while giving support for those struggling with addiction. Although he has long since retired from Asuproz, he will be remembered for his contributions. The accomplishments are significant and numerous for this ninety-three-year-old. Now it is my pleasure to invite our guest of honor and his family to come forward for the unveiling of his star."

The mayor stepped away and followed his aide to an awaiting car as Robert wheeled to the podium. The family maneuvered around him. Spencer hurried directly behind his grandfather and clasped his shoulder, which Robert shook off as he started to stand.

The entire family froze. Spencer's series of instructions didn't include his hunched grandfather standing. Spencer stood back and rubbed the faint patch of discolored skin on the side of his neck. He turned away, only to see Hank's mother hiding off in the distance. She jumped back, too late to avoid being spotted. Spencer rubbed his neck even harder, another part of his plan gone wrong.

Robert steadied himself with both hands on the podium and nodded to his great-grand-children to do the honors. Family and guests applauded as photographers captured the scene of children pulling away the fabric cover. The news cameras rolled and the gleaming star sparkled. Robert began his speech as his contributions to the world appeared engraved under his name.

11

Actor * Businessman * Philanthropist

Robert captured everyone's attention by standing and by the tenor of his oration. He concluded by thanking his family and invited the attendees to the reception at his home. As the applause ended, Hank ran to the front and helped his grandfather back into his chair.

"I've still got it."

"If you mean the ability to shock us with your actions, true. And nice speech, Granddad, you're magnificent."

"You've got that right."

"What the hell were you doing?" Robert's health aide responded in a less cheerful way. He handed Robert a bottle of water and put two fingers to his patient's carotid artery. William also jumped in to check on his father. The aide demanded that they get Robert to the air-conditioned van. Otto joined his younger brother William as they both fended off gracious attendees greeting the honoree. In all the commotion, Hank returned to his bike and sped off down the street.

3

Before the After Party

HANK APPROACHED THE EXTERIOR of The Dwelling. The home stood within an imposing boundary of white open lattice breeze-block with flowering bougainvillea and fortified security gates. His grandfather had told stories of first visiting the midcentury mansion in the 1950s. He and a group of young actors were day guests escaping winter in Hollywood for the warmer temperatures of the desert. Robert's dream home eventually turned into reality. Living there checked off another personal goal for the honoree. Hank paused with his bike at the walkway gate, always cautious about entering the compound. Lea, who handled everything at The Dwelling, spotted him.

"Hank, what are you waiting for? Get in here."

"Big party today?" he greeted her.

"As if you didn't know." Lea straightened her outfit.

"How did your son do on his science project?"

"Hank! I have a million things this minute and no time to talk. What are you doing here early and where are your father and grandfather?"

"They are still loading up in the van. Now tell me about your Rico."

"He's doing fine. His robot got an A, thanks to your help. I need to make sure everything is ready. Come with me and bring your bike to the back, away from the entrance. This is the welcoming area and not a bike rack."

Hank followed Lea toward the back of the property where a flurry of workers prepared last-minute touches. The caterer finished unloading a caravan of vehicles at the property's rear entrance beyond the tennis court. Food, linens, and countless boxes flowed into the service building. Hank and Lea continued toward all the activity, passed newly placed urns of hydrangea, orchids, and jasmine permeating the backyard with their fragrance. High-top tables covered in gold tablecloths and matching floral arrangements polka-dotted the pool area.

The first person exiting the service building was Lea's mother Leandra, adorned in a black waitress dress with a white half-apron, matching her daughter. They both broke out in laughter seeing their mirrored image and did curtsies like two members of royalty. Leandra then turned to Hank for a big hug before explaining how she and Lea made their own executive decision about the catering for the event.

"In this heat?" Leandra said. "We told the caterers they would be circulating with trays of appetizers and not placing all the food out in a buffet."

"A buffet?" Hank asked.

"That's what your brother wanted," Leandra continued. "Your grandfather would be mad as the devil if he saw a table of food spoiling in the heat."

"Si, claro," Hank responded.

"Of course! You should have seen Spencer here this morning with his surprise inspection before he went to the event. He demanded *opulence* for arriving guests and media."

"Mama, stop," Lea begged her mother.

"He acted like Lea didn't know what opulence meant, so he started waving his hands while instructing my baby. He gestured the image of towers of food and shouted, *Think cruise ship.* before he left in that noisy car. I told him he was going to sink the cruise ship."

"Mama."

"My Lea has run *this ship* for the past fifteen years and I before her. We know how to create a successful event. Spencer with his third-generation status doesn't carry any weight here."

"Mama, basta!"

"And Mr. Spencer, the big planner, didn't even tell us the number of guests."

"Mama, get back to the main house and turn everything on: the music, the fountains, and open the driveway gate."

Leandra hugged Hank one more time and went to the house. Lea and Hank continued through the grounds and stopped by the bar area set up.

"My mama can get emotional, especially when defending her daughter."

"I know the feeling. You have been as protective of me."

"Well, you're like a nephew."

"And you, Auntie Lea, are like a tiger auntie."

They both started to laugh, then her phone buzzed with a message. The family and guests were leaving the event and would be home in fifteen minutes. She notified the bartender to start opening bottles. With a hand motion to her mother across the yard, the message had been sent, the show was about to begin. The high temperatures meant the wood fire ring would go unused although the landscaping crew constructed a combination of hickory and cherry per Robert's preferences. No fire meant one less thing for Lea to clean the next morning. They continued to the catering building where Hank left his bike outside and they entered for Lea's final review.

The staff were prepared in their black and whites. She recognized some faces from local restaurants. Thomas and Reese stood near the back and got additional instructions. Robert required his events to hire some of the workers from local outreach programs. Lea marveled at the impact of a fresh shower combined with a crisp white shirt and black pants. The untrained eye wouldn't discern between the experienced waitstaff and the outreach workers. Lea caught Thomas and Reese waving to Hank, but before she could take another step, her phone signaled again. The triple-pulse placed her boss a quarter-mile away. Robert insisted on the GPS notification alert to ensure Lea or his aide was ready to help him when he reentered the property. She pulled a handkerchief from her pocket and wiped her forehead.

"Hank, your family will be here in minutes. Now get to the main entry with the rest of them. We both must get to our stations. Now vamonos!"

"Claro, Tia."

Lea left Hank at the entrance of the service building to continue her final touches. Hank looked around at the waitstaff and spotted the cleaned-up Thomas and Reese as they completed staging the food. He felt more comfortable with this group than at the front of the house and decided to go home. As he rode down the street, he caught sight of the line of cars arriving at the main entrance. The party was about to begin.

4

Let the Party Begin

THE CUSTOMIZED VAN pulled up to the front of the mansion. Robert exited on the mechanical ramp, assisted by his sons, William and Otto, leaving the aide to drive the van to the garage. In the back seat of the next car sat Robert's daughter, Adela. She quizzed her grandchildren on their week out of curiosity and as way to give a break to the parents up front. Her air of contentment created a glow of a woman nowhere near seventy years. The rest of Robert's family followed in a string of cars, parking outside the gate. The trail of relatives strolled up the drive to the front of the house and formed a receiving line. The rank order positioning of family appeared as regulated as the British monarchy. Everyone knew their spot. Adela took the role of matriarch, standing next to her father. This fulfilled her default position of welcomer and sometimes trusted spokesperson for the company.

A brief frown ran across her face as she pondered being passed over as president by her nephew, and in the past, by her brother. She conceded her current age was enough reason this time, but in the past, she would have relished the role. Instead, she left the family business to become the leader at the local addiction recovery center, her real realm. In the receiving line, she understood her father and brother saw her as the equivalent of a store greeter. *And yet here we are,* echoed in her head. It was the phrase her grandchildren used as a joke about similar ironic situations. Adela frowned again, realizing her stylish blue dress mirrored the color of a warehouse store worker's vest.

The guests arrived and brought almost never-ending handshakes and halfhearted embraces. Adela managed occasional laughs at cocktail-party level jokes and listened to small talk she had heard far too many times. She loved her life, but at that moment, the flash of anger from being passed over made her want to take a swing at something. She imagined slamming a bat at a piñata in the shape of her president-of-the-company nephew's grinning face, only to produce an explosion containing confetti covered with all the 'what if' and 'should have' possibilities in her life. She let the thoughts of floating scraps of paper dance around as a calming distraction.

Once she had enough of greeting guests and living in regret land, she moved away from the party. Her role for the day completed, she exiled herself to a chaise lounge under a distant pergola. Facing away from the event, she sipped an Aperol Spritz, hoping the digestive bitters might help her swallow all the inequity the business world fed her over the years. The star event and party, along with the early spring heat, had zapped Adela's energy as the lounge welcomed her into a secluded slumber.

A duet of "Nana, Nana" from her grandchildren interrupted her impromptu nap. She sat up and reached out for hugs from the smiling children. Her son, Steve, followed in pursuit and asked them to set their grandmother free so she could leave but Adela pulled the two in closer for a tight squeeze. He asked if she needed anything before the ride home. She looked up, shaking her head *no*, saying she had everything she needed as she kissed the two children.

5

What a Drag

ADELA SAT AT HER GLASS-TOP DESK at the recovery center, savoring the remaining warmth of her spiced tea while looking out at the courtyard, blanketed in morning hues lighting the blooming lupine and verbena. The meeting at the top of the hour made her wish the ritual of a morning cigarette (or two) still fit her repertoire. Seeing a group of patients through the window settling into their calming breaths of nicotine made her fidget more. She fumbled with a pen as one of them took a long drag. Adela returned to her mug to breathe in the last of the aroma. The hints of ginger and cinnamon had to carry her through her first meeting.

A few weeks ago, at her father's recognition event, her brother William pulled her aside. He said he wanted to have a meeting. *A meeting?* The next morning, Adela received an email invitation. The new formality surprised her because the two usually handled business updates during their personal time or through a phone call. *Had the world changed that much since his son Spencer took over his nepo baby corporate leadership?* She still had connections at Asuproz from when she worked there and wasn't going into a potential ambush meeting without preparing. Adela set up a couple of social calls with her past Asuproz colleagues for informal reconnaissance of any information she could glean about her brother's meeting request. She uncovered Spencer leveraging his father to set up a meeting and her nephew's plan involving her organization. A couple of days before the meeting, William added Spencer to the invitation and a note about him brainstorming ideas. Adela started to take a drag from her pen while pondering this new formal interaction of Asuproz with the recovery center. She took a final glance out the window and wasted a wish to have a moment among the outdoor smokers instead of being committed to her calendar.

Adela entered the conference room thirty minutes before the meeting start time set by her brother and greeted her executive team, all in place. None of these attendees were on William's invite list. She invited them and already held individual discussions about Spencer's plan. She confirmed they all knew their assignments as they settled in for the meeting. William opened the conference room door and his expression adjusted to a broad smile as he greeted the group. Spencer froze in the doorway at the sight of the unexpected audience as Adela beckoned them into the room.

"Thank you for coming to *our* location this morning. I realize you've met this crew before but I like to start with introductions for any *guests* of Desert Recovery. My team was available, and doesn't the best brainstorming involve diverse expertise?"

They exchanged names, and William's smile grew even bigger as he nodded to his sister. Spencer found a chair and pulled a computer from his satchel.

Adela continued, "It's your meeting, William. Lead the way."

"Thank you, Adela, and thank you all for being here. For today I am turning things over to Spencer."

Spencer glanced at his father as he rubbed his neck.

"Because Spencer is now the president of Asuproz."

Adela jerked the pen away from her lips upon realizing she somehow brought it to her mouth for the second time that morning.

The entire team focused on Spencer as he connected his computer to the projector and tapped the tabletop to gain attention.

"Not everyone is going to fly to Palm Springs for treatment," he said while scanning his notes. "Expansion is key for growth. You . . . all of you . . . all of *us* here, we have a good thing here.

The brand name is solid and what you do, what we do is solid. Be proud and grow the business."

"Nonprofit," replied Adela.

"What?"

"This is and always has been an independent nonprofit, not a for-profit business."

"Aunt Addie, you know what I mean. Let's grow the brand and the footprint of this thing to be really big. Let's make this reputation known globally."

"Robby—" Adela replied, as she pushed the pen away from her grasp.

William stood and produced a series of coughs while he moved in a slow cadence toward a tray of beverages. The coughs continued until all discussion ceased, and he opened a bottle of water.

"Adela . . . I think Robert Spencer may be getting caught up in his own excitement. Last month you and I discussed your idea of setting up satellite locations across the country to benefit patients returning home, right? They could continue getting support in their hometown while being helped by the same quality of care you've established here."

Adela relaxed back into her chair. "Keep going."

The heads of IT and legal counsel glanced at each other and returned attention to their computers.

"Spencer will take us through leveraging the technology from Asuproz to improve . . . well, even if there is no room to improve, possibly expand quality across more staff and to remote locations." William continued, "This is your sandbox and your call. We simply have some helpful thoughts. But I don't want to take away from what Spencer has put together. Let's hear what he has to say about helping your patients improve their journey."

Adela made eye contact with each of her team members before turning her attention to her nephew as William returned to his seat and motioned to his son.

Spencer's introduction slides covered Asuproz's success in recording real life situations like customer service calls and using them in future training. He started outlining how Desert Recovery could implement recording their customers. Adela signaled the attorney, who immediately interrupted.

"Are you implying Desert Recovery should start videotaping clients, who in this case are patients? This sounds like a HIPAA hornet's nest in the state of California and beyond. I want some time before giving feedback of a state-by-state analysis. To be clear, you're proposing recordings between a therapist and patient? Your proposal is for these private sessions to be used in public training films?"

"I can show you outcome improvements from real-world training," Spencer continued. "There is a jump in comprehension when real-situation training videos are implemented."

Adela looked over at the Medical Officer who instantly joined the discussion.

"Even if this is legal, and excuse me, Lilly, for interrupting your legal concerns, but even if it is, I would want to gauge the comfort level of our staff to understand their acceptance. It's not only a matter of the patient concerns."

The side of Spencer's neck started darkening as his rubbing increased. Adela didn't even need to cue the controller.

"Where would the budget come from for equipment costs? Do you have numbers for training expenses? Are we adding headcount?"

Spencer worked his keyboard and flipped back and forth between slides. No answers came quick enough for the barrage of questions, which wouldn't have mattered. No one listened to him as the IT manager brought up more concerns. William leaned into the table and smirked at his sister. She returned a nod. He had shown up to her sandbox and made the mistake of bringing his rambunctious son, who tried to build a castle with her sand.

Neither the father nor the son prepared for the reality of Adela and her posse being loaded with water balloons and squirt guns aimed at Spencer's creation. William replaced his fake-cough approach with a long and hard laugh as his white flag of surrender. Adela, with one subtle motion, stopped the verbal soaking of Spencer's proposal.

"Thank you all." William's forced laughter dropped off. "These are all good questions and we will take them into consideration." He motioned for his son to shut down the projector. "We will build on your concerns. If there isn't an immediate opportunity to use our technology for your training, let's consider possible use for one-on-one sessions to support the patient. We could evaluate this as a pilot program at Desert Recovery. And yes, Jason, I see your hand. Is yours a question about budgets? Asuproz will pay for this as a test. Does that work for you, Adela?"

Adela stood up from the table.

"So, William, your company will pay to set up recording equipment with secured storage, supply training, and a technician to manage everything? I am sure we can find a way to use this generous offer and identify a few interested test patients. That will work for Desert Recovery. Robby, did you get that?"

Spencer kept his face down as he put his computer away and left the room, followed by Adela's team. William waited for the last attendee to exit before looking up and laughing again.

"Addie, my intentions are pure. I want to bring the technology here because you are the one person who will know if it's viable for this industry."

"Keep going."

"Yes, finding an application in the recovery industry will help Asuproz grow, but you can see the possible joint victory."

She smiled at her brother. The gloves were off. William's petulant presenter and her reinforcements were long gone.

"William, I'm not a new client you are pitching. I'm your

sister. What were you thinking to come in here with an ill-prepared idea and so many loose ends? You had to know the legal and financial gaps."

"Sometimes you need to test the waters to see how a concept will sound."

"Training videos of actual patients going through recovery? That wasn't your proposal. Your ideas are vetted twenty different ways before they leave your office. Don't use Desert Recovery as a training ground for your son to learn how to sell a concept. If he's ultimately going to run the company without your guidance, test him out on other people. Don't waste the time of my leadership team."

"This meeting wasn't a complete waste for your organization, was it?"

Adela shrugged.

"Somehow, I've committed to cover the installation costs of recording equipment and other support to make this place even more state-of-the-art. How did you manage to pivot Spencer's presentation to such a degree that I ended up giving away so much?"

"Like father, like son, or in this case, like daughter. Our father taught us both about negotiating."

"Skills I am instilling in my son. Sorry for testing him here so I could do some situational training."

Adela headed to the door, pausing to put her hand on her brother's shoulder.

"Maybe the training was for you on selecting leaders."

6
Namesake Mistake

WILLIAM LEFT the recovery center and withdrew to The Dwelling. He demolished part of a bag of potato chips before pulling out sandwich ingredients for lunch. In a matter of minutes, everything he needed for a peaceful meal sat in front of him: a sandwich, the remaining chips, a beer, and silence. The chips lasted longer than the silence, as his father entered the main house from his casita and started on Robert's topic-of-the-month, Spencer. William looked down at his sandwich as his father approached.

"My star recognition event was a disaster."

"So you said at breakfast and possibly every meal for the last four weeks." William took another bite of his sandwich.

"To be succinct, how will Spencer ever be able to run Asuproz if he can't handle children pulling a piece of cloth off a star? The mayor told me Spencer was an A1 pain-in-the-ass and apologized that he couldn't stay due to the short notice from your son. Several industry people sent their regrets and let me know they were invited the day before."

William took a swig of beer and another bite of his sandwich. Talking during the meeting with Adela cost him company funds. He didn't want to provoke any more losses. Besides, his father didn't wait for answers to his questions.

"I won't stand by and watch anyone take down my company. I used to be angry he didn't use my name or at least Robert Spencer. Now I am relieved he doesn't. We're going to make an office visit tomorrow to your president-son."

"To Pasadena? You're going to Pasadena?"

"We're going to the headquarters we created."

Robert demanded the two of them go to Asuproz's main office the next day to hear Spencer's vision. As much as William tried, he couldn't convince his father to cancel a drop-in meeting. He finally persuaded Robert to make a trip to each location of the family's major investments. He hoped to decrease the focus on Spencer or to tax his father's attention span enough that he'd cancel the drive to Pasadena. They'd start in Palm Springs at Desert Recovery.

William relished subjecting Adela to a *friendly* visit from her father after what she put him through with Spencer. The next stop would be the nearby research and manufacturing site. Then, the two of them would plod the two plus hours to Pasadena in Robert's van. William checked corporate calendars to assure his son was on site and then told his father they'd begin the tour immediately the next morning.

🌴🌴🌴

The following morning, they arrived at Desert Recovery at 7:30 a.m., catching Adela in the middle of reviewing her morning emails. She directed a wry smile at her brother as she graciously welcomed her father for the update. The discussion went without a hitch, and Robert gave her a high-rated performance appraisal for a situation where he had no authority. Adela sat up in her chair upon hearing her grades and winked at her brother. She escorted them to the front door and sent them on their way in less than an hour.

At the Asuproz Technical Center stop, William expected his father to wander down a rabbit hole of questions about the latest discoveries. At the receptionist's desk, Robert surprised his son with news he had placed a call the day before, requesting Hank be part of the update with the technical director. The call allowed enough time for the director to have a brief presentation and prototypes assembled in his office for the discussion. Hank worked at the tech center as a summer assistant while in college and Asuproz hired him full-time after graduation, allowing him to continue in his grandfather's inventive spirit. The discussion sped along with Hank listening and only commenting when Robert directly asked him questions. There were no easy questions from Robert, who enjoyed hearing Hank get into the details of his project. To William's surprise, the discussion lasted only forty minutes, at which point Robert's loud "okay, thank you" and clap of his hands signaled the meeting was over.

They reached the Asuproz Pasadena location a bit before noon and entered president's office, from where they both had led the company. One step up from the rest of the room sat a large wooden desk with eagles carved at each corner, as if they were pillars supporting the oak top. Robert looked at the company name on the wall.

"Asuproz. A great and timeless name. Does Spencer even remember it is from combining the Latin *supero*, conquer. I added an A at the beginning and a Z at the end."

"We conquered everything from A to Z," William added. "Although I thought it sounded like a brand of antacids."

"It works, like this desk I got from that movie set in exchange for dubbing work. A desk I never worried about you taking over as president." Robert said, looking at his son sitting at the desk, now bearing a newly added nameplate engraved with Spencer's name above the title of president.

"You sure put me through my paces to earn the title."

"Well, you never should have assumed it a foregone conclusion you would be president. I wanted you, Otto, and Adela to prove yourselves."

"And we did! We all understood each project assignment had its strict measurements. And you threatened to take the position back if I didn't produce."

27

"I don't know why I am telling you this now," Robert paused before continuing his thought, "I thought Adela had the skills and ability to outmaneuver you or any of the other candidates. Sadly, she didn't fit the business culture in the '90s. Our employees wouldn't have accepted a woman, even a family member, in charge of everything."

"Our male client base would have made life tough for her."

"Did I ever mention her telling me she could handle the job? She constantly dropped newspaper and magazine clippings on my desk about the success of women like Katherine Graham at the Post. She even brought up Anna Bissell's work in growing her vacuum cleaner company after her husband's sudden death. I didn't listen. I picked you as president to sit at that desk. And neither one of us needed a gawd-damned nameplate saying we were the president."

William grabbed the nameplate to see what it said.

"William, you've done a good job, but neither of us occupies that desk anymore."

"Dad, I want to keep leadership in the family as much as you did. And there were four options."

William didn't continue with his thoughts. He wanted to step away from the presidency earlier than his father and keep leadership among his children so he could decrease his role and enjoy his free time. He decided to stay on as chairman and act as mentor until Spencer could handle everything on his own. He also expected his son to rely on him for all big decisions; he never wanted to put the pressure on Spencer that he had felt. William's children all worked for Asuproz during points of their lives. Even his nephew, Steve, had taken on a role in contract negotiation and had closed several successful deals. When looking for candidates, Willow had the business savvy and worked in the finance department, but William decided a transgender president would be ineffective, not realizing he followed the same criteria as his father for not picking Adela. Willow saw through this early on and moved her career away from Asuproz. Hank shined on the technical side and had led customer meetings but fought some of the same addiction demons as his mother, along with being younger than his siblings and cousin. Spencer, the sales account manager, knew all the big clients and their needs. He became the logical or possible default choice.

William looked up from the president's chair and caught the stern gaze of his father.

"It's not working," Robert said.

"How's that?"

"Your boy isn't cutting it. My grandson isn't delivering."

"It's been about a year. The numbers look good."

"The financials don't worry me. We're still doing well based on the plan you put in place."

"Then what's the problem?"

"You're the chairman. Tell me. What's the problem?"

"He has no growth ideas of his own."

"Bingo! My grandson can sell if he doesn't piss off the client. But I don't hear him talking about the future. He spends more time promoting himself. I wish he would use the same energy to grow the business we created. Damn it! That I created."

Both their heads turned as the office door opened and Spencer entered while talking to his assistant.

"You could have told me they were *both* here. Dad! Gramps! What a nice surprise to see you both. Gramps, what are you doing all this way from home?"

Robert adjusted his wheelchair and pointed toward his grandson, "*Robby*. Your father and I are here to talk about the future of my company."

William shook his head. He had already tried both his cough and laugh interruptions within the past twenty-four hours to break the sour mood of a meeting and he didn't have the energy to fake an interruption again. The business side of the discussion had not even started and Spencer already irritated Robert with the gramps comment. William thought back on the drills his father had put him and his siblings through to be professional and balanced during meetings. Each memo, phone call, and meeting were a test of their composure. But this current president continued to miss his chance to shine. William wondered where he had gone wrong in his training of Spencer. He knew his father's thoughts: Robert's expression declared the need to get someone else in place to save the company, grandson or not.

William watched his son fidget in the doorway as Robert's eyes bore through Spencer's skull. His grandfather blocked any path to the president's desk, and William didn't offer to move from it. Spencer plodded over to the meeting table and sat.

"Let's get closer together over here and be more comfortable." Spencer pulled out a chair as an invitation to his father. He thought back to his Aunt Adela's morning call to alert him of his father's plan to make a visit. Although it allowed enough time for him to leave the golf course and clean up, he hadn't heard that his grandfather would also be there. *Why had his Aunt Adela withheld the information?*

With everyone at the table, Spencer reached for the speakerphone. "Let me get you something to drink. Coffee, some juice, lunch?"

"We're fine," William countered. "We want to hear your thoughts on the direction for next year. The annual board meeting is coming up."

Spencer looked toward his desk and then toward the door. "What if we get Steve in to do a contract summary, or Jennifer from finance? They can get you up to speed quicker than I. They will be able to answer any questions directly."

Robert looked toward his son; his expression conveyed someone searching for the ejection button on Spencer's chair. William took over the conversation and prodded his son with leading questions to discuss his longer-term vision.

Spencer was gun-shy about discussing the failed idea he pitched at Desert Recovery. He avoided talk about recording patient sessions for training and instead ran through a list of advertising buys with him representing the company in a variety of videos and print. Spencer commented on options for promotional signage inside the Los Angeles basketball arena or for the baseball and hockey teams. He continued with opportunities on social media along with sponsorship of a golf tournament he had attended. His grandfather got more perturbed as the discussion continued. Spencer listed every standard marketing idea he had seen in the last six months. William tried to steer the talk toward growth by launching new products and services. Spencer just stared blankly until William broke the silence with an offer to spend the rest of the time brainstorming growth ideas. Spencer remained quiet and William gave a grim look to his father.

William and Robert used to hold brainstorming sessions for hours, inventing numerous outlandish ideas to be narrowed to a few gems. No ideas were coming from this meeting and Robert had mentally checked out. William couldn't tell if the noise was intentional, but his father fidgeted with the joystick of his powered chair causing it to roll back and forth, banging against the table. Finally, Robert completely stopped engaging. He didn't ask questions and directed his attention to some of the legacy recognition awards on the wall. William knew the time arrived to get his father out of there.

Robert's powered chair once again made a loud bang against the table before he wheeled to the door, followed by William. Spencer stayed behind, staring at the desk of the president, the tipped-over nameplate, and the empty chair. He didn't hear his grandfather's parting comment to William.

"You need to act or I will. Take me home."

7

Memorial after Memorial

FROM THE FIRST DAY he married her until the day she died, William took pride in his role as protector to his first wife, Matilda. The enthusiasm grew with the addition of their two children. He relished his role as a 1980s father until the loss of their third child and Matilda succumbing to postpartum complications. He lost the title of husband and had no plan for his children, so he focused on maintaining her memory. This meant regular family visits to her grave for birthdays, holidays, and the anniversary of her death.

He paid the extra groundskeeper fee for perpetual maintenance but they didn't meet his expectations. The first few years consisted of William retrieving lawn tools and a bottle of water from his car trunk. He removed weeds around the headstones and washed dirt off the surface, the remaining care he could supply them. Once he finished, he stayed on his knees with a child on either side, and together they said a prayer or two. With an arm around each of them, he squeezed them close during the final amen.

The gatherings on the anniversary of her death started simply enough but grew in complexity each year in proportion to William's financial success. During the third anniversary, his executive assistant invited William's siblings and father, and coordinated two flower arrangements and a violin player while the pastor from Our Lady of Guadalupe Parish led prayers.

As the priest ended his prayers, Robert turned to William and gave his assessment.

"This gathering has turned into a street show and is scaring the birds at the cemetery."

"Dad, I am trying to show respect and help the kids."

"I am not sure scaring the birds is what anyone wants."

Enough was said. William changed back to memorials of only him and his children, but he never considered the impact of Matilda's death on them or himself. Each anniversary they returned. Not to celebrate her life, but to cling to it. Adela and Otto hoped William's marriage to Tiffany would change the memorial visits but hadn't considered the additional strain of adding a stranger. Tiffany bowed and mimicked those around her during the prayers while Spencer took offense to an infant fussing and crying near his mother and sister's grave. Tiffany and baby Hank lasted a few visits before she and Hank stopped attending. The memorial visits returned to only attendance by the two children with William. He continued to clean the headstones, followed by bowing his head in prayer to ask God if he did enough for his deceased wife and baby and his living children.

8

Never Again, Never Ever Again

WEEKS HAD PASSED since Hank and his counselor approved Adela's request to record five of their one-on-one counseling sessions. The sessions would be used to test if patients could learn more about themselves by seeing their reactions and possible progress over time. Hank understood Adela wasn't a proponent of the idea. She honestly explained that her goal was gaining access to technology and funds from Asuproz and convincing William to try a separate idea of hers. As for this project, staff remained skeptical if recordings could help patients to enhance their journey.

Asuproz utilized their expertise to hide signs of microphones and cameras in one of the tranquil meeting rooms of the recovery center. The first two sessions for Hank were clumsy, with the counselor and patient struggling to act natural. For the third session, Hank had already started his part of the discussion as they walked down the hall to the room.

"But what about everyone else?" Hank asked as he sat at the table.

"This isn't about everyone else." The counselor replied, closing the door to the room.

"But they don't get drunk, or at least they don't black out."

"Hank. We've discussed the dangers of comparison. We're here to discuss your path."

"But—"

"Hank, this has led to challenges in your mindset in the past."

"Why don't they have to deal with any of this? Others don't

have any regrets."

"Hank!" The counselor closed his notebook, leaned forward in his chair, and calmed his tone.

"Let me tell you about others. Let me tell you about regrets, big and small. Perhaps moving forward, you can take a moment to think about what is behind the faces of those around you."

The counselor took another pause and waited for Hank's full attention. "Here are some of the regrets about *not stopping* or having the feelings of *never again* behind the smiling faces you see. Everyone is dealing with something. It's the marbled steak grilled to perfection or the favorite five-star spicy Thai dish at the special-occasion restaurant. Starting with a stomach grumble and turning into unbearable indigestion and pains the doctor cautioned could lead to a hospital visit. There are at least three times during the sleepless night of swearing never again. Then, for the next milestone birthday or anniversary, they do it again."

Hank listened to his counselor.

"The person who goes on one more unmentionable fling with the known bad boy or crazy chick even though he or she has been sworn off for life."

"I mean real regrets."

"These are real regrets even if they are not significant to you. The actions may impact that person physically or emotionally. A person stands on their bathroom scale and sees nine pounds return after losing four. There's the smoker, vowing it's the last cigarette for the seventeenth time in seven years, only to be greeted by their chest x-ray. There is the regret popping into your head now. One too painful to say out loud. The consequences may need rectifying or an apology given."

Hank looked down at his feet.

"Or the action with no consequences and yet the thoughts of what could have gone wrong demands the vow of never again. The never-again pledges accompany a need to crawl out of your skin or stay in the shower trying to wash away the bad decision and to try to forget. *Never again, never again, never again* being the chant while sitting on the shower floor hugging your knees, surrounded by the reverberation of water never cleansing deep enough."

"But that's not the same. You don't understand," Hank slowly shook his head.

"Then what are you talking about? Could you please stop looking away and talk to me."

Hank sat searching for a way to speak of his own recent regret. He never thought he would drink again, even months after the DUI, and yet it happened. There were not drinks in the plural sense. Not even a full drink, but he drank alcohol and drove. Never again. He also drove without a license. Never again.

"I couldn't sleep all last night," Hank started. "I was with my mother."

He stopped as his mind filled with consequential images because he had drunk alcohol. The counselor asked him to continue.

"No one got hurt. I drank some wine with my mom and drove her home. Nothing happened. I got her home safely instead of her driving."

Hank started repeating himself about drinking and helping his mother.

"Hank, let's go over the triggers you've identified around drinking."

Hank reviewed the three areas of typical anxiety. Work: colleagues and drinking events like happy hours, golf outings, and the martini lunches with clients. Dating: going out to meet women at bars. And Tiffany: specifically, being with his mother when she was drunk and her pushing for them to drink together, which started in his pre-teens.

"Hank, those are the situational triggers. You've discussed feeling inadequate as one of your internal triggers. You've told me drinking isn't the solution in those situations. We've also discussed successful sober businesspeople in the world. Let's focus on what happened yesterday. Tell me what transpired."

Hank told of his mother's request to meet at a clubhouse for lunch with her friends after they finished golfing. They'd have time together and she could do one of her favorite things, show off her son. Hank started the morning having coffee with Reese, Thomas, and Kate, and the usual conversations until he said he was seeing his mother for lunch. The discussion stopped.

"Family is important," Hank said to fill the silence.

Reese responded, "'You are my son Dantés! You are the child of my captivity,' is how Alexandre Dumas would say it."

"My mother hasn't been in captivity," said Hank.

"Maybe in our type of captivity?" Thomas added.

"What do you mean by that?" Hank replied.

"Great, more of Reese's book quotes with coffee." Kate jumped in. "When is lunch and how are you getting there?"

"Noon in Rancho, at one of the golf courses."

"Let me take you."

The ride turned less than pleasant with Kate mentioning her frustration with who Hank became after he returned from any visits with his mother. She said he regressed into a middle-school-aged boy. The tempers between Kate and Hank didn't cool before reaching the clubhouse. Kate's parting words were that he had an unhealthy relationship with his mother that hurt him and the people around him. He slammed the car door in response.

Hank entered the clubhouse and went on to the restaurant where he found his mother at an outside table. Tiffany sat with a near-empty glass of rosé and a few dirty place settings at the other empty seats.

"Angel, you have perfect timing; the girls left me here all alone. We were having a hysterical time." She said as he pulled up a chair and moved the dirty napkin from the seat.

Hank asked if he misheard the time.

"Well, the girls ended up taking an earlier tee time, and then we continued with lunch. It's all Marlene's fault. I knew we were supposed to have lunch with you, but Marlene needed to golf early so she could leave, and after all, her club membership got us in. Then the rest of us decided to go directly to lunch. Honey, you understand."

The waiter came over with a full bottle of rosé and a clean wine glass. He filled the new glass for Hank and topped off his mother's. Tiffany pushed her half-eaten club sandwich in front of Hank and motioned for him to eat.

"See, we are having lunch together . . . sorry I destroyed the potato chips." She started on her refreshed rosé.

Hank heard how his mother began her day with mimosas at Marlene's before joining the others at the country club. Too early for them to be drinking on the course, one of them brought some pot she had gotten from her son.

"Hank, we had such a good time on the course; I swear I was at par. Marlene said my game was on point, and she never compliments me. But why am I going on about golf? I know you aren't any good at it. If you would concentrate more, you would be good at things like golf."

Tiffany went on about her foursome having the munchies so badly when they finished their round. They immediately needed food. Hank looked at the disarray of remaining items on the table and imagined the group's stoned antics on the course and during their meal. He pulled his mother's plate toward him and took a bite of one of the remaining quarters of the sandwich. His mother continued about how the girls felt chilled rosé was the best way to take the edge off and get rid of their cotton mouth.

"Honey, have a sip; it's delicious, and it's only rosé."

Hank's mother lifted her glass and made a toast to her son with the exclamation that she loved him more than anything in the world.

"Come on, my baby boy, you have to toast to that!" as she

extended her glass toward him.

After the fight with Kate and being stuck in the sun-drenched heat discussing his apparently terrible golf skills, having a sip of wine to quiet his mom didn't seem terrible.

Hank told his counselor how they ended up finishing the bottle of rosé. He didn't clarify that his share was half a glass to his mother drinking the balance. Instead, he focused on the triggers. The counselor encouraged him to say more.

"Being with my mom when she's drunk is a huge issue because we used to drink together when I was a kid. I felt grown up."

"And what, Hank?"

"And . . . included."

Hank continued with how she had pushed him to be more involved in the family business. Another trigger. She said the business was as much his as any of his siblings. The pot, too much sun, and an indeterminate number of rosés drove the tone and pointedness of her comments as she continued.

"What's wrong with you that you aren't an executive at that Asuprozo? You could be as successful as Spencer. Are you trying hard enough?"

The conversation completely shut down. Hank had enough *life coaching* from his mother's increasingly slurred words. They both got up and left the clubhouse. On the way to her car, Hank asked for the keys.

"Oh honey, you can't drive. You're illegal."

"I'm not illegal. I don't have my license. I know how to drive. You are not driving in your state."

"What state, Califrownea? I am fine. I have my drivi-lisssins."

"Give me your keys."

Hank took the keys from her hands, and they continued to the car. The situation of waiting for a taxi or car service at the golf course in the middle of the day would raise Tiffany mania

39

and cause Hank to explode even more. He also feared leaving her would mean she would try to drive or go back and drink more.

Hank continued explaining his feelings to his counselor. "All the triggers were going off and I wanted the quickest way to get out of the situation. Isn't that what you told me to do?"

Saying the words aloud made him realize it didn't make sense. The counselor reviewed other options available without driving or drinking. Away from his mother and sitting in the meeting room, these all seemed so logical to Hank. His entire body drooped.

"I shouldn't have been drinking."

The counselor remained silent.

"I shouldn't have been driving. I shouldn't have been drinking. I shouldn't have been drinking." Hank repeated to himself again and again.

The session ended with remarks from his counselor and confirmation of their next meeting. Hank left the office thanking the counselor while in his head thinking he would never drink again, never again.

9

Cleaning Day - The Araby Home

EACH FRIDAY, Lea's cleaning schedule shifted from The Dwelling to William's former house in Araby Cove, now owned by Spencer. Somehow, Spencer decided his house purchase included weekly cleaning. Lea took on the extra work, but unlike Spencer, she winced at the thought of her services being part of the house purchase. She did it as a favor to William and it was an easy task as the home remained empty for the most part because Spencer's family lived in Pasadena. Still, Spencer demanded the home be in top shape in case they came out for the weekend or he decided to entertain friends after a round of golf in the desert. If the family visited, he sent a list of food to fill the refrigerator and a reminder to make sure everything was *extra clean*. Lea had received an *extra clean* request message from Spencer the night before and a second message to expect him there before 9:00 a.m. Lea wondered if he'd forgotten to send the typical request to stock the refrigerator, but frustrated enough at the excessive morning messages, she didn't follow up. She got to the house at dawn and kept cleaning until she heard the front door open.

"Lea, are you finished?"

"I am in here, Mr. Spencer."

He yelled from the entryway. "I will be reviewing the entire place to check your work when you are done. Let me know. I'll be outside."

He went poolside to make calls and returned when a florist

arrived with three large arrangements. The Murano glass pendant lights lining the hallway twinkled as Lea cleaned them. She tried to imagine an occasion requiring so many flowers and no guests. Typically, she saw such arrangements at a wedding or a funeral. Her mother's voice popped in her head, 'With Spencer, it's better not to know.' Spencer wandered off and directed the placement of the flower arrangements.

"Are you finished?" Spencer echoed his earlier question as she got down from the step stool. "Let's see how you did."

Either Lea or her mother had been cleaning this house since Spencer was a child, and yet he seemed to take an odd pleasure in critiquing her work. They started with the kitchen. Oven doors were opened and the footrests of the bar stools checked. Spencer ran his fingers along the tops of cabinet doors and inspected sink drains, window frames, and light fixtures. The bathrooms and bedrooms received the same level of attention. The audit continued through all the living spaces until he tried to open the door adjacent to the great room. Spencer tapped at the keypad and opened the office door.

"Mr. Spencer?" Lea said. "In here? The room was locked, so I didn't clean."

Spencer frowned in disbelief and reiterated his expectations for every room, letting her know she should have tried the keypad. The room was immaculate except for a light layer of dust. Spencer told Lea to make sure the office looked as clean as the other rooms before he returned to the patio. Having worked straight through the morning, Lea was ready to be done. She grabbed her supplies and attended to every flat surface in the office and reached the closet door. Another keypad she unlocked. The room lights switched on with the movement of the door, revealing audio and projection equipment from the 1980s to the latest technologies. The closet contained the brain center of the media throughout the property. Lea looked around and decided. The room hadn't been part of her responsibilities and it wasn't going to be. The shelves of dusty records, discs, and tapes along with the file cabinets were not getting cleaned. She put away the supplies and exited to her car, avoiding any chance of being spotted by Spencer and having to clean more for an unknown event.

Spencer called for Lea and then saw her car was gone. He did one more check of the home and turned on the lighting in each room. He readjusted the flower arrangements so the fullest side faced the entry to each room in preparation for a photo shoot. Another magazine spread meant more publicity for the company. An Asuproz marketer got assigned to set up regular press for Spencer. The marketer called Spencer that morning with an overview of the shoot while he waited for Lea to complete the cleaning. The marketer had sent pertinent information to the magazine in advance. It covering the architect and property details along with the provenance of the furniture and art.

Spencer requested the photo of the owner be of him leaning on his newly detailed car in front of the house instead of the typical poses in the living room or by the pool. Sybil and their children hadn't attended photo shoots in some time. Their participation extended the time to settle the children, and Sybil expressed her distain of being directed on how to improve her makeup or fashion choices.

The magazine crew arrived and explored the property, preparing their plan. In past photo shoots, the magazine representative read the fluff copy to Spencer to check for accuracy. This time differed. The reporter discovered Spencer lived there as a child. She asked questions about his memories growing up in the house trying to discover the personal angle. As they continued down the hallway, she stopped at a small room not scheduled to be photographed and asked if they were looking at his childhood bedroom. His face reddened when she popped the idea of getting a photo of him in the small room and asked if there were any similar photos of him as a child in the same space.

"My gosh," she exclaimed, "maybe a side-by-side retrospective. There could be a photo of you and your mother and one of you now in the same spot."

Spencer froze. The request for a photo of him with his mother created a mental image of having to fan through a stack of family photos as they ignited childhood flashbacks. The limited number of remaining pictures were either boxed in a storage closet or discarded. He leaned into the doorway to hide his face from the others as they moved down the hallway without him. They continued to chatter between themselves about additional photo ideas while making notes.

Spencer entered the small room and collapsed into a chair. The reporter hadn't investigated everything because the room wasn't his but would have been his baby sister's nursery. The house renovation removed all traces of his sister and their mother. Especially true for the owner's suite where Spencer completely reconfigured the layout so the sleeping area and bathroom were unrecognizable from their past. Nothing remained in the house as reminders of his mother until today.

Somehow, the reporter had tapped into layers of memories of his mother and his never-to-be-seen baby sister. He rose from the chair and rejoined the group. They were ready to start photographing and decided to change the shot order to take advantage of the sunlight. Everyone moved to the front of the house to capture the happy owner with his new car. Except Spencer felt another jolt running through his body as he stood in the front driveway, the last place he saw his mother's body being taken away in an ambulance, never to return home again.

🌴🌴🌴

Spencer recalled his active young mother. Matilda, or Matti to her friends, ranked high as an amateur league tennis player. Spencer attended the tennis club as her cheering section when they lived in LA. He enjoyed sitting along with the smart and chic set of the Hollywood wives and their children. But after the arrival of his younger brother, Willy, they stopped attending. His mother seemed slower and stopped wearing the short pleated skirts altogether. Spencer recalled his father being at work most of the time and Aunt Adela fighting with his mother about the amount of time she spent with her "coffee neighbor." Spencer never forgot his mother's comments after Aunt Adela left one day. Matilda told Spencer that Adela didn't want her to have any fun and was trying to take away her best friend. Later that week, Spencer saw his grandfather Robert appear for a meeting with both of his parents. Adela also arrived and took Spencer and Willy out for ice cream. Soon after, the family moved to Palm Springs.

Spencer recalled his parents telling him he should be excited for the new desert house with a pool and a baby sister. He felt even happier getting to be his mom's little helper in painting and finishing the new nursery. Together they adorned the ceiling with stickers of clouds with glow-in-the-dark stars and sparkling rainbows while elephants and teddy bear decals danced across the walls.

Matilda expressed her love to her sons at every opportunity and shared her joy about naming her baby. Spencer gave a smile or frown to each of the girl names his mother considered. He also heard how his mother didn't get to pick Willy or his name, but she did choose his middle name, Spencer. Matilda and Princess Diana Spencer were born in the same year and on the same day. They both had two boys, and Matilda told Spencer of how Diana was the epitome of motherhood. She, like the princess, picked her moments to fight against Robert's *suggestions* for raising the children. She sent them to public school and tried to put the boys first. She didn't accept the options of private school, tutors, or childcare. Spencer and Willy garnered all her attention, and she *knighted* Prince Spencer be her protector and he vowed to do so.

10

Marge

ASUPROZ'S TECHNICAL DIRECTOR entered the main doors of Desert Recovery with a utilitarian backpack and metal briefcase. William's additional financial commitment to Desert Recovery happened months ago. In the weeks after that, Adela convinced her brother to invest resources in her idea, a way Asuproz's technology could expand into the recovery industry. The technical director was assigned funds and research hours to make a prototype, and it was time to show Adela. He paused at the atrium fountain and took in the sense of tranquility overlaying the functionality of the medical complex. He checked in at the welcome desk where the receptionist directed him toward the administration wing and to Adela's office. The description on both of their calendars had the single word, Marge. Adela stood at her doorway and took a moment to be thankful for Spencer sparking her idea with his question of how Asuproz's technology could be used at the recovery center.

"Is that Marge?" she asked about the metal case, as they entered her office. He set it on her desk and unclasped the latches.

"This is indeed Marge, and this is the first time I've taken her outside the lab. Let's get her out of this case so she can show her stuff."

The opened container was foam-lined and held a small metal box with a switch, one dial, and a few electric ports on the side.

"I'll set her up, and you can be the first person to try her out here in the wild."

"With no disrespect, Marge looks a bit rudimentary."

"I know we discussed a beta version. Let's say this is a few Greek letters away from beta, but she works."

With the last connection completed and a flip of the switch, a red LED light changed to green.

"Ready?" Adela leaned in with excitement.

"We'll know soon enough. The green light shows the modulator is active. The knob allows you to change your voice to one of three different intonations. The past technologies for movie post-production work optimized the actor's familiar voice while enhancing intonation. Marge cloaks the speaker's voice and creates a unique and replicable modification, completely masking any recognition while adding the specific tones you requested for a compassionate helpline worker. Between Hank and me, we tapped into past inventions and kicked this out in no time."

"Hank?"

"Hank did most of the heavy lifting on the new stuff while I dug into some of our old technology to help."

"Why isn't he here?"

"Neither of us is keen on these family business meetings and would rather be in the lab."

"Well, you're doing fine. Show me what we've got."

Adela spotted a sticker of the animated character, Marge, from a popular cartoon show, on top of the invention. The technical director explained how they used Marge's recorded voice to test the device in the laboratory. The equipment modulated the voice in real time to a generic tone with no trace of the distinct cartoon character. Adela looked at the green light and asked if they could start.

The director turned the knob to setting three and nodded yes. She picked up the receiver and dialed her brother's assistant at the Asuproz offices and they put the call through.

"This is William; how may I help you?"

"Hi, I'm calling regarding an interview for an article about famous business siblings in Palm Springs."

"Who's calling, please?"

"One of the smartest interviewers in the Palm Springs area."

"Who is this?" The ire in William's voice increased with each word.

"It's Adela! It works. Marge works."

She looked to the technical director, who flipped off the switch.

"Adela?"

"Could you tell that it was me?"

"There you are! No, I had no idea. So, you are trying out Marge. What do you think?"

"This test worked and it's easy enough to operate, but your director here says we'll test it with a few other pilot users. Your donation of technology won't be used for training sessions, but based on this test it will work for the helpline. Dad already volunteered to be a guinea pig. We finally have a response to his constant requests for more involvement in both organizations. We'll also be able to help some of our more famous patients find a way to volunteer or to use the device if they want to call in to get support without revealing themselves."

"Addie, it's a pleasure to help. But let's circle back. What about doing recordings for use in training? Spencer's idea. Are we still pursuing training videos?"

"You're going to have to tell Spencer that's a dead-end idea. I've gotten a couple of patient-counselor pairs to agree to the recording of their sessions for improving their individual growth, but no one would approve the training concept. Our legal team put together a brief if you're interested."

"No, that's fine. I'm glad we may have practical uses in your industry. That's great news, and especially if Dad gets something to do, an unexpected bonus. Still sharp as a tack at his age. Let's hope we are so lucky. When do you see *the big boss?*"

"We are headed there now. Wish me luck!"

🌴🌴🌴

Adela knocked on the door of her father's casita as the director fidgeted with his backpack straps.

"Dad, are you ready for us? We're here to do the test."

Adela heard a bellow from her father for them to enter. As she opened the door, she found Lea in the archway welcoming them. Adela led the technical director across the room to her father, sitting in his wheelchair reading the newspaper. The director eyed the shelves on the back wall filled with the company's original prototypes, along with framed patents, two Emmy Awards, a Grammy, and an Oscar for technical contributions. The magazine rack beside his chair contained a mix of *Popular Mechanics*, *Variety*, and *Vanity Fair*.

"Thanks for letting us try this on your phone," Adela said as she pulled the *Wall Street Journal* out of her father's hands. "We're testing the technology without exposure to the public. We don't even want to get much beyond the family at this point."

"Anything for you, Addie. Now tell me what this does?"

The technical director went to the phone, connected the box, and made a couple of trial calls while they talked.

"It's quite simple for the user. We want to do test calls coming to you from our staff who will pose as helpline patients seeking support. The testing will evaluate whether the calls are clear on both ends and assure the voice modulator works."

"How is my voice being modulated?"

"The reason we want to modulate your voice is so it can't be recognized by patients calling in to the helpline. At the same time, the device adjusts tone to give an emotion that is more in line with our best counselors."

"Like my inventions did with actors years ago."

"With the exception we want to mask the voice in addition to changing the tone," Adela replied.

The director nodded.

"Why would anyone care what my voice sounds like? And I didn't ask *why you are doing it*, I asked *how* it is being done. Do we have any new technology in this?"

The technical director hesitated before attempting to answer.

"The *how* is leveraging some of your original technology and some new concepts we have been wanting to try, although there's not enough time to give the description any justice. And if anyone should tell you about the technology, it is Hank. He did most of the work."

"Hank? My grandson?" Robert said.

"Yep, Hank and some others have spent months adjusting some of our newer technology to create this prototype. He has a knack. If all goes well, this electric box may be a worthy addition to your shelf of inventions." The technical director looked toward the living room wall.

"Well then, where the hell is he? Why isn't he here?"

The technical director continued, "We wanted to keep this to a smaller group for today. Let's focus on getting this set up and tested. And your specific voice doesn't have anything to do with today's test, as famous as it is to those of us in this room. The goal is to mask the speaker's voice to anyone on the other end of the call."

Adela took over the discussion, seeing her father's growing frustration. "Desert Recovery and Boarding is becoming so renowned that we now have musicians, actors, and lawmakers wanting to protect their anonymity."

The technical director continued, "We are going to have people call you to see if the connection is clear, regardless of the phone they may be using. We also need to check if the modulating equipment creates an unrecognizable voice in a reproducible way, so the tone of the new voice can be recognized by callers."

"So, you repeated the same thing that my daughter said three minutes ago."

"I guess I did . . . um, from a technology standpoint, this fits under some newly filed patent protection. We're thinking of applications for the recovery industry and other markets. This model currently produces three unique voice modulations for each user."

"I am going to want a full review from Hank later. Let's get this going. Are you ready? What's next? I don't want to spend my entire day doing volunteer work for the company I started."

11

VIP

IN THE END, EVEN ADELA JOINED the Marge trials before she signed off on the official launch. Robert enjoyed the role-playing so much that he trained to become a helpline volunteer with the coordinator scoring him high during his training. Adela and William loved the shift of his mentoring away from them to others. They weren't surprised by his ability to handle crisis discussions but marveled at his high scores in compassion. Robert chided Adela and William to get moving on the launch so he could start his volunteer work with the latest Asuproz invention.

With the final approvals completed, Adela contacted Calvin Moore, as the first user of Marge. Calvin came to prominence in the 1990s when cable companies invested heavily in children's programming. *That's Todd* led the ratings as one of the hottest shows of that era. Its child star brought in major brand sponsorships and two Christmas specials. Calvin Moore fit a perfect model of the adorable black child who could produce an angelic smile, a puppy dog pout, or a mischievous giggle within a minute with believability and relevance to the show's storyline. The Todd character lived in a hectic sitcom family hardware store while serving as the show's voice of reason. Todd wrapped up every episode by looking directly into the camera to recite a quip with a life lesson which caused all the surrounding characters to stop and say, "That's Todd!" Then the show credits scrolled to everyone's content, especially the network producers and sponsors. Calvin's popularity grew as did his screen presence where he appeared as a celebrity guest judge, or commentator in other shows, and as an advertising spokesperson for several products. Every scripted word he spoke was filled with purity, leaving Calvin fighting to discover himself. All this occurred while his parents pushed for as many jobs as possible, concerned their money train would end sometime after his puberty.

Calvin's introduction to drug use started at the same time he filmed public service announcements telling kids to eat their vegetables instead of candy. He, on the other hand, was snorting cocaine at underground parties. His parents used him as a golden ticket at exclusive gathering, standing in front of the bouncer, pointing to their son, and saying his tagline "That's Todd." In retaliation for being used by his parents and then being ignored, Calvin found his way into the darker corners or on the dance floor. Coke became his escape. Soon people on the television set started complaining about the new attitude of the lead actor. Most chalked the erratic mood swings to Calvin entering a brooding teen phase. No one imagined Todd to be anything but America's darling child. He certainly wasn't buying coke off the costume coordinator during lunch breaks. Except, he was.

Whispers began around the show about an actor needing makeup reapplied under his nose after breaks. The rumors stayed within the studio until the sixteen-year-old got caught by police, and a few neighborhood security cameras, running naked down the streets and through the yards of Brentwood with lit fireworks in both hands. The show went on hiatus for two months while Calvin entered a court-ordered celebrity treatment center as a way of avoiding stricter sentencing. The production company completed the remaining three episodes of the season with Calvin. He finished with treatment, although he hadn't finished with cocaine.

Brother and sister twins joined the cast for the final episodes to take the focus off the star. Summer meant another treatment center check-in, accompanied by a press release stating that Calvin reentered of his own accord to obtain additional support. One article referred to the time as a tune-up and not the actual studio ultimatum. When the next season's filming started, Calvin lasted two episodes before he got caught by a tabloid photographer misbehaving. The magazine cover photo showed Calvin in a compromising position under the heading "That's Todd!" The incident led to an immediate release from the show for being erratic, disrespectful of coworkers, and for behavior inconsistent with the values of the series.

The show changed the title to *That's Mod*, and the twins went on to be the next influencers of the youth generation. Calvin and his parents were no longer welcome anywhere in Hollywood, and after a decade, the industry completely forgot them. The break allowed Cal to do real recovery work and to sever of all ties to his parents. As an adult, he decided to seek help for the first time by his choice instead of a studio or a court order. He became appreciative of his life through his enrollment in Desert Recovery and Boarding. During those first days in treatment, Calvin, or the adult Cal, feared having to deal with the shame of being recognized, only to face worse: an internal emptiness when he realized no one knew of him or the character Todd.

Over time, Cal gained appreciation for the anonymity and used the privacy as his new strength instead of letting his ego tell him otherwise. He used his time in obscurity to redefine himself. He and the cable network company had both put *That's Todd* in the past. They decided never to show reruns, which meant no residual checks but also allowed a fresh start. He reentered the entertainment industry slowly in West Coast theater productions and, after a few years, returned to television. The adult Cal began with bit parts on criminal procedural shows. His childhood stock expressions transformed into the brooding criminal, the intellectual forensics expert, or the distraught young widower. These small roles evolved to lead characters and progressed into movie offers. His acting income fed a startup production company and recording studio. Cal and his business thrived, and he decided to give back to Desert Recovery for their help in the process. Cal went public about his addiction journey and wanted to do more.

He dedicated time as a sponsor and worked on the helpline at Desert Recovery. He enjoyed volunteering and found reward in being an ear for people at their dark moments. As his fame rose, participation became more difficult without creating a scene. Cal's charm and presence changed the energy in a room. While working the helpline, his caramel-smooth voice was easily recognized. Incoming calls began requesting Cal, often by someone offering a script or movie deal. Adela needed a way to protect him and other celebrity volunteers. Spencer's poorly thought-out presentation on recording patients inspired Adela. She came up with the concept for a new type of voice modulator for stars like Calvin.

Adela grinned, again remembering her grandchildren's expression, "and so here we are," and thought about how the statement literally applied to where she stood. After weeks of Marge trials, Adela and the Asuproz technical director were in front of a solid aqua blue door, completely framed by a 10-foot ficus hedge walling off the yard and home from street views. She rang the doorbell and a light on the camera started to glow. A buzz signaled the lock opening, followed by a polite, "Adela, please come in," over the speaker. The two guests followed the canopied sidewalk up to the home's front doors, sitting wide open and framing the host. Cal and Adela hugged as the technical director admired the familiarity. Cal led them to his office while the director took a deep breath and tried to decipher the home's unique fragrance, finally deciding on the smell of opulence. He went to the desk and began the task of connecting Marge to Cal's phone as Cal and Adela stepped out and sat on the patio.

There she told him how calls from Desert Recovery's switchboard would be forwarded to his number during scheduled times. Adela noted Cal's interest and went into more detail about his participation.

"And you will be our first person to use the modulator as a finished product," Adela said.

"I am glad to be back volunteering on the helpline."

"Cal, I appreciate you doing this and must admit there's a lot riding on its success. This project centers on trust with the people on both sides of the calls, so please let us know your experience with it."

"I'm happy to help."

Adela paused and then decided to continue with the question she had wanted to ask for some time. "Why do you do it? You're a major success in several parts of your life and can pick and choose what you do for the rest of your life. Why spend your time on the helplines?"

Cal rubbed his hands on his thighs, stood up, and took a deep breath. "Here's the thing," he started slowly, pacing as he responded to Adela, "At times, and believe me, I have been told never to read your own press, but at times I stop and read the articles. I suppose it's human nature. So much is projected upon me of how others perceive my life. They intrude to the point of deciding my mindset based on my movies, the box office revenues, salary, my girlfriend, and the cars. They list the values of the Malibu house and the place in New York, or they show an aerial shot of this place in Palm Springs and discuss my happiness as if it is theirs to decide. There are actual articles on who the top twenty-five happiest celebrities are and I'm typically near the top. Maybe they are right . . . maybe not, but if so, it's not for the reasons they list."

He returned to his chair next to Adela.

"My childhood consisted of a path full of takers. My parents. My employers. Everywhere I looked there were takers. Do you want to know what's funny?"

Adela nodded for him to continue.

"I still yearned to please them and get their attention. I was broken. But, thanks in part to the help of your organization, I learned my addiction, well . . . it wasn't my fault. This may be my situation or at times my burden, but it's not my fault. It is my actions that are my responsibility. I was a celebrity with everything at a young age and lost everything: the fame, the money, the career. Here I am back on top and could lose it all again."

Cal stared at Adela with his dark eyes. "All this success can still vanish in a moment so I decided to give more than I take. Be a helper and fill my voids created by all the past takers. So, thanks. Thank you for creating a way to give back to people who struggle the same way I do. That's what makes me happy."

Adela reached over and put her hand on his, "and we're thankful for you."

"And now here's my question." Cal put his other hand on top of hers. "Why me?"

"Why *you* what? I am not sure I'm following."

"Why did you take such good care of me when we first met. Was it because of the *That's Todd* show?"

Adela started to laugh and then pulled her hands away and put them to her face as she blushed.

"Cal, my laughter. I shouldn't have. My laughter was intended toward me and not a reflection of you. My son . . . Steve, he often accompanies me to various fundraisers. He jokes about how he must quiz me on who the VIPs are and their reason for fame. He puts articles on my desk from tabloids as homework. I live in a world where the son cuts out articles and gives them to the parent, and not the other way around. I didn't know who you were because of who I am, not because of you."

She straightened up, keeping her focus on Cal as she continued. "I've stressed the importance of ensuring the organization treated everyone who came through the doors the same. You probably recall this from my welcome statement whenever I spoke to new patients. The three main parts are: sincere appreciation for trusting Desert Recovery with their journey, a reminder of Desert Recovery's goal to instill hope through support, and to remind the patients that Desert Recovery may not be the solution for everyone and this will be discovered together."

"I've heard you say that a couple of times." Cal smiled.

"I stand behind those statements and they apply to all our

patients. But I felt something the first time we met, not your celebrity. There was something about your story and your parents' neglect. When you first arrived, you were so . . . I could see the impact of your parents' behavior. We see all sorts of people from less-than-ideal upbringings, but there was something about you, about your eyes. It's just, Cal, you are a special person."

The tech director startled the two with his greeting to say he was ready. They returned to the office desk where Cal picked up the receiver of the desktop phone and dialed. The first call went to his girlfriend, who didn't respond immediately after hearing the voice greeting her.

"Hey hon."

"Hey hon? Who is this? Cal?"

"It's me. I'm trying the voice thing I told you about. It works."

12

The Third Generation

'Robby' (Robert Spencer), age 7 – 1989, Independence Day Weekend

The elder Robert decided to check in on his son William's family on what he considered an unnecessary vacation day on Friday. He wanted to see how the family was settling into their new home in Palm Springs. Robert fidgeted to find a comfortable position in the lawn chair beside the pool while studying his two grandchildren. He savored his bourbon old-fashioned and tried to determine how much a distraction the youngsters were for his business-partner son.

Matilda, William's wife, declared the Independence Day holiday weekend started on the Friday before the actual Tuesday holiday. She also added her birthday, which fell on July 1, as part of the multi-day celebration. Robert continued his mental calculations of the business impact for not working for five consecutive days, birthday cake or not. This holiday got added under the liability column. His daughter-in-law seemed calmer living outside of the LA area. An asset. William settled into the Palm Springs home might have been an asset for Robert and yet his son still bounced between the desert home and an apartment near the Asuproz headquarters in Pasadena. Robert paused to consider the appropriate column as the children amused themselves playing. Before Robert could decide, a flash and a cry came from his namesake grandson, Robert 'Robby' Spencer.

William jumped to his feet, "Well, this isn't the promised relaxing weekend."

Robby's hand went to cover the area where the fireworks nicked his neck. Matilda screamed about the possible loss of fingers or an eye. She struggled to get out of the patio chair while supporting her belly and the soon-to-be youngest member of the family. Robert didn't know what to think about his son's parenting skills, except he didn't like the chaos which meant more items for the liability column. William tried to calm his own laughter after catching his wife's ire.

"All I am saying is that he will learn more about life through consequences."

She didn't respond as she reached down to check on her son's burn.

William turned to Robby and remarked how years from now the girls would love to see a scar. Then speaking to no one in particular, he continued, "Didn't Charles Bronson have a scar on his face or Steve McQueen? All the tough movie stars have scars."

Leandra rushed out of the kitchen with a paper towel in hand and reached Robby, relieving his mother. She applied the towel to the wound. Robert had orchestrated Leandra's schedule to be at William's home each Friday, in addition to tending to his own place on Monday through Thursday. From the day William arrived in Palm Springs, Robert noted his son's home being in disarray and wanted to help by stepping in and supplying Leandra. In her exhausted state, Matilda didn't object, so Leandra became part of their Friday.

Robert visited exclusively on days she worked. He found mayhem like the fireworks supported his decision. Leandra calmed the crying child. With a magician's slight-of-hand, she got a piece of chocolate into Robby's mouth and tended to his neck while Matilda collapsed back into her lawn chair.

William went on about Robby's need to make smarter choices, to be more confident, and to stand on his own with less mothering. The paper towel against Robby's neck became damp from pus. Leandra removed her hand to see the burn and the start of a crimson tone on the skin.

"Jeez, Robby, are you trying to ruin our holiday?" William put down his drink. "Get him to the car. We're going to the hospital."

Matilda shot him another look, filled with a mixed disbelief and exhaustion. "This is your version of parenting?" With little remaining strength, she pulled Willy close, out of the commotion.

"Stay with me, Prince William; Leandra will take care of your brother." Matilda hugged her youngest.

Leandra tried picking up Robby to bring him to the car. He pulled away and grabbed the paper towel from her, looking toward his father at the garage door.

"That's right, Robby. Don't let anyone baby you. Be a real man like your father and grandfather."

Leandra stopped the boy and looked at his neck again. The seven-year-old's tears had ended and so had the bleeding. He wiped his face dry and put the towel back on his neck. Leandra grabbed William's tumbler, filled with gin and ice, and held the cold surface to Robby's neck as she carried him into the house. There wouldn't be a hospital visit.

During Robby's teen years, high school girls didn't notice the discolored skin, but the rouged mark greeted Robby in the mirror every morning for the rest of his life. As an adult, the patch of hair on his neck emerged stark white, so he always stayed clean shaven and wore a high collar. The disappointment of his father greeted him in the mirror each morning for the rest of his life.

'Willy,' (Willow, once William Jr.), age 7 – 1991

William, the second child and namesake of his father, started being called Willy at an early age. His mother, Matilda, decided neither William nor Junior felt right and had less excitement about Will, Bill, and Billy. She didn't get to see Willy turn seven but did notice differences from the disposition of other children. Matilda tested Willy for possible issues with hearing, vision, and even autism. In the end, the doctors diagnosed the behavior as a phase. Robert and William looked for signs of an inventor in Willy, but the child spent less time with the building blocks and found more interest in his mother's shoes. To keep her children from bringing the desert sand into the house meant a 'shoes off at the door' policy. More than once, Willy would take off his shoes only to replace them with his mother's shoes and then try walking through the house. Willy had the protective eye of his mother until the year he blew out five candles on his cake. She did all she could until she was no longer of his world to help him with his unknown challenge.

Matilda's death preceded Willy's conscious understanding of his yearnings to be Willow. His clues went unseen by the rest of the family, and even by the teenage Lea, who often was a sitter for the young children in the absence of their mother. At seven, Willy didn't know what he felt, except the shape reflected in the mirror did not match his feelings of self. During childhood, there weren't many moments to test the waters of femininity. The chances to be alone in the bathroom and wrap a bath towel or shower curtain around the torso to soften his form had to suffice. He also grew longer hair, refusing any form of a cut or trim. His father attributed the style to a coping aspect around Matilda's death and didn't consider it as his son's attempt to find a more relatable image.

Willy's search for his true self didn't emerge from behind the bathroom door during his youth. He didn't know how to share something indescribable and found no additional clarity in the world. The fluid gender appearances of Boy George, Annie Lennox, and David Bowie were dismissed by Robert with his comment, "This is all an attempt for fifteen minutes of fame," and then added, "no matter how disgusting the deviancy has to be for their parents." The patriarchal message hit Willy at his core. No matter how successful the individual, coloring outside the gender norms was wrong. Willy didn't know the definition when Grandpa Robert referred to those people as an abomination, but he knew the word didn't sound good.

Hank, age 7 – 1999

"Why are we moving here?" Hank asked as Tiffany darted from room to room, assessing their new home.

"What's that, honey? Put your things here. It's your new bedroom; it's going to be hysterical."

"Why aren't we moving with Willy, Robby, and Dad?"

"Allergies. They didn't like the cat."

"But why did we have to move? Where is Boots?"

"Honey, stop worrying about that mangy cat, and your dad only lives a couple of blocks away. You can visit whenever you like. Now come and see your bedroom."

Hank was too young to notice the friction between his parents, typically ignited by Spencer's disrespect toward Tiffany which transferred into fights between Tiffany and William. These escalated to battles ending with Tiffany sleeping in one of the guest rooms or leaving the house for the night, all unseen by Hank. The relationship strained to a breaking point during the same time William took over running Asuproz. The logical decision for William involved moving most of the family into The Dwelling, closer to Leandra, while the stepfamily members did not.

Instead, Tiffany and Hank set up their home in a nearby two-bedroom house with a clean design and slab patio in the front. The yard created a place for Hank to play and Tiffany to sun herself in a tangerine bikini on a chaise. She stayed there in a layer of baby oil, hoping to catch William's eye when he drove by the house. None of the neighbors made a point to stop and talk or even greet her. The young, attractive, single mother didn't fit in with the wealthy, married, and private community of Old Las Palmas.

Over time, the invites for Hank to visit his siblings decreased, and Tiffany never pushed the issue. At the same time, Hank began experiencing a new set of visitors to the small house. Even at seven years old, he heard Tiffany say she didn't plan on spending the rest of her life single in a Midcentury Modern cage. After all, Tiffany would lament, she looked every bit a woman in her prime.

Hank's introduction to new house guests started with his mother being picked up by dates and him being left home alone. The dates evolved into evenings when a gentleman would spend the night. There were awkward moments when the visitor ran into Hank the next morning. So, Tiffany directed Hank on the importance of not making her guests feel uncomfortable. Hank was instructed to be in his bedroom and out of sight whenever one of his *uncles* appeared. Once, Hank pushed back, claiming his right to all parts of the house whenever he wanted. Tiffany snapped back, stating the men paid for Hank's toys and for his mother's nice outfits. She questioned if he wanted everything to go away and for them both to go hungry.

Hank only knew Tiffany's dates as uncles because she never used names around him. He spent evenings alone or on rare occasions Lea would see him playing in the front yard and stop to chat, leaving her special ginger cookies. The solitary time consisted of dining from a container of restaurant leftovers or a bowl of cereal and then cleaning up before going to bed. The uncle visits didn't happen every night and the uncles didn't change each time. The relationships could last anywhere from a few dates to a few months and Tiffany didn't completely hide Hank. There were a few photos in the house and other small signs. Tiffany told her son not to scare off the uncles for no reason. He understood he was the "no reason."

Hank lived his invisible life while Tiffany cycled through

emotions that were predictable, even for a child. He experienced his mother's start of each relationship, excited and upbeat. The dates progressed to overnight stays. The appearance of new dresses or jewelry, and occasionally a toy for Hank followed. Then, without notice, came some remark about the uncle not returning. Most of the jewelry faded from view, and Hank later learned Tiffany sold the bobbles for cash and returned most of the dresses for credit.

Hank mastered his mother's patterns but couldn't decide which phase he liked the least. While dating, Tiffany barely had a moment for him. Between dates came periods moodiness and depression with Hank not knowing how to comfort her. He learned at an early age how to make gin gimlets as a tonic to dampen his mother's more extreme moods. Neither the complacent nor the depressed mother frightened him as much as the third version.

This occurred the evening of a last date when Tiffany arrived home sobbing. She went straight to Hank's room, crawled into his bed, and hugged him like a drowning victim clutches a life preserver. Her breath smelled of rum and cigarettes as her tears hit the back of his neck. Tiffany muttered about never finding anyone to love her while embracing her child.

On those nights, Hank eventually slipped away to the couch, leaving his mother in bed, still in her dress and shoes. Often, there were skin indents on his cheek or arm from where an earring or chunky bracelet had compressed against him. Free from her grip for the evening, Hank found himself crying for his mother and oddly missing her embrace.

Steve, age 7 – 1981

Steve couldn't remember the first time he asked his mother about his father, but her responses were usually terse. Early on, her comments were distractions to other topics. The question was handled like others from the child. For example, he asked why he had dimples but she didn't and why he had a birthmark on his hand.

But, by the age of seven, Steve became serious and pushed for more of an answer. Adela hugged her son and began something she had practiced many times. Steve heard three messages: his mom would always love him, she and his father agreed he wouldn't be a part of Steve's life, and Steve needed to focus on determining his true self, without concern for his father or even the rest of the family. It was okay if he didn't know who he was at seven, although his life's mission should be to discover more about himself each day. Then Adela hugged him and repeated her love for him.

He asked a few more times over the next years and the answer remained unchanged. Each time, his mother's response ended with a hug and his lessening interest in his father. The topic became as uninteresting as the birthmark on his leg. The entire exchange even made him less interested in his mother's past. He rarely heard her mention her childhood or life before him. He learned instead to be ready for her questions. They would cover his future goals for the week or even the year. From a very young age, she started each dinner with them each stating one positive, one humorous, and one challenging event from the day. Then, before starting to eat, they would have a moment of gratitude.

As an adult, Steve could never find the parenting book where his mother discovered this technique, but he continued the process with his children. In his youth, he asked his cousins how they responded to the same meal rituals and got blank stares for responses making him consider the uniqueness of his path compared to theirs.

13

Help and Hope

DESERT RECOVERY WAS THE PERSONAL PIVOT Adela needed after leaving Asuproz those many years ago. Her role as director of negotiations had become a Sisyphean cycle of bids and contracts. She won the deal or declined the bid and moved to the next one. Adela felt no sense of larger accomplishment in the family business even with all her successes.

The original recovery center consisted of a modest, mostly volunteer staff when Adela joined. The organization offered help, although limited to managing schedules for addiction counseling and group meetings at a rented office space. Starting first as a volunteer and then a full-time employee, Adela didn't take long to feel a sense of reward through the impact in those coming through the door. Over the next years, she migrated to a leadership role, and as president, she hired a specialized staff to increase the breadth and quality of the offerings. Adela's connections to the business world and access to her family resources helped sponsor her team's vision to create a full campus in Palm Springs. The completion of the campus was a major accomplishment, and yet she continued to desire more for the patients. The round-the-clock campus logically supported the addition of a twenty-four-hour helpline, and that drove the addition of the Marge modulator. Adela was a builder.

As a sign of good faith, she attempted Spencer's idea of recording patient sessions for the recovery center's own use. She was thankful for Hank and his counselor as first testers before dropping the idea for all the anticipated legal reasons. Adela admired Hank's participation and was relieved the recorded sessions weren't a source of challenge to his sobriety.

The creation of Marge, and even some of the other added programs, were small victories in comparison to the next expansion in the works and the topic of her next meeting. Adela and her team focused on ways to supply help and hope to the patients. Hope was a word she cherished. She believed in doing the hard work at Desert Recovery and had a framed quote on her office wall. "I don't think man was meant to attain happiness so easily. Happiness is like those palaces in fairy tales whose gates are guarded by dragons: we must fight in order to conquer it." — Alexandre Dumas, The Count of Monte Cristo

Adela reminded staff that hope may be all a patient had left and was worth the effort. Armed in her spirit of hope, she left her office and ran into the project leader of her next meeting.

"Jason, are we set? This will be the final approval for the biggest expansion the organization has seen in years."

"All good. Do you still want to give the opening comments? I'd be happy to take over from there."

"Yes, I'll take the intro, but jump in if I miss anything."

"I doubt that, and besides this meeting is only a formality, we should be good. Everyone has seen the information packet you signed off on last week, and I've gotten no pushback. We may get some financial-impact questions from city council members, but we are set."

"Thanks for your leadership. Let's get this done."

As they entered the meeting, Jason confirmed the attendees in a hushed tone to Adela. "Everyone's here: our operational board, the development board, and two members from the city council as a courtesy, who can question but don't vote. This shouldn't take long, but we need the formal approval for the size of the expenditure. Even representation from Asuproz's philanthropic board is here, minus the president."

"Spencer skipping a meeting invite where there's no photo

opportunity? Shocking. But the foundation pre-approved their funds?" Adela queried the project lead.

"Everything is approved and budgeted for the first of the next five years. We're good."

Adela's voice went from a whisper to presentation mode as she kicked off the meeting.

"Welcome, everyone. Could we start with introductions before the discussion on this next milestone for Desert Recovery and *Boarding*."

Adela couldn't avoid an ever-so-small wince each time she stated the full name of the organization in public. She didn't know when the name and abbreviation of DRAB would change, but the need sat high on her to-do list.

Years back, when the expansion to a full campus occurred, a critical financial tie to Asuproz and its corporate philanthropy was created. At that time, one Asuproz director joined the operational board of Desert Recovery and another to its fundraising development board. One of these members was her father, Robert.

The creation of a campus involved significant planning on so many points. Little interaction between the recovery center and its development board of directors occurred beyond the primary task to raise funds. Robert rarely attended. He made appearances on occasions when he felt the need to show support. When the campus added dormitories, the team decided to rebrand and create a more comprehensive name for the organization. On decision day, Robert appeared and wanted to help. His support came in the idea of a name having the solution right in the title.

Robert declared, "If potential customers are looking up treatment centers, they should find this organization among the list. We'll have a name that states exactly what we do. The name is Desert Recovery and Boarding!"

Shocked, Adela couldn't speak. Her team had investigated a list of names that felt welcoming and didn't sound like the patients were horses. Her father won that decision although she would declare losing by default. At that time, she didn't have the experience to say no to her father or his money. She was railroaded by Robert's mode of operation of sweeping in with a flare of chaos and a firm mindset. He ignored any research data and the months of investigation to make a *man-gag-imous* decision. Adela's term. These decisions were the opposite of or a mashed-up version of magnanimous and she made sure to emphasize the 'man' and 'gag' part of the term she created.

Back during the name branding meeting, like so many other times, her father sat silently through half or less of the meeting. Then, without any warning, he stood, pushing the office chair away with the back of his legs, and proclaimed his decision of *Desert Recovery and Boarding*. Robert reinforced his decision by saying, "Did everyone get that?" and then exited without waiting for a response. Over the next board meetings, Adela learned how to bring her father back to the discussion before he left and refocus those in the room to continue with the original plan. She couldn't always persuade them, and in that first instance, she lacked preparation, so everyone around the table confirmed the name: Desert Recovery and Boarding – DRAB.

To her relief, Robert's involvement in the business diminished. She missed his ability to stand and walk out of any room but not his additional "help." With the funds he supplied back then, she evolved the nonprofit to the twenty-acre campus. Desert Recovery and Boarding consisted of the detox unit, separate women's and men's dormitories, the outpatient building, a central structure with a dining hall, fitness area, crafts department, an auditorium, and business offices. There were also plenty of public outdoor areas, including a meditation path that wove throughout the entire campus. Despite the name, the campus was a success and poised for the next big step.

Introductions wrapped up, and Adela continued with her part of the presentation.

"You all know the end goals of this project. I will start with the rationale for what this investment will do, and Jason will get into the details." She took a pause, making eye contact with each attendee as she spoke. "We have seen patients be more likely to maintain their sobriety when they continue their relationship with Desert Recovery, whether through local meetings or use of the helpline. The importance of longer-term connectivity has gotten our team to investigate ways for a smoother reentry to mainstream life. We've identified patients who could benefit from an intermediate step between their treatment here at the recovery center and returning home. The concept is to create an additional structured environment in their post-treatment months, outside of the campus."

Adela beamed as she spoke on the new way they would help their patients. The preparation for off-site sober living involved two years of investigating patient integration into the Palm Springs community. Desert Recovery's medical and counseling departments evaluated the model of care and consulted with industry experts across the country. City council and community groups were brought in for planning meetings. Adela tested the interest of local businesses in hiring occupants of the sober homes. Desert Recovery had also bought three houses, using them as short-term rental properties while designers evaluated possible enhancements to fit a sober house community. The investment risk was low as the properties produced a positive cash flow as vacation rentals during the evaluation. Adela continued speaking to the group.

"As I wrap up my section, you will see in this map that all three houses are within walking distance of the campus. If there are no other questions, I will turn things over to Jason, our project leader, to review the financials and call for the final vote."

Jason's discussion was receiving approving nods when the door swung open and in sauntered Spencer. Adela straightened in her chair while Spencer blathered about how they should keep going and he didn't mean to interrupt. Two minutes into his attendance, he asked Jason to stop, leaving the project leader looking to Adela for direction. Spencer leveraged the pause into a sign of his turn to speak. He produced a series of questions on the short and long term cash flow impact on Desert Recovery. He blurted a comment about the costs for the helpline and how it was already having a negative impact on financial numbers. Spencer described the start of a downward spiral demanding more funds from the family and the Asuproz foundation.

"DRAB is moving into a tenuous financial situation."

Adela sat initially dazed hearing the erroneous characterization. She didn't wait for a pause to respond. "Spencer. What numbers are you referencing for these com—"

"Everyone, I've gotten access to the financial numbers on the rentals for the three houses. Well done! This is the big shift that Asuproz needs."

"Gotten access? Spencer. We're here to finalize—"

"Asuproz will be making major investments in rental homes up and down the desert valley to create a new branch of the company: Asuproz Rental and Real Estate!"

The room sat in silence, trying to determine the meeting topic and who was in charge. Adela stood to take attention away from Spencer at the other end of the table. She knew how much the sober homes meant and had put her personal credibility into the community to create acceptance. The addition of off-campus housing would improve success rates and bring the patients hope. Her face grew dark as she considered each of these facts.

"Spencer! Our goal is to sign off on the already approved funds for—"

"Therefore, DRAB will not go ahead with this expansion . . . "

"Robert Spencer! These funds have already been approved, and there are contracts in place."

"I have final say over the Asuproz philanthropic funds funneled to this organization. I will be diverting resources for the next few years to create the new vacation rental and real estate branch of the company. You should sell those three houses to Asuproz because you won't need them." He reached the door and focused in on Adela as he said, "did you get that?" and walked out.

"Robert!" she shouted to the door closing behind her nephew. The eyes of the room turned to her. She gathered up her things and headed toward the doorway.

"We'll resume next week," she said and left the room.

As Adela traversed the building to the parking lot, she realized her frustration with herself. How did her nephew tear the bandage off a raw nerve from years ago? The vivid memories of the business decisions she lost with her father came to the surface as she continued down the hallway. She slowed her pace to calm her breath as Spencer sped away in his sports car. She had spent a career growing this site and hadn't let anyone's ignorance get in the way. She was the planner who made community connections and built consensus before moving forward. Her team had done an excellent job, and the discussion wasn't over.

Adela filled her journey back to her office with deeper breaths than a child inflating their pool floaty.

"What's going on?" her assistant asked as Adela dropped her things on the desk.

"It's that obvious?"

"I haven't seen you this flush in some time. A Code 21?"

"Hell yes."

The assistant opened a bottom file drawer, retrieved an envelope, and handed it to her boss. Adela grabbed the envelope and headed outside. The courtyard walkway took her past several sculptures of varying styles and through the garden area, to an avenue of chimes. There she opened the envelope and took out the pack of cigarettes and lighter, putting both to use.

After one long inhale, Adela looked up at the art installation created by a past patient. The series of thin-walled metal tubes hung from crossbeams of a path-shading pergola. The breezes moved the wind-catchers of the acoustic tubes and drove strikers of the airborne xylophone, sending tones from each chime. The music filled the surrounding area with deep melodic percussions.

Adela remembered the first time she experienced the installation. She had enjoyed having the artist lead her through the fifty-yard-long walkway. He described how each group of chimes represented a different chakra, starting with the root of the body and moving up to the head. The supports of the structure consisted of framed panels of mosaic glass. Their colors caught sunlight and were aligned to hues representing each of the body's energy zones. The chime tones sung out like Tibetan copper bowls.

Adela stood alone on the path and took another drag to facilitate her own chakra adjustment while she admired the complexity and simplicity of the musical avenue. She stood at the start of the path and thought back to the meeting and Spencer. She knew he couldn't handle the complexity of his proposal and wouldn't stay focused to start a new branch of the company. She shouldn't have gotten angry and would find a way to make his idea fade like the tones from the surrounding chimes. Adela took one last deep breath of nicotine and then stretched her arms out as she strolled under the pergola. Her fingers caught and released each of the strikers as she progressed through the waves of chimes. The tones washed through her in a cleansing choir as she traversed the installation. Refreshed and ready with a plan to address the chaos of her nephew, she decided to check in with the person who used to push her buttons better than anyone. Adela decided she would test her argument against her toughest sounding board.

"Addie?"

"Dad, how are you?"

"I'm fine. Did we have a call scheduled?"

"No, I just got out of a meeting with your namesake."

"My what? Oh shit. You mean Spencer? What happened?"

"He's messing around with future funding for Desert Recovery and Boarding and wants to pull Asuproz's donations."

"He what? How did this happen?"

"During the meeting about the satellite housing project—"

"Addie, I saw the packet on this. The logic is clear. The first phase of the project has been approved by the foundation. What happened? Never mind. I'll take care of it."

"Dad, I have an idea to address—"

"I've got this. Addie, I owe you. William never should have picked Spencer as president and frankly . . . damn it. Adela, I was wrong about picking William over you years ago. I am sure you have some good ideas for handling Spencer, but frankly this is my mess to clean up and you have the recovery center to run."

"Dad, I can—"

"It's done. It's time for me to pay you back for my past bad decisions."

14

Do Not F This Up

SPENCER RACED away from Desert Recovery. The car music blared in celebration of his victory over Adela. This was the start of his imprint on Asuproz with a change from antiquated ideas to a fresh outlook. He turned up the volume and revved the engine as he merged onto the 10 heading toward Pasadena. Spencer tried to think of whom to call and share his victory. Sybil was volunteering at their children's school and Willow didn't care about the business. His mother would have loved to hear of his success. Without that option, he pressed down on the accelerator and swerved through traffic to get back to the office.

Halfway to his destination, Spencer received a call from the perfect person to hear his news.

"Gramps! I'm glad you called. I have something to tell you."

"Spencer, we need to talk."

"Let me go first. I pivoted. I listened to you. You wanted to hear my next ideas for the company. I pivoted."

"What the hell are you talking about? Please don't say you are referring to that real estate concoction."

"How do you know? The meeting just happened."

"Spencer, what are you trying to do by turning my company into a discount hotel chain or making us become slumlords?"

"I had the finance guy run the numbers. There are going to be new revenues."

"What are you thinking? Now you're making public

corporate statements about future investments of Asuproz before getting shareholder approval?"

"This is going to be—"

"There were city council members in the meeting and other business leaders. Did you think about that? How do you think you can make this into a financially sustainable business? How will you differentiate it from anyone wanting to buy up rental property in the Coachella Valley and underpricing you? Who at the company knows anything about property management and rentals? What has our legal counsel said? You love marketing. What will be the backlash from pulling committed donations away from a major non-profit? Asuproz has given press releases about our five-year commitment to Addie's project."

"Aunt Addie called you?"

"I know everyone who was in that room. Don't you think they all are calling me and your father?"

"I'm the president of this company," Spencer declared.

"Did you think of looping us in? Spencer. This rental thing is dead. Your father and I are not approving it, and I would guess Adela and Steve are a no. You need shareholder approval for moves like this. Has your father taught you nothing?"

"I can put something together."

"You aren't spending any more time on this except to send a clarification to Desert Recovery of Asuproz continuing the planned funding. You may also want to apologize to your aunt. All the rest of your time should be focused on the new client presentation next week, which is our real company future. The one your father and brother created. That needs to be a win. Do not F this up!"

15

Colored Toes

A FEW DAYS AFTER Spencer's attempted decimation of Desert Recovery's expansion, Adela received a call from her father. Robert began with one of his typical status reports.

"Addie, Spencer has far too many other Asuproz priorities to create a real estate branch. I confirmed with him that the corporate donations would continue. Also, Spencer will send a representative to your board meetings, not him."

"Dad, you know I can handle Spencer," Adela said calmly in a tone her father taught to each of his children.

"That's not the point; you shouldn't have to deal with—" Robert raised his voice.

"Dad, that is the point. You need to know I can deal with Spencer and I learned how to deal with you years ago."

"I am well aware of that, Adela." Robert's pace slowed.

"Besides," Adela continued, "I've spent the last few days going back to the entire board, including the Asuproz members, to assure the project stays the course."

"Addie, I've never doubted you, although I can't stop trying to help. You're doing important work, and I have grown to appreciate your impact. This is clearer after working on the helpline. Thank you for bringing this into my life."

"I am glad you like it. You surprised me. It seems a bit out of character."

"I love it. I'm back on the front lines of something. By the way, it wouldn't hurt the image of your place to name the call center after me."

"There he is! He's back. The father I know and love."

"I'm only saying I would be fine with the recognition. Besides, helping on these calls gives me something to do besides watching your brother sneak his girlfriend in and out of this place while he thinks I'm asleep."

"Dad! He's what?"

"You had to have known he was seeing Tiffany again."

"There have been a couple of comments at O'Donnell, mixed in with the regular country club small talk. Are they seeing each other again?"

"Well, she always arrives here after dark, and the cameras show her leaving before sunrise. William has forgotten the gate alerts show on our phone apps, He probably turned off his notifications. Chairmen don't worry about such things."

"Dad! Good for him. His vague schedule makes sense now. I'm glad he is focusing on something besides business."

"Bite your tongue, Addie. I raised you better." And then Robert let out a laugh. "Seriously, I am happy for him too. I want all my children to enjoy life and be successful. It is not as if you don't have your own dalliances."

"Dad."

"You both are having your fun, even if I need to focus on Asuproz. The business isn't going to be an afterthought."

"Dad, everything will be fine. My Steve, Hank, and even Spencer on a good day will keep your baby going. And frankly, getting Willow back on the team would help."

Adela ended the call with her father and pondered the new insights about her brother. She had seen Tiffany and William's romance ebb and flow over the years. The new information made her recount how her relationship with Tiffany had decayed from sisters-in-law to barely acquaintances. She maintained the past social distancing rules for Tiffany that she thought William wanted. Apparently, those restrictions were over, so she contacted Tiffany.

She chose pedicures at the Parker Hotel with Tiffany as a reacquaintance time with some structure. Her text message invite was quickly accepted. They met in the hotel lobby and continued through the common area of large-scale white pottery, shag rugs, and macramé wall hangings for a combination of Midcentury and Woodstock-Chic vibes. They exited the hotel into a courtyard of blooming shrub lined paths to the desert spa named the Yacht Club. Palm Springs devoured irony.

The elite pampering location provided sophisticated treatments, couples massages, and even post-Oscar awards rejuvenation retreats. Adela booked the appointment for a private room. Tiffany and Adela, adorned in plush robes, tapped fluted glasses of champagne as their feet soaked in a lavender bath.

Tiffany kicked off the conversation by expressing her gratitude for the invitation.

"I've received so few invites from William's family. I mean . . . that came off as rude. Let me start again. I'm grateful for today and wondered if you had any advice on how to improve my relationship with Spencer and Willow, and with you."

"I didn't realize you felt isolated. Maybe I did. Let's look forward. I want to get to know you better. As for Willow and Spencer, that is for them to say. Do you speak with them?"

"It's been rocky from the start, since they were kids. I got thrown into their lives and brought Hank into *their* home. I never tried to replace their mother, but William didn't help by being the absent father figure to his children. Let me stop. I'm not here to speak badly of William."

Adela smirked. "The apple didn't fall far from the tree between William and his father."

"How do you mean?"

"Let's just say Robert wasn't always around for us either."

"That makes sense," Tiffany continued. "As for the kids, I was the only adult in their home for most of the day and tried instilling some discipline and support. The children were confused by my role and resented me. William never let them know who I was supposed to be. Frankly, he didn't clarify roles to me, either."

"So, things started out bumpy and got worse?"

"And how. I tried versions ranging from firm parent to the best friend, which was exhausting, and Spencer took offense at any interaction. He treated me like I killed his mom. In the end, I chose avoidance. Robert must have noticed and took his form of action because Leandra started showing up more often to manage the house, and her daughter Lea was a regular sitter. They started taking care of the children's immediate needs while I found reasons to be busy in my room or went out. I was rarely with them except for holidays and birthdays, and William was too busy with business in Pasadena to notice. Hank got stuck not being one of the original kids and not old enough to escape with me. He was in better hands with Leandra and Lea. I think Lea was more a mother to Hank than me during that time."

"All I've ever heard from William was that it didn't work out. What finally happened?"

"We stayed together for some time, but I saw the strain on Hank and the other children. William even announced once how coming home from work felt more like entering a circus instead of *his* castle. Leandra and Lea added more confusion of roles into the mix. The distancing started when I began taking trips away from Palm Springs with Hank. My son and I would have a weekend at Disneyland or go to the Santa Monica beach. The ending happened when William took over leadership of Asuproz and moved into The Dwelling with Spencer and Willow. Robert left the main house to make room for William's family and moved into the casita. Hank and I moved into the small house down the street."

"All William told us is that he was done with the relationship and done with the topic," Adela replied.

"Well, I heard the same. Hank turned seven when William moved us into the separate house. Hank would see his siblings if they passed by our home, and not much more."

Adela agreed there had been a bad start to Tiffany and William's relationship. She wondered who could survive so soon after Matilda's death and William becoming president of Asuproz. Adela couldn't tell if William loved Tiffany then or if he had made a human resources replacement for an empty position at his home. Tiffany had been self-supporting for most of her life and yet she seemed to lack direction or sense of self. Adela decided she had dipped too far into unpleasant memories and shifted to a more upbeat topic and asked how Tiffany met William and what she liked about him.

"He caught my attention right away when I was working at the restaurant in the country club. Him, with his confidence, and the admiration of others in his foursome."

Adela imagined a work outing with either vendors trying to get business or William's employees vying for attention. Tiffany wouldn't have distinguished courteous laughter and attentive listening as a business obligation of his team.

"I worked the day shift and spent a big part of that afternoon serving the group's lunch followed by their post-meal drinks. I made sure to be at his table as much as possible. At the end of their meal, he left a large tip and signed the tab with a note saying, 'Thanks for brightening my afternoon, William.' He must have talked to the manager and returned near the end of my lunch shift a few times during the next week. The relationship path from there to moving in with William and the children happened in a flash."

Adela had never heard this story and nodded for Tiffany to continue.

"During those lunches, we talked a whole lot. I asked all sorts of questions about what he did. I had no idea."

Adela smiled, picturing how her brother would have enjoyed the exchange.

"Next, there were dates followed by dinners to meet his children, and somehow during that time I got pregnant."

Adela marveled at her candor and tried to ask if they planned to have children, but Tiffany's storytelling lacked focus and soon Adela heard how Tiffany came home with Hank from the hospital and moved into William's first Palm Springs home. Tiffany interrupted herself to talk about young Hank breaking an expensive vase and adopting a cat, all woven into other mini dramas. Tiffany wrapped up by saying William decided she should move to a separate home with Hank and the cat.

She turned to Adela and asked, "Did you know your brother is allergic to cats? Apparently, so is Hank. We had to get rid of the cat. Unfortunately, after William got rid of us."

Adela looked down at the new polish on her toes and became resigned to the reality of not understanding the past or current relationship between William and Tiffany. Her skill in reading people didn't work in this case. She decided to invest more in the future relationship with Tiffany and Hank. Hank had some rough edges, and Tiffany had more, but Hank and her son Steve could be good cousins for each other in the same way she got along with her brother.

The spa technicians wrapped up the session and directed the two clients to the exit.

"I enjoyed this," Adela said. "We should set up a lunch."

Tiffany smiled back, "I'd like that."

16

The Chrysalis: Willow Emerges

DURING WILLOW'S CHILDHOOD as Willy, she recalled her Aunt Adela saying, "As the twig is bent, so grows the tree," and then would smile at Willy and say, "but butterflies always appear from change." Willy desired change throughout childhood and finally emerged as Willow. In adulthood, she had become a sleekly dressed woman with strong jewelry and killer sunglasses that protected others from her Medusa stare. Although not made of snakes, her flowing hair caught the attention of everyone in the room.

As a child, still named Willy, the moments to find true self or at least a true form were few. On one occasion, visiting his grandparents' home, he got into a storage closet at the back of the house and found his grandmother's wig boxes. Although she had passed, they remained on a shelf. He took down a glossy black box with raised gold lettering and it felt exciting to hold. Inside the box, on a Styrofoam head form, sat a wig. The ten-year-old carefully pulled on the blond locks, and after a few adjustments, the wig sat just right.

A powerful charge electrified his body as the boyish exterior softened. Willy also found clip-on earrings and a gold necklace. He discovered the shoe boxes next. A pair of high heels wrapped in the original tissue paper made his heart race. He removed his tennis shoes and slipped into the 1950s lizard skin heels. Across the storage room Willy spotted the full-length mirror. Initial attempts to walk while maintaining balance mirrored a newborn giraffe standing for the first time, although confidence and skill grew with each step.

His feet slipped around in the shoes while everything else felt like a fit. With a slow movement and focus on balance, he reached the mirror and saw the combination of full hair, jewelry, and the two-inch heeled shoes. He always remembered the taste of those tears as they streamed down his face upon seeing the reflection. Emotions stretched from the joy of a more feminine face to the disappointment of seeing a boy's body in a baseball shirt and denim shorts. He removed his grandmother's items and returned them to their place with the realization he needed more of the feelings, although unsure what they were.

Few opportunities to be alone in the storage room occurred for several years. The chances for those transformations ended when Robert sold his home to William, and all the clothes belonging to Willy's grandmother were taken away, except the wig and a pair of earrings smuggled out by Willy. Those few experiences helped during puberty, as hormones produced even stronger visible male aspects of his body. Any new costume escapes were limited to wrapping towels and shower curtains around his body while alone in the bathroom.

By Willy's teenage years, trying to be a boy became the actual costume covering his internal feminine being. With each year, the duality got more difficult, and high school brought on alpha-male classmates and few hiding places. Willy didn't feel comfortable in a male form during those years and had no way of creating a female one.

*** *** ***

Willy, like most sixteen-year-olds, had the goal of getting a driver's license and the associated independence. The ability to drive came secondary to having a legal identification. With the ID, he got something other teens didn't want or even know about. Willy immediately went to the post office and registered for package pickup away from home. The world of being almost an adult had its rewards, and Willy did everything possible to have the best sweet sixteen for himself.

Sixteen meant the clarity of no longer feeling like a boy, even if the male form stared back in the mirror. He needed a new name and got inspiration from the movie *Willow*. Although a male character, Willow was a sorcerer, and the sense of magic fit the feeling of transition. With an account at the post office, he ordered a dress and the potential to change the image in the mirror. After years of scanning magazines and Sunday newspaper ads, Willy or Willow found a women's clothing catalog selling all sorts of appealing options and even offered unmarked packaging for gifts. Therefore, everything got sent together, creating a single interaction between a minor and a federal employee. The newly minted sixteen-year-old had the ability to pick up a package from the post office without needing a parent.

Willow placed the order, and after a few days, he went to pick up the transformative items. The first visit occurred right before closing time and consisted of a long customer line. Willow used the time to practice the interaction. If anyone nearby paid attention, they'd have seen Willow's lips moving while rehearsing. Each step closer to the window increased the anxiety. She imagined handing over the ID and the worker disappearing behind a wall. Next, the alarms would be screeching while security guards appeared with the opened package and all its feminine contents. The counter worker would be calling Willow's father, as the postal manager cut the driver's license into pieces. With only two people in front of him, Willy ran from the post office.

The second attempt happened the next day, right after school, and no one stood in line. Willow marched right up to the service window with the driver's license in hand and pushed the plastic card across the counter.

"I am checking for a package."

The worker grabbed the card and disappeared, only to return with news that no packages had arrived.

During the third try, Willow found a line of four people and an elderly man at the open window. The individual couldn't understand how to ship a package, confused by the need to check the weight. The options of different delivery rates and possible insurance coverage baffled the customer. The postal worker listened to proselytization on the failing postal system's need to ask for insurance on packages they were responsible for delivering. The others in line exchanged frustrated glances as the volume of the old man's voice revealed he'd probably left his hearing aids at home.

The ever-so-slow process continued with each person having special requests until the woman in front of Willow stepped up and requested a single stamp while putting her exact change on the counter. The postal worker's smile let out a crisp thank you as the customer left. The quick turnover left Willow fumbling with the license. The well-rehearsed script faded from memory as the ID fell to the counter with a blundered request of, "Package?" The worker went behind the wall and returned with a brown paper package and an accompanying approval form. Willow signed the paper, accepting the package and the gateway to her future. The first signature made with a W, on an official document, not containing the name Willy or William truly made the day feel like her new birthday.

Willow returned the license to its wallet and went to the car. The package in the passenger seat created a moment like being a child spotting the biggest Christmas present under the tree containing their name. The plan succeeded in acquiring a dress: set up a pre-pay debit card, get a driver's license, set up an account at the post office, place the order for a birthday gift, and pick up the package. All the steps completed. Where to open the package and try on the items was not part of the plan.

She started the car and drove through town, past the turnoff for home and continued beyond the welcome signs to Palm Springs. The journey progressed to the highway with a goal to get away from everyone. She drove for thirty minutes before exiting at the town of Cabezon. Willow had gone there in the past with a group of high school rejects to get stoned at an abandoned warehouse. She followed the dirt road around the back of the structure and parked near a dumpster. Willow panned the vacant surroundings while reaching for the package. The sun started to set behind the mountains and the entire energy changed around her as the heat of the day dissipated and her eyes adjusted to the twilight.

She couldn't wait any longer and tore into the packaging, removing the cover and interior wrapping, exposing the dress. The next moments were a blur as Willow hopped out of the car, pulling off shoes and clothes to put on the dress and heels. Bracelets slid onto wrists and she completed the crowning blond wig of grandmother. The most important thing didn't get considered for the plan, a mirror. As the sun continued to set and the shimmers of light over the top of the mountain faded, Willy, no, Willow stood alongside the car viewing her image in the side view mirror. She stood back to get her entire self into the frame. The distortion of the mirror, along with the twilight of created the perfect filtering of the new image, the new body, the emerging Willow.

She looked into the mirror and sang happy birthday to the person looking back in the reflection. Her entire essence filled her body to the point of pushing out tears and this time she knew they were of happiness. When the song ended, she threw all the packaging into the dumpster. The clothes were carefully placed into her school backpack, while class books went on the car floor. Willow drove home and hid the new treasures in the back of her closet. She rarely wore them, but knowing they were there was enough on most days.

🌴 🌴 🌴

Senior year of high school didn't arrive soon enough. Willow's long hair flowed even further down her back. Everything else externally presented as Willy, while internally the sense of being Willow grew more complete. The dresses and accessories remained in the back of the bedroom closet, under a stack of sweatshirts, inside a package for an old video game. The viewings occurred during rare 2 a.m. closet mirror fashion shows. As thin as Willow tried to stay, larger dresses were eventually needed, and a particularly elegant one arrived right before the weekend of her eighteenth birthday. The excitement of the new dress and of becoming an adult drove the need to have a weekend alone.

The family planned a Los Angeles trip to the annual auto show and rented a beachside house for accommodations. The sunny forecast built everyone's anticipation for a getaway weekend. Spencer was especially keen to attend the auto show and pick out his next set of wheels. Adela even invited ten-year-old Hank. Everyone planned to go.

Willow pushed back, claiming the privilege of adulthood as the reason for staying home. William Sr. liked this sign of manhood coming from his namesake. He eagerly agreed to his son's request, saying, "And don't have any girls over," then whispered with a wink, "without using protection." Willow gave a double thumbs up, creating the dude persona he thought his father wanted.

Departure day arrived and everyone met at The Dwelling for breakfast before driving to LA. Willow fidgeted and paced the entire time until the travelers grabbed their bags and went to their respective cars, each waving goodbye as they drove away. With the cars out of sight, Willow spun like a cartoon princess in an animated musical. The plan worked and Leandra scheduled vacation, but not before she spent the morning cleaning. She finally grabbed her bag and headed toward the door. While escorting Leandra to her car, Willow detected a feeling of suspicion, confirmed by Leandra's departing words.

"Be sure to clean up after your party. I want spotlessness before I come back. Happy birthday."

She gave a hug and a swat before driving off.

The backyard felt warm for a January afternoon as Willow

entered the patio carrying the previously hidden box of women's clothes and an appropriated bottle of champagne left over from the family's New Year's Eve party. Patio speakers blasted "You Are Beautiful" by Christina Aguilera as the champagne cork popped into the swimming pool. No one would be home until Monday, so the entire property was Willow's domain. There would be plenty of time to recover corks and any other evidence from the weekend.

Willow upped the energy by stacking extra logs on the burning fire. This was her day, listening to Christina belt out the anthem of *different* people. The song played on a loop as night skies darkened and the crackling blaze sent embers floating up to join the stars. Willow set down the emptied champagne glass and opened the box from her closet. She cast aside her clothes. All the feelings of being complete returned as she pulled the dress up and tucked the remaining signs of masculinity between her legs before letting the dress flow down to the new pair of stilettos. Discarded socks filled the bodice. Her true form glowed in the light of the fire.

More champagne tickled Willow's nose as she looked at her face in the mirrored surface of the tray holding the bottle and fluted glass. She used the tray mirror reflection to apply makeup. Lipstick went on slowly with attention to keep the dark crimson tone within its place. She picked up her t-shirt and blotted her lips like she had seen Tiffany do with tissues. The clumsy trial of brushing on mascara took longer than expected but eventually the lashes became long and defined.

Willow looked into the tray mirror. The makeup helped. The lipstick and mascara were the only two items on hand. Then Willow recalled Tiffany's personal commentary she used to give while applying her own makeup. She would turn to Willy and lecture on how, when a lady is caught without the right makeup, she could pinch her cheeks to bring in color or use a bit of lipstick to rouse them. Willow tried this technique with uncertainty about where and how much to apply, leaving bright red circles under each eye.

The third glass of champagne felt mature and brought excitement seeing the lipstick marks on the rim of the glass. Willow poured another and started to dance with the bottle and glass in hand like she was a character in a music video.

She sang out the lyrics about being beautiful and ignoring what others say and then spun around with a flourish and spraying of champagne across her dress. She stopped in a bit of panic, put the bottle and glass down, and then carefully removed the dress. The lyrics continued blasting through the backyard and the fire roared in response, reinforcing that no one could bring her down because of who she was.

Willow looked at the spill on her dress. It would need a soak, but the weekend still belonged to her as she sang louder—until the music abruptly stopped.

"What the heck is this?"

Spencer shouted from the patio doors. Willow stood caught in a combination of her past and future spirits, the clumsy naked younger brother with a face full of lipstick and a blond wig, standing in high heels while holding a champagne-stained dress. Spencer reached Willow.

"It's bad enough I had to cancel my trip to not spend time with Hank! What exactly is going on here?" Spencer pulled the dress from his brother, standing completely naked, moving his hands to cover his crotch and chest.

"I figured I should check on you but didn't expect to find this. I don't even know what *this* is." Spencer started to feel the champagne soaking through the dress to his hand.

"For effin sake, what's on this? It's all wet!" he said, as he threw the dress into the fire. Naked and shattered, Willow ran into the house. Spencer's shouting reverberated off her back until she reached her bedroom and locked the door. She went to the bathroom and scrubbed every remaining bit of femininity from her face and threw the stained hand cloth across the room. She checked the lock on her bedroom door before burying herself in bed, clinging to herself while the lyrics of "You Are Beautiful" faded from her thoughts.

As the sun rose the next morning, Willow peeked from her bedroom and didn't see any sign of Spencer. The patio door sat open. The champagne bottle and broken glass lay on the pool deck with the lipstick and mascara. The wig floated in the pool and the dress remains were a mix of cooled ashes and parts of a melted zipper.

Willow picked up the t-shirt from the chaise and rubbed her fingers across the smudge of lipstick. She gathered the shirt, wig, shoes, and the other treasures into a bag and drove to the closest gas station where she threw them in the outdoor trash bin. Spencer never discussed the occurrence with the rest of the family. But he held the secret over his sibling for years until the wings of the butterfly finally completely emerged, removing any power Spencer thought he had.

The evolution from Willy to Willow took years, borne out of a determination to define self along with access to specialized surgeons and psychologists. The fear of getting caught had long vanished, as had the male body-image discomfort. She had no role models and no clarity between wearing drag and being transgender. Laverne Cox and Chaz Bono were years from becoming public figures during Willow's early struggles. The determination came from moments in front of the bathroom mirror searching for the real self. With no choice for Willow to be anyone but herself, she created the body to match her soul. She directed her own path and became her own mentor, one step at a time.

17

His 'Just Desserts'

ADELA AND WILLIAM FINISHED OFF their shrimp cocktail and gin gimlets at a corner table of Melvin's, continuing the second-generation sibling birthday tradition ongoing for most of their adult lives. Otto sent his regrets from his home in LA after reports of terrible highway traffic. The attending revelers started their entrées with a check-in on the well-being of each other's children and a status report of their businesses. Adela chose to keep her personal struggles with Spencer to herself during her brother's birthday celebration. As the meal progressed, William jumped to the next topic with a lack of decorum fitting of a younger brother.

"Any news on your woman cancer test thing?"

"The woman cancer test thing? William, sometimes I wonder how you run a company. Can you retain any details outside the circle of your concern?"

"You are in my circle of concern. I apologize for not remembering the name of the test."

"The BRCA test for breast cancer? And it's not exclusively *a woman thing.*"

"But you are doing the testing because of Aunt Emma?"

"Yes, I am doing a comprehensive genetics review because of our aunt. She tested positive when they found her cancer. If mine comes up positive, you should be tested too."

"So, no results yet?" William asked.

"No. And while we are speaking of things in our circles of concern, what is the status with you two, you and Tiffany?"

"Ah, the Tiffany question. I was wondering when that topic would show up."

"It's just that—"

"It's just that you and Tiffany are becoming better acquainted and you are realizing how lovely she is and you know how lovely your brother can be, at times."

"Yes! A person as lovely as my brother, *at times*. Is there something going on with you two?" Adela laughed as she picked up her Malbec, took a sip, and relaxed back into her chair while cradling the glass between her hands. She let the question linger in the silence between them as the aroma of fermented dark berries greeted her nose. A jazz quartet played as the singer crooned "Strangers in the Night," trying to recreate a 1950s ambiance. William continued to cut his steak and took a bite, followed by a pause.

"She's cake all day," William answered.

Adela made a familiar shrug, her response to her brother whenever the clarity of his assertions wasn't completely clear as they traveled from his brain out of his mouth. She took another sip of wine and let their silence continue. William cut another piece of steak and set the piece on his plate.

"Remember when we were kids," William continued, "and we couldn't wait for our birthdays to pick the flavor of cake? Mom would be so excited to make the cake of our choice, and we could have as big a piece as we liked?"

Adela nodded but didn't show any sign of understanding.

"Tiffany is like that to me. She is like having cake all day. I loved getting chocolate cake for my birthdays and eating such a large piece with ice cream that I felt sick afterward."

"So, she is cake?"

"It's not that she is cake. It's that she's too much of a good thing. She is always there for me and supportive. She is great at . . . we enjoy each other. She thinks I'm amazing."

"Sounds terrible." Adela returned her glass to the table.

"Here's the thing. Tiffany is the mother of my son and that's a wonderful gift. She has so much love for me and for Hank, but she doesn't know who she is. I'm worried this may be part of Hank's issue as well. When she and I were first together, I got too caught up in how much she thought of me and missed how she didn't think much of herself."

"So why do you see her now?"

"I still like cake! Just not cake all day." William's face filled with a childish smirk; the type of face made to a sibling after saying "Mom likes me best." Adela kicked him under the table and sat up in her chair. William responded by picking up the piece of steak and popping it in his mouth.

"She's too good for you, even if she's searching for herself," Adela said in defense of her friend. "I hope you're not giving her mixed messages or confused expectations. I enjoy our time together and I don't know why I didn't appreciate her sooner."

William continued with his meal and listened to the song lyrics coming from the singer about yearning for love.

"She *is* too good for me, as *lovely* as I am. I think we both can agree on that. I wish she could be better to herself. She is nothing like Matilda. Matilda wasn't cake but instead the entrée, vegetables, a starch, and a beautiful mother to our children. She was not dessert."

Adela listened to her brother and for the first time thought about the difference between Matilda and Tiffany, complete opposites in several ways. Matilda embodied the definition of matriarch, a strong mother to their children while bringing out a softer side of William. She also brought her business savvy and family connections, which accelerated Asuproz's success. Adela continued to listen to her brother.

"We met when I was a nothing and Asuproz faced financial

95

challenges. She had everything and was such a gem. Matilda's family being one of *the* families of LA. Matilda . . . Matti and I were a great fit. Matti and Billy."

"Oh my gosh, Matti and Billy. I forgot the *Billy* years. That's from a different era. You were a different person."

"It was. Was I different?"

"You certainly were."

"I guess so. Matti and Billy. We knew how to be there for each other. She was the stronger of the two of us in so many ways, and we were such a good fit."

🌴🌴🌴

In the second half of his twenties and still single, William accompanied Robert to a Golden Globes after party. Over the years, Robert learned the impossibility of making business connections during award shows, while after-parties allowed everyone to relax and mix. Robert used a few business favors to get into one of the bigger parties. Asuproz was no longer the new fun technology in the television industry, and they did even less in movies. Times were lean, so they got relegated to a back corner of the party while many of the actors mingled with producers and directors in the VIP areas.

Robert used the event to gain new contacts and thought William could be the younger face of the company. He sent his son off with the mission to meet the young people in the room to talk business without directly talking business. The two of them parted ways in the hunt to establish new opportunities for their company.

William tugged at the pinching shirt collar and readjusted his cummerbund before facing the crowd. He scanned the room several times before seeing her, possibly a new star of television, or maybe from a movie he hadn't seen. William stayed current on industry news but there were always a few unknowns. The entire room buzzed about someone named Pia Zadora, who won an award that evening for best acting in a movie even though no one knew her. The lovely woman in his gaze could be another unknown star.

She carried herself with confidence and, unlike many of the industry people, showed indifference to the multitude of celebrities. She met his glance and smiled, occasionally looking up as William wove through the crowd of tuxedos and evening gowns. With one final polite push through a group holding awards, he found himself right in front of her.

"Hello, you know how to navigate a room."

"Hello to you," William motioned to the group of globe holders. "Did you win tonight?"

"I . . . no, I . . . hello, my name is Matilda, Matti."

"I'm Billy!" William responded, although he was unable to recall the last time he had been called Billy. "It's William, but please call me Billy."

"Billy, it's a pleasure to meet you."

Matilda's smile washed away any nerves William was experiencing and melted his forced public face. She politely revealed being her father's date. He was in publishing. She then shook her head and corrected herself to use her father's new moniker of *media and entertainment*. William caught a blush when he revealed he thought she was a movie star. She pulled William to the empty seats at her table and showed a bottle of Dom Pérignon, tucked away with a champagne bucket.

"I hate having to wait at the bar."

They both laughed and continued their introductions. He learned she finished her finance degree at Stanford and spent summers in her father's business. They were kindred spirits working for and with relatives in family businesses. While everyone else at the after party celebrated their victories or searched out new ventures, Matti and Billy were locked in each other's attention. The evening turned into a taxi ride back to

William's home in Santa Monica. The next few weeks together flew by with each day presenting new aspects of Matti that set her apart from other women. Her confidence outpaced any of his past dates and she didn't take any nonsense from him. She understood working hard and the pressures of a demanding family. Besides her professionalism, she made him laugh. She made him feel young by introducing all the things he missed during his twenties because of his career. She quit her family job and married William within the year, followed by the birth of Robert Spencer a year later.

🌴 🌴 🌴

William reflected on the Billy years and smiled, realizing how much Matilda had changed his life. He looked up to his sister and continued his thought.

"We had the movie love story and she got along with everyone and admired you, Addie. Yes, really admired you."

Adela looked across at her brother and searched for the right words. "She certainly brought out the best in you."

"I would have done anything for her. She was given such a weak body. I couldn't help. The doctors couldn't . . . "

Adela wondered how much her brother's perspective differed from hers. She didn't recall a weak body as much as a troubled spirit. The entire family was devastated by her miscarriage and subsequent death. Did the sadness cause William to block out Matilda's drinking, or did his position of never speaking ill of Matilda to his children overpower his own memories? He had to recall Robert almost demanding the family move to the desert to get Matilda away from her drinking buddy neighbor, Phyllis. He couldn't have believed building the technology center so far away from LA was only due to the cost of land.

The move to the desert and Robert supplying household support from Leandra was a last hope to keep Matilda healthy in her final trimester. William was right; he couldn't help her and neither could the doctors at that point, but William may not have had a clear memory about the reasons. In the end, Adela had reaffirmed her perception of how much her brother liked the shiny facade in his relationships, often missing the rest. She understood Matilda filled his need at the time for what he called meat and potatoes. She had a strong personality, an understanding of business, and connections to the industry. Adela realized back then that William liked to devour the entrée, but now he mostly liked *dessert*.

"I'm not sure if I'm the person to help Tiffany find her way or at least get out of her own way," William said as Adela took her last sip of wine. "Maybe you can do that for her in a way I never could. You can show her how to find what she wants out of life."

Adela realized her friend and her brother were two halves that were never going to make a whole, but she still cared for them both. Wasn't Matilda one of the reasons she got so involved in the recovery center? She didn't know how to help Matilda back then, but the relationship spurred Adela to help others. She wondered if any of her support for Matilda back then helped, or only pacified her own conscience. The family thought they were doing what they could by moving out to the desert as a way to help Matilda and her baby. Adela thought about her brother's request to help Tiffany, a woman he called cake, and she decided she needed time to differentiate helping from meddling.

The singer ended the set and the quartet left the stage as the room filled with polite applause.

The Tiffany topic ended. Adela understood the relationship between her brother and his current girlfriend as much as she could and possibly more than her brother did. The waiter returned to the table with dessert menus. Adela looked at the offerings and laughed as she ordered a piece of cake for her brother and asked them to add a birthday candle to celebrate.

99

18

Tech Review

THE CUSTOMIZED VAN made its way down the interstate from Palm Springs toward Pasadena through the cooling November air. Robert rarely went into Asuproz's headquarters but made his second visit that year based on mounting frustration with Spencer and concern about the new-client meeting. William failed to talk his father out of making the trip, so he and Adela's son, Steve, sat up front as Robert sat in back, perched in his retrofitted power wheelchair. Robert's appearance in a navy-blue suit resembled Charles Xavier, the Professor X, from the X-Men movies. He didn't have Patrick Stewart's shining bald head, but he could pull off a steely cold stare. Robert didn't like being strapped in but relished the chauffeuring aspect of the ride which left him to reminisce about the start of his business and the various evolutions.

Robert's movie acting career in the 1950s consisted of bit actor parts, so he spent his free time on the studio sets trying to get pulled in front of the camera for any last-minute needs. He also used the time to understand the workings of the studios. He gained insights into the expenses incurred due to rework, such as off-camera noise interruptions or instances when actors failed to achieve the desired emotional tone. The Hollywood industry prioritized the rapid production of movies. Crew and studio time were the commodities most in demand.

The prerequisites for the lead actors typically meant glamorous looks and an American sounding voice, even if they couldn't master their vocal expression. Robert observed frustrated directors needing numerous retakes of scenes, trying to coax an emotion from the actor's voice, only to end a day's work with an exasperated, "That will have to do." Robert enjoyed learning the studio's needs and then investigating solutions in science and technology magazines. From it all he created a voice-modulating electronic solution. The new equipment allowed directors to focus on the visuals, then end filming with a, "We'll get that in post-production." Robert calculated the difference between studio time versus a small room with the director and a couple of technicians modulating a voice recording to get the desired results. He turned post-production editing into a profitable business for Asuproz.

Robert supplied cost savings to the movie industry and used his access to studios to gain clients. Studios kept these enhancers a secret, worried about negative publicity. The combination of cost savings and Oscar wins drove Asuproz's success. Robert got invited to the awards ceremony by one of his studio clients. He sat near the back and listened as the starlet spoke of her gratitude to the director who helped pull the character out of her. The director and Robert both wished the modulator was connected to the podium microphone so her voice reflected the emotion she wanted to convey. Robert's life had gone beyond anything he could imagine; the failed actor had no regrets in his new life.

"Everything okay back there, Dad?" William broke his father's daydreaming. "Steve asked you about how you ever decided to come out to LA from the East Coast. I told him because you are always networking. Right?"

"Waiting tables at the Rainbow Room in Rockefeller Center was the difference. That's where I got to first meet a movie director dining with two other big names, all of them caught up in an animated discussion about some future Broadway show. The director pulled me aside and asked if I was interested in being on the stage. Thanks to that moment, I got to try acting. Then he convinced me to follow him to California to be in movie musicals."

"That's right. My dad. The movie actor," William replied.

"The timing was bad. I got to Hollywood on the tail end of a rush of actors arriving from New York. Background dancing was never going to be my strength, but had I gotten to California a bit earlier, I could've been a Hollywood star."

"And that's when you learned the importance of shifting or pivoting?" William probed.

"I realized that when I first moved to New York. Always watch for—"

"—what's next?" William and Steve both completed Robert's mantra.

"Exactly. Always watch for what's next and keep good connections. Remember that. Acting wasn't for me, but it got me to California, and time in New York libraries is where I first read about voice synthesizing. As for connections, that famous director helped with the initial funding. Although, I think he mostly wanted a way to make his job easier."

"You started in your twenties? I am falling behind you," Steve chimed in as a compliment to his grandfather.

"That's right. There were expectations back then to have a career, a marriage, and children. Those drove me to expand into television and create a higher quality of laugh tracks to grow the business and feed my three children. And William was a big eater!"

"Dad! Let's get back to your TV acting career," William said.

"What are you talking about now?"

"*The Monkees.* Didn't you make a cameo on the TV show *The Monkees*? Steve, did you know your grandfather got asked to do cameos, or he asked for roles in the TV shows where they used our laugh tracks. Dad? Did they really ask you or did you ask them so you could keep your SAG card?"

"I liked being around the action. That's where the new ideas came from. I wasn't likely to get an Emmy Award for being an extra but the company garnered a couple for technical contributions."

William continued sharing Robert's success story with Steve, even though they both knew it by heart.

"Some of the musicians at the television studios requested modifications to the new electrical instruments. Your grandfather, the acting extra, got talking to the musical director on *The Monkees* and brought in adapters for the electric keyboards and we were into music synthesizers."

"You were a teenager. How do you remember all this."

William laughed, "It was rock music! And besides, Addie and Otto were interning and talked about it every night."

"Asuproz tried other markets like the emerging text-to-voice stuff, but other companies beat," Robert grumbled. "We couldn't go up against their size so we differentiated ourselves by providing in-person service and making modifications quickly. We watched for what was next!"

"You needed to pivot! What happened?" Steve fed his grandfather the hook, knowing they had about an hour more of driving and the backseat stories would fill the time.

"Shifting to the music industry carried the company for years. We went from synthesizing instruments to using a similar technology to modulate pop music singers' voices. A good reminder to you both to anticipate the new trends."

"Got it!" Steve smiled into the rearview mirror.

"Steve, your mom is more like me. She liked watching for trends but she didn't like dealing with all the BS of Hollywood and the music industry. She was like you and found her niche in negotiating contracts."

"I guess that's where I get it from. And how did you get all your grandkids to work for you?"

"I'm happy the business gave you all jobs," Robert puffed his chest. "I was thrilled when Spencer, Willow, and Hank followed their father into working at Asuproz. Hank and his love of problem solving helped him in the tech area and Willow with numbers. Are you enjoying yourself working on contracts?"

"Don't forget my chauffeuring skills," replied Steve. "I enjoy taking over for Mom. I even go to her for pointers when things get complex like today's contract, which we should focus on as we're getting closer to the office. We have Hank and his team to thank for dissecting frequencies of a voice track to change the accent from a British/Indian dialect to a midwestern American while also editing sentence structure in near real time. It's our big selling point."

"One of you run this by me again. I want to make sure I am completely prepared." Robert said.

"Steve, I'll take this. You focus on driving. Dad, this credit card company has call centers in India and the Philippines," William started the overview. "The company can't hire and train workers fast enough. The strong local dialects are one of the biggest barriers. Hank's solution modifies the Indian or Filipino tone to an Americanized voice while simultaneously analyzing the worker's response and adding or removing typical words differing between an Indian and American sentence structure."

William reviewed the examples Hank would use during the meeting.

"Definite articles like *the* are added into the conversation and the British pronunciation of words like al-u-min-ee-um morph into al-u-min-um. Some filler phrases get added to the response during the software analysis to fill pauses and make the experience feel like a gap free conversation. If the phone bank person were to say, 'She received an al-u-min-ee-um knee replacement at hospital,' the output would start with filler words and then convey changes. 'Thank you for your time' gets added to the start of the response while the computer modifies the response with, 'She received an *aluminum* knee replacement at *the* hospital.'"

"And in a tone like the call was from Iowa," Steve said.

"The current version catches about 70 percent of the common differences between the two dialects," William continued. "This equates to improvement seen after six months of training new hires. Our tech center ran trials and even set up testing in India and the Philippines."

William summarized the key deliverables of the client meeting and the expectation of Robert to represent the decades of knowledge. Steve jumped in to describe the signs he would be looking for from the clients before he could finalize the details of the offer. The discussion ended as they pulled into the parking lot.

Although William had turned corporate leadership over to his son, he managed this account and brought in all the key leadership for this meeting. They gathered in the most prestigious presentation room. The technical leadership was ready. Every aspect of the customer's visit received the white-glove treatment, except an absent president. No Spencer. A receptionist slid William a note stating he got stuck in traffic and to start without him. This triggered William's broad smile as he invited everyone to take their seats while he extended his gratitude for their time. He then turned the discussion over to the technical director and Hank, who worked as a perfect duo in navigating the presentation slides and prototype. Finally, Hank began the demonstration. With the assistance of his engineer, noticeably of Indian lineage, they took their places at the phones. Everyone around the table leaned in as Hank showed how a person representing a call center worker would respond and how the output would come from the speaker in the center of the table reflecting what a caller would hear.

The president of the credit card company started the mock phone call saying he wanted to question a charge on his credit card. The engineer answered from the script in a strong Indian accent and phrasing. With only a short delay, the voice coming out of the speaker gave a response. The conversation went back and forth for about a minute when the executive stopped the script and started laughing, "Well I'll be, if I didn't think I was talking to someone from our Chicago office."

Steve and William remained stoic, conveying the confident expression that yet another Asuproz solution performed as expected. Based on the reaction from the customers around the table, the demo was a success. Steve took some notes on his laptop. Hank started discussing steps for implementation when Spencer came through the meeting room door. The room turned as he maneuvered himself to the remaining seat next to his grandfather. He waved one hand as he sat down and asked everyone to please continue and to not stop on account of him. Spencer leaned to ask his grandfather how the meeting was going and got no response from Robert.

Hank wrapped up the demo and Steve scheduled a meeting to sign the final contract. Everyone left in good spirits and Hank returned to Palm Springs to notify the technical team of their success. Robert got back into the van, feeling the same way he did years ago at the Oscars, able to see the success of the next iteration of the company he started. Steve once again took the driver's spot. He turned the drive time into a dissertation of his takeaways from the meeting and started to verbalize a proposal for the final contract. Robert caught William's eye as he looked to Steve and nodded. X-men telepathy superpowers of Professor Charles Xavier weren't needed for Robert's thoughts to enter William's mind. William caught his father's pride in Steve and Hank's contributions and decided not to think about Robert's opinion of Spencer.

19

"One Moment, I'll Connect"

HANK TOSSED IN BED, feeling a mix of excitement from the successful client meeting and stress from mentally listing the next steps needed to meet the final performance specification. It all sparked a fury of personal demands he had for the coming weeks. The pressure grew. He looked at his phone and placed a call. Available twenty-four hours a day, every day of the year, the receptionist on the Desert Recovery helpline made connections between callers seeking support and a welcoming ear.

"One moment, I'll connect."

Hank's thank-you came too late; the receptionist's voice had already been replaced by canned music. The familiar soft classical melody wafted out the phone speaker. Hank spoke with his regular counselors during in-person meetings but valued the off-hours calls and enjoyed having some anonymity. The music continued in its mix of hopeful and solemn melodies until he heard the transfer click.

"Hank, is that you?" asked the voice, replacing the music.

"Yes, I hope I didn't wake you." Hank felt relieved he got connected to one of his regular helpline volunteers.

"Not a problem at all, we've talked about this before. I keep odd hours and the helpline doesn't ring unless we mark ourselves as available. Why did you call?"

"I didn't realize the hour, we can talk tomor—"

"Hank. It's fine. I'm awake. What's on your mind?"

Hank no longer thought his topic important enough to call at such a late hour, and trying to say the topic out loud felt all the more trivial.

"Thanksgiving is next week."

The pause was endless until the voice broke the silence.

"Hank, I appreciate the declaration of holidays. Should I be taking the turkey out of the freezer?" The response was slow and metered. Anyone else could say the same thing and push all Hank's buttons. The trust and comfort had grown with time. The voice continued, "And what is coming up for you this Thanksgiving?"

"The same as always, a big family gathering. Everyone will be there. Four generations of judgment over a long holiday weekend, and don't even think about being late. It's the start of the flood of events: Thanksgiving, the annual board meeting, followed by Christmas, New Year's Eve, and the cycle starting over again in the new year. On top of everything, family time started early this year because we are in the middle of landing a new customer, so it's all hands on deck for the family."

"Sounds overwhelming when said all together. Don't let it be. How do we eat an elephant?"

"Great. Are there elephants in the room I am supposed to worry about as well?"

"Hank, you know what I mean. You called about Thanksgiving. Why are you're thinking about Thanksgiving."

"The dinner will be at the family compound here in Palm Springs. There will be the regular sniping and a few vying for power in all ways. With my brother's new role as president, there's his constant attempt to assert authority, even at Thanksgiving dinner. It's exhausting."

"You've said your brother started running the business. What do you think about the changes?"

"Oh, I don't know. My brother is the president. My father is still an adviser and ultimately running the company. I don't think he'll ever quit. He'll hang on as long as my grandpa did or longer. Even during family gatherings, my brother finds a way to discuss his title as president. I honestly don't know what he does, which is frustrating because I want to keep working on the technical side to avoid interactions with him and family politics. I am not sure I can describe it. You wouldn't understand."

The voice allowed for another pause. "You started by talking about Thanksgiving, and yet we are talking about office politics. Is everyone in the family the same?" asked the voice.

"Not everyone. At least not to me."

"Let's get back to eating that elephant. So, are there people you want to see? You called about Thanksgiving and not about every holiday and business meeting between now and your retirement. What is your plan for Thanksgiving?"

"My grandfather and father host at their house. The place used to be owned by a movie star."

"Do you like the home?"

"Oh, it's swank. Think old Hollywood in the best possible way. The Dwelling is one of the biggest properties in old Palm Springs. There are four or five structures and the main house, all surrounding the pool area and the fire pit. I'm sure the landscapers and pool people are going to be there first thing this morning to get everything ready for the holiday."

"Your grandfather must have done well for himself to own such a big home and to have a staff."

"I *think* he owns the place. Like everything else, there are complexities and there is some legal thing about my dad being the owner. I don't know. Yeah, my dad and grandpa, his dad, built their business from nothing."

"That's great to hear. But we were talking about Thanksgiving. Hank, it's your dime. We can talk about whichever you want or both, but let's go with one at a time. You said 'everyone' will be there for Thanksgiving. Who is everyone?"

"Well, let's start at the top: Grandpa, his three kids. My dad, who also lives there. My Aunt Adela, with her son and his family. And their brother, Otto."

"Will his family be there?"

"He's single and doesn't have any other family. I remember hearing word of him having a child somewhere, but no recent discussion. It's a forbidden topic, like so many things."

"You're saying you have another cousin?"

"Only Steve. I guess. I don't know. A while back I heard talk of Otto and a child. With all the other family dynamics to deal with, and so many of us working together, not asking questions about whispers means one less thing to spark an argument."

"Let's get back to Thanksgiving," the voice coached through the phone.

"So, it's my grandpa, my dad, Adela and her family, Otto . . . that's eight. My sister, Willow, will be there."

"Is she bringing anyone?"

"Who, Willow? I don't think so. Not right now. And it's Willow, so there are her complications as well."

"Okay. Are you bringing anyone?"

Silence.

"Are you seeing anyone?"

"I shouldn't see anyone. You know. First year sobriety."

"Shouldn't? But are you? Is there anyone you would bring or want to bring to Thanksgiving?"

Hank laughed. "I'm not sure I want to go, so why would I bring someone else?"

"Is there someone?"

"There might be someone. I met her in treatment. We get along well, but everyone says to wait on dating."

"Okay, okay. I am not pushing you to go against your program. Who else will be there?"

"That's everyone. My siblings. So, Willow, me, and Spencer and his family. That's Spencer, Sybil, and their kids. That's fourteen. That's everyone. Every casita will be full and most of the rooms in the main house. My grandpa's tradition is for us all to stay on property for the weekend."

"What about your mother? We've talked about her and the rest of your family before."

"I think my dad invites her because she says he does. Spencer treats her so badly. She can't handle disrespectful prodding at meals and wouldn't last the entire weekend like the rest of us She ended up running out mid-meal during her last visit. I get infuriated when Spencer needles her at every chance he gets."

"What does he say?"

"He finds indirect ways to say she's only my mother and not a part of the family. She's my mother and belongs there as much as I do. I swear, I don't know why I go most times. I probably should just—"

"You brought up a lot of family members. Do you want to see any of them? What about your grandfather? Do you both get along?"

"He is so smart. He started an entire company. Everyone knows him in town. I don't often see him, and he's rather stern and stays to himself."

"He sounds like a good man. Maybe you should try talking to him more. And as a reminder, you are attending Thanksgiving. You're going to dinner, not to war. Who else do you look forward to seeing?"

"Well, I do enjoy getting to—hold on. One second." Knocking continued at Hank's apartment door. "Hey, I gotta go. There is someone here. Thanks." Hank ended the call as the knocking at the door got louder.

20

Cans

"HANK! OPENNNNNN THIS DOOR!" came a too familiar voice as the knocking turned to rhythmic drumming.

Hank jumped from his bed and rushed to stop the late-night rattling. As he opened the door, a combination of body odor and rancid food announced the uninvited caller.

"Do you believe what people throw out? Well, do you? Didn't you say you needed a coffee maker? Your lights were on. What are you doing up? Look, the pot isn't even cracked. This looks brand new. Let's plug in this beast."

"Do we need to do this now?"

"Time, dear friend, time brings round opportunity; opportunity is the martingale of man. The more we have ventured, the more we gain when we know how to wait. Except not for coffee makers, at least not tonight."

"So, quoting another book is your version of yes?"

"It's Dumas." Reese pushed through and continued into the kitchen, searching for the nearest outlet. Hank closed the apartment door and followed to watch his guest shove countertop items to the side and plug in the new find. Reese's maneuvering continued; a faucet turned on, the coffee pot filled, and then its contents poured into the appliance reservoir. Within seconds, hot water began filling the pot. He raised his hands like he had stuck a perfect landing from a pommel horse.

"It's a ten! Nothing broken here. It works and jeez. . . thrown out. Hank, it's yours, retrieved from a blue recycle bin. They threw it in the wrong bin. Now I look in both the recycle and the trash bins because people are too lazy to put things in the right containers. They don't care about the world. So, what do I find? This perfectly good machine."

Reese's nocturnal life meant the length of his greeting correlated to the depth of the night. The people in town nicknamed him Cans, based on pre-dawn sightings of him going through bins on trash day, pulling out aluminum to exchange for cash at the recycling center. By sunrise, he could be mistaken for a bizarre parade vehicle with four to six bulging lawn bags of recycling hanging off his bike as he pedaled through town. His sense of balance astounded the early morning dog walkers and involved skills of balancing full bags of recycling, and on occasion, a coffee maker.

"Hey, I didn't find any coffee filters and damn, I stink! Sorry, man, I didn't realize how bad 'til I got indoors. Mind if I—" and with that he disappeared into the bathroom. Hank unplugged the coffee maker, dropped a clean towel on the bathroom countertop, and returned to bed.

The next morning, Hank woke with the need for caffeine and conversation. He knew where to get both if expectations were set low for the coffee. As he trudged toward the bathroom, memories of the previous night returned. Clothes of his late-night visitor dried on the shower curtain rod. Everything else sat in its original place as if Reese never had used the bathroom. Hank wondered where the owner of the garments could be. The entrance to the living room revealed a naked form strewn across the couch and half covered by an old Afghan blanket. The image reminded Hank of the times he had seen the same body draped over the edge of an adjacent twin bed during the month as roommates at Desert Recovery and Boarding. Hank recalled the conversations they had on the place's name. Didn't anyone realize the acronym was DRAB? Hank spent his first few days at Desert Recovery in an unshared room until his rehab roomie checked in, the same person as his current overnight houseguest. They both were court-assigned to those thirty days together, a both rapid-paced and never-ending month where Hank and Reese tried to decide how drab their lives were. After leaving recovery, they tried to stay in contact, even if it meant the odd 2 a.m. reunion. For anyone else, this late-night interruption would have been a rude overstep, but Hank didn't mind and instead felt support from his rehab friend crashing on the couch. A crucible is sometimes needed to create ties that bind, even a DRAB crucible.

The motionless body of lean muscles and scarred ebony skin still showed signs of the former college gymnast. He slept with one arm through the strap of his patch-covered backpack. The largest decal declared *Reduce, Reuse, Recycle.*

Hank placed one of his sweatshirts, some clean underwear, protein bars, and a few dollars at the end of the couch. In a bit of a surprise, his typical light-sleeping guest didn't move. Hank headed out the door, quietly closing the handle behind him, only to be greeted by four large plastic bags of cans and a locked rusty bike on his patio. Hank paused and wondered what else he could do to help. *Should he have left more cash? Should he have not left any? Did the family business have a position open for Reese? What crossed the line between helping and trying to change a person?* Hank started to question his own need to change. The morning filled with even more personal questions until Hank sat with a group in a circle of metal folding chairs and said, "Hi, I'm Hank, and I'm an alcoholic."

21

Box Lunches

SPONTANEITY OCCASIONALLY WORKED. That's how Adela got William, Hank, Steve, and even her father together for a last-minute lunch at the outdoor commons area of the recovery center. An impromptu celebration of Asuproz's successful client presentation along with Desert Recovery's start to refurbish the rental houses into transitional homes served as the excuse. Adela's secondary reason involved a promise to Tiffany, and to herself, to get Hank and Steve together socially to strengthen the bonds of the next generation. She still wasn't sure how her father got invited, but his uncharacteristic upbeat mood added to the gathering as they enjoyed their box lunches.

"She's there, under the pergola," Adela's assistant pointed toward the group.

"Addie?"

The entire table turned to see Calvin Moore striding in their direction, every bit the movie star/producer he appeared to be when on talk shows and in movie theaters.

"Cal, what a nice surprise. I didn't realize you were coming today," Adela said as she jumped into executive mode, making introductions between Cal and her family.

"I'm here to get those promotional photos done that I promised the recovery center."

"Mr. Moore, I admire your business acumen." Robert moved his chair to be at Cal's side.

"Well," Cal replied, "I think I am using some of your

company's technology to volunteer on the helplines."

Adela let Cal know he and Robert were both volunteers and Cal's was one of the famous voices that needed disguising.

"You do have a distinct voice," Robert said. "Did you take vocal training or singing lessons?"

"It's from growing up in the Midwest and being raised with that universal dialect, along with demanding parents who wanted me in show business, so I got on-the-job coaching at a young age."

"I was born in the Midwest as well. We are kindred spirits."

The discussion continued until the photographer arrived to take Cal back inside.

"How about a group shot with the family?" the photographer asked Adela and Cal.

"Sure, let's," Cal said, so they all gathered around Robert for some quick photos.

Adela smiled seeing Hank, Steve, and William kidding around as they posed for photos. She caught a glimpse of the 'Billy' side of her brother not seen in years. It was a moment of comfort bringing her family together. She looked forward to the next get together with Tiffany to share the moment.

22

The Early Birds Special

WEEK AFTER WEEK, Kate and Thomas arrived first to the Musketeers' gatherings. Punctuality drove Kate, and fear of missing out drove Thomas. Hank and Reese arrived in an unknown range of five to twenty minutes late, while the two punctual members filled the time with first sips of coffee and idle talk. This time, Kate looked up at the cloudless blue sky and decided to go beyond morning surface chat to ask Thomas about life with Reese.

"All I'm saying is it looks like you passed the friendship stage months ago. What is your stage? Not stage . . . I wonder . . . how everything is, you know, with you two?" Kate asked.

"Lady, what are you trying to say?" Thomas replied, while confirming Kate's suspicions with a big smile. "To be clear, we haven't tried hiding anything, but I don't have a relationship definition for you. We've checked the sexually active box on your questionnaire. Is that what you're sniffing around for?"

"Well, no, but yes."

"We aren't about labels or exclusivities," Thomas studied Kate's face and continued, "but what?"

Kate fidgeted with her coffee cup.

"What's the follow up question?" Thomas asked. "This feels more like an interview than normal coffee time."

Kate blushed. "I think I might be interested in Hank."

"Shocker. I'm glad I am sitting down because that's news

to—nobody!" He continued his not-so-gentle prompting with an elongated, "And?"

Kate rolled her eyes. "I don't want to move too fast, and I don't know what the next steps are. I don't even know if either of us is ready." She looked at her feet and changed to a new topic.

"And then there's Reese's homeless situation. How do you handle that?"

Thomas laughed and sipped some coffee.

"Situation? So, this is the moment our coffee chat shifts from fluff to the Oprah Winfrey type questions and you make me cry? Relationships and homelessness?" Thomas continued. "Well, Miss Oprah, I wouldn't say he's homeless. He's spent more than a few nights on the streets from what he's said, under bridges on the north side of town and sleeping on poolside furniture of the vacant homes of snowbirds. He still stays out occasionally even though I ask him not to because it's not safe. He tells me there are times he needs the outdoors to sleep. After the abuse in high school gymnastics and residual paranoia from the codeine, he trusts about two and a half people."

Kate shook her head. "Is there any way he'd go back to college now? He's so smart."

"He's ancient compared to kids starting, and could you see him sit through lectures? The gymnast scholarship back then created his means of affording college. His injury changed everything."

"I know, but I want the best for him, for both of you. How does he get by?" Kate asked.

"Reese isn't called Cans for nothing. Collecting recyclables and finding jobs from construction and catering helps. He's come a long way since we all met. Somehow, he manages to connect a series of places to live, like crashing at Hank's. He doesn't want people to know where he sleeps and barely lets me know. He says I talk too much. As if."

Kate smiled and nodded in support.

"A lot of times he sleeps at construction projects so companies can leave their tools. He calls this his symbiotic relationship. It drives me a bit crazy, but he feels safer there than in what he calls being caged by walls and a ceiling."

Kate caught her breath. She didn't like walking in her own shoes on most days and couldn't imagine Reese's path.

Thomas continued, "The world has treated him like shit. You've heard some of his stories at DRAB and in our AA meetings. He keeps reminding me that his brain fires differently than mine. Still, he's trying to make the world a better place. He tries to make us better, but his attempts to zhuzh up my knowledge skills drive me nuts."

"What do you mean?"

"He brings me books he finds in the recycle saying they are only the ones he's read before, but I swear he reads everything. Our four Musketeers' names came from one of those books. I thought of the *Three Musketeers* candy bar, but no. He's read that book a few thousand times and has it memorized. He gave me a copy and it sits on my nightstand, all 700 pages. He's the kindest person I've ever met and he'd do anything for me, you, or Hank. He's one of the most active volunteers at the desert meal service agency and gets me to go at least once a week. He says the organization needs helpers who are relatable to the people coming in."

Kate looked down. "He never asked me to go."

Thomas finished off his coffee. "I don't think he'd have asked me if it weren't for his counselor saying acts of service together would help our relationship. Reese said it was his good deed stuff and didn't want to force it on you." Thomas tried to take a sip from his empty coffee cup, then removed the plastic cover and tipped out the remaining drops.

"And as for us, as for Reese and me," he looked around for any signs of the other Musketeers, "although we haven't defined our relationship, we do like our naked time together but also decided not to have sleepovers. We're staying away from anything close to creating a home. Kate, neither of us thinks we should live together right now but Reese keeps quoting that 700-page book to me and says, 'Everyone knows that God protects drunkards and lovers.' So apparently Reese and I are covered. As for you and Hank, you're not Reese and me. Whether we work or not doesn't mean you'll succeed or fail. You don't need to talk to me. You need to talk to Hank."

Thomas looked up to see Hank coming toward them and turned to Kate, saying, "And now, Ms. Oprah Winfrey, let's welcome your next guest to the show. What questions do you have for him?"

23
Love at First Sight

LOVE AT FIRST SIGHT and the other messages from rom-com movies didn't stand a chance with Hank against the trail of his mother's uncles-dates. *But, did Kate just smile at him again?* The Musketeers sat around a table in the coffeeshop courtyard as Thomas extolled his magnum opus on the reasons reality television stars are actors and should be nominated for Emmy Awards. Hank's thoughts drifted back to actors in sappy romance movies. He couldn't understand why people watched the genre when they knew the disinterested pair would end up in love. Never a surprise ending, and yet the audience kept watching. The viewers would see the two characters get locked in a supply closet or other situations sparking their unbridled love as they became enveloped in violin music triggering the movie credits.

Was he in a rom-com with Kate? His helpline counselor had asked if he was dating, and he wanted the answer to be yes. Each time the Musketeers got together for coffee, he found himself staring at her and taking in her smile and sparkling eyes. Except there was no meet-cute, or the meet started with their shift scrubbing lobby bathroom floors at a treatment center, not the movie version of returning to a high school reunion. The details of their first encounter were lost in the fog of his early days in treatment, a haze that felt as confusing as his growing feelings for Kate.

The thirty days overflowed with the conflicting urges of being fully committed to sobriety and the desire to escape out the door to the nearest bar. The importance of structure and normalcy in treatment didn't help Hank remember when he met people at DRAB or their names, yet the moments with Kate had flashes of joy. He recalled a calmness when they were together even though every past moment of his life trained him to not trust the feeling.

Post-treatment, gatherings with Kate included the other Musketeers. This meant a mix of Reese's literary quotes and Thomas's pop-news updates. Hank wasn't sure if his attraction to Kate occurred at their first meeting. Over time she held returned glances and some intentional bumps. He relished her leaning into him when she laughed.

"So people from the *Big Brother* and *Top Chef* shows should be winning Emmy Awards!" Thomas made his closing argument.

"You should start a petition!" Kate winked at Reese.

"I would, but my emails to *People Magazine* didn't change how they pick the Sexiest Man Alive. I swear they have no point system or criteria at all!"

"Don't give up the fight." Kate laughed and leaned into Reese.

All the rom-com cues Hank thought Kate gave him were the same interactions she had with Reese and Thomas. Maybe none of it meant anything special. Except her hugs felt warmer than a perfunctory one from friends. He had heard hundreds of people say his name over his lifetime but never with the same effect as when said by her, and she seemed so interested in him. The morning with friends left him more confused, so he ended the personal rom-com running in his head and returned to Thomas giving his criteria for the sexiest man alive.

Hank looked at his group and smiled, thinking of how the Musketeers got through Desert Recovery and stayed connected. They began meeting at the coffee shop with no exact expectation except that they missed the informal conversations and even Thomas's hot topics. They were regulars and sat in the shade of a rusting 15-foot iron statue of Don Quixote. Reese enjoyed meeting near the towering replica of the famous dreamer. He quoted Cervantes about optimism and pointed to the statue, saying how even Don Quixote found his love, Dulcinea, and he had found Thomas. Then he looked at Kate and smiled at Hank.

Hank questioned if Reese saw something between him and Kate or was smiling about Thomas. He wondered what Kate thought. He'd heard enough about the energy around addiction transferring from liquor to work, fitness, gambling, and even sex. He tried not to get too buried in work, but what about his focus on Kate? During their sessions at the recovery center, Hank recalled how he and Katie described hitting their addiction bottom. She had a string of embarrassing blackout stories, but nothing matched his DUI. He could hear his counselor in his head, 'Who hits the lowest bottom isn't a contest.' So, Hank swore to follow all the directions and not drink again.

"Hank. Hank! Wouldn't you agree they picked right this time with Idris Elba instead of the time they picked The Rock as the sexiest man?" Thomas looked for support.

"Idris Elba got picked for an Emmy?" replied Hank.

"No, no, no! And besides, Elba is Oscar awards material. We aren't talking about awards anymore. Hank, your participation is a requirement of this group. Is Idris Elba sexy?"

"I will defer to your expertise on this topic."

"Another yes vote for Idris. My work is done here." Thomas wrapped up the impromptu presentation as the group finished their drinks. Reese and Thomas headed toward Thomas's car and Kate followed Hank as he left the coffee shop courtyard.

The two of them reached the enclosed archway of the courtyard, and Kate stopped him.

"I've been thinking," Kate said, looking into Hank's eyes. "Thomas was saying—"

"I'm sorry for not listening. I was thinking about something else. Is this about Idris Elba? I didn't have the courage to tell him I don't know who that is."

"No. I was talking to him about us."

123

"Us?"

"About you and me. I was wondering what you thought about us going out together, the two of us, maybe as a date."

Hank remained silent while looking up and finally sputtered, "I don't know. Do you think that's smart?"

"Right. Okay." She turned and rushed to her car.

Hank stood there in his silence not meaning to end the conversation, but he didn't know what to say. Restless nights followed until deciding he owed her a better answer and proposed they go on a 'meet up.' It sounded better than a date, but he wasn't sure why.

The scheduled day arrived, and they drove to Thousand Palms Oasis to hike the nature preserve. Kate picked up Hank for the thirty-minute drive to the trailhead. It didn't take long for the 'meet up' to turn into a definite non-date. The first minutes of the journey were silent, except for filler questions reserved for two strangers. Attempts to have a conversation consisted of comments about the weather and if their takeout coffee tasted bitter. No topic sparked more discussion until Kate questioned how Hank slept. He stared out the passenger window and began an unending sentence consisting of all the concerns around their meet up and how he had a terrible night's sleep. To his surprise, Kate had the same experience.

"I barely slept at all and was going to cancel. I thought I had forced you into this," she said.

Hank remained looking out the window with his shoulder pressed against the door. The silence continued.

"Did I?" Kate asked.

"It's just that I keep getting told to focus on my sobriety," Hank replied. "I don't want to mess us up. I don't want to mess up our friendship. I don't want to mess up the Musketeers."

"I don't either."

"Kate, my counselor from the helpline asked if I was seeing

someone, and I said no. I wanted to be able to say I was seeing you."

"You talked about us to your counselor?"

"No. Maybe. It was the helpline, and that was all I said."

"I haven't either, unless you count Thomas as my counselor."

"I am sure he does."

They both laughed.

"So, neither of us has talked to our counselor about this?" Kate asked as she turned off the route and pulled the car into a fast-food parking lot.

Their first date turned into a two-person recovery meeting. In place of the hike, they sat in the car talking and eating snacks meant for the hike. They agreed that any real date would be preceded by discussions with their support system and decided to avoid being alone together in socially pressurized moments like New Year's Eve and Valentine's Day until they had a better sense of what they meant to each other.

24

The Second Non-Date

HANK AND KATE'S FIRST NON-DATE ended with criteria allowing for phone calls, which often meant extended goodnights outdoing any high school couple. The dynamic led to an additional rule of no phone sex. One evening, Kate called Hank after a sunset run. While talking about rubbing lotion on a leg cramp, she noticed she had brushed close to the restricted topic. Upon realizing this, she changed the topic to how she thought the statue of Sonny Bono, in the center of town, was covered in bird poop. They both started laughing and chose Sonny Bono as their safe word if discussion ventured out of bounds.

Hank occasionally substituted Sonny Boner, which made them laugh even more. After numerous phone calls, they decided to try a second non-date. Hank picked a public spot. Palm Greens, a vegan restaurant off the radar of friends and family. He scoped out the restaurant earlier and figured they would sit at one of the tables in the center of the place, but instead, the hostess led them to a private high-topped booth.

"Will this work?" she asked while setting menus on the table.

"Yes?" Hank answered, happy to see a confirming nod from Kate. Their legs touched as they sat, and neither moved away. Kate looked at Hank and asked, "Sonny Bono?"

He reached across the table and grasped her hands, saying "Cher."

The wordplay wasn't perfect, but Hank didn't want Kate to move away. There were no rules about touching legs at a restaurant. Hank continued holding her hands and smiled.

"I don't want to lose this," he said.

"I don't want to lose this either. We shared so many serious topics at the recovery center. Can you tell me something non-recovery about you? What do you do at Asuproz? I know your job is technical, but what does that mean?"

"It's like playing with puzzles, electronic puzzles," Hank said. "My father and grandfather look at the needs of the entertainment industry and try to figure out if Asuproz can solve them."

"What is your part?"

"The puzzle is typically about altering music from an instrument or how a voice sounds when it comes through a microphone. Right now we are doing even more, where we can move around the words spoken into a speaker."

"That sounds incredible."

"I don't do it on my own, but I have been messing around with this stuff for a few years."

"Have you met any musicians?"

"Some, but not anyone significant. My dad and grandfather have."

"That is so cool. The only thing new with me is that I've started talking about you and me at the meetings I attend in Encinitas. I feel more comfortable talking to a group that doesn't know you. I've also told my counselor here."

"Well, I've told Willow about you."

"Really?"

"She said she'd only approve of us dating after she met you."

"Tell her I look forward to it." Kate smiled.

Hank and Kate compared notes and decided to complete the twelve-month period before any real dates. The sharing went well until Hank shared the wine-drinking experience with his mom.

Kate jerked away and pushed her body against the back of booth.

The restaurant sound system started playing Cyndi Lauper's "Time After Time" as Kate gathered her thoughts.

"You've been drinking?"

"I took a few sips. The wine has nothing to do with my relationship with you. I've told my counselor."

"We've talked about your mom. Why didn't you tell me or any of us, and what are a few sips?"

"I didn't want to make you angry. No, that's not it. I'm embarrassed."

"Don't you trust me?"

"Yes, of course I do. That's not it either. I said I told my counselor. I trust you. I'm not sure I trust the impact on our future."

They both went quiet as Kate reached out and clasped Hank's hands. "I'm not sure I understand the difference."

She started to say more and stopped. The silence filled the booth until a waiter stopped and asked if they knew what they wanted. They sat up in the booth, legs and hands no longer touching as they both responded, "Sonny Bono." The fading lyrics of the song lingered in the air, a reminder of their commitment to each other, time after time.

25

We Got the Contract

HANK RUSHED from his work lab space into the technical director's office to hear a choir of familiar voices coming through the speakerphone. Spencer, William, and Steve called in from Steve's car with news while talking simultaneously. Then, from a third line and overriding everyone, was Robert's gruff tone.

"Okay, you've got me dialed in. Who's in charge of this circus? What's the news? Did we get it finalized? Just one of you speak. Steve, what is the status of the contract?"

Spencer jumped in. "Gramps, sorry you couldn't be out here in Pasadena, but it's done. I got a verbal approval in this morning's meeting. Both companies did the final electronic signing before we left. My final push got the agreement."

"Anyway," William interrupted his son. "Steve figured out the content of the final contract and it's signed. Everyone pulled together, and Hank even dialed into the meeting from Palm Springs to give input on some final technical specs. They signed the contract, and we wanted to get the word out."

Spencer talked over everyone. "Now that our job is done, it's time for you guys in the tech center to deliver!"

Robert continued. "Spencer. Our technical director and Hank have the next steps under control. This call is done."

"It's party time!" Spencer yelled through the speaker as the call ended.

Hank got up to leave the technical director's office when he stopped and asked his boss for a celebration. The technical team deserved a victory moment as much as the people calling from the car. The director agreed, and Hank sent an email to all involved at the Palm Springs location for a gathering later that day. The milestone involved months of Steve managing contract negotiations while Hank's team tweaked the product capabilities. Years of development and filing for patents preceded that. Hank's on-and-off participation due to time in treatment never stopped the engineers from advancing.

The afternoon started simply enough. Hank represented the family leadership and was the person to throw the credit card down for everything. He knew his mother would approve of him taking on this role and chose the bar area in the iconic La Val'erise restaurant. The jazz quartet started the first set with their rendition of Dave Brubeck's "Take Five." The bartender popped corks and poured champagne into a line of glasses for the attendees. Hank celebrated each person by noting their individual contributions. A touch to the lips with each toast became Hank's solution for tiptoeing down the social balance beam of sobriety at a work event. For each toast made, there were others wanting to share their gratitude in return. One of the bar staff eventually searched the restaurant cooler for more chilled bottles.

The technical director left to attend to his daughter's soccer match, and a few others followed. The happy hour continued well beyond its sixty minutes, and the group wasn't winding down. With the technical director's departure, Hank became the senior attendee.

When did the scotch come out? Why did he leave the restaurant? The head of software design had some good cigars and they couldn't smoke in the bar. *Is that why they went outside?* Hank's head hurt. He couldn't move without his entire body hurting. *Where was he? What time was it?* He dared not open his eyes. *Tacos and tequila shots? Where was Kate? Did he have his phone? Spencer called?* They all were laughing. *Reese was there? Did he call Kate? When did Reese show up?* Jen, from the voice-mod team, was hungry. Some of the group went for tacos and toasted with tequila. *Why was Reese at tacos?* Still a blur. His head hurt. *Tequila? When did the work people leave? Dancing with Jen, and singing?* Slow dancing, swaying to the music. *Were they kissing? Did they go to the biker bar before the tacos?* Hair of the Dog for another smoke. His mouth, stale with cigar smoke, yearned for cleansing, but the urge wasn't strong enough to convince the rest of his body to move. *Where was he?* They all were howling at the full moon as they stubbled along. "Let's go to Hair of the Dog, aaaaahoooooo, werewolves of London, aaaaahooooo."

He sensed a body in the bed next to him. *How did he get back to Kate's place? Was he at Kate's?* Hank opened his eyes for a flash, confirming his apartment. *Did they have sex? Did he remember having sex?* Again, memory flashes of champagne toasts. *Kissing? Toasts of tequila, maybe some scotch?* Howling. Why wasn't he part of the contract signing? Spencer called during the team's celebration. Hank was lining up shots of tequila at the bar. Kate was going to be so angry with him when she woke up. *Did he fall off a bar stool?* His arm hurt. She was going to be angry that he drank, angry that he started drinking. His body shook from chills. Sweat broke out across his forehead and down his back. He couldn't turn over and face her, not that morning, not in his condition. He opened his eyes to see a gleam of morning light. The brightness made his eyes burn. Thankfully, he was in his apartment. The shivering got worse. He couldn't stop the chill from surging through his body. Then came a kiss on the back of his neck as two arms reached around to warm him and help stop the shaking. Two muscular black arms and a familiar voice said to hang in there. Reese held him tight.

26
The Ride

HANK HAD NO IDEA how much time had passed while he slept. A fever sweat soaked his bedsheets only to be replaced by waves of body-shaking chills. His stomach turned, still unsure of any remaining contents to expel into the nearby trash bin. The buzzing in his ears reverberated through his brain. He opened his eyes enough for the alarm clock to come into focus. A red digital 2:17 and sunlight. Afternoon. A noise at his apartment door jarred his head. He grabbed a pillow to muffle the noise. Movement and voices in the living room continued after someone opened the door.

"We need to talk. Now." A voice said.

"We need to help a friend," Reese replied.

"That may save your ass for now, but what—tell me exactly what happened!"

The voices dropped to a whisper, but the rage reverberated through the walls. Hank struggled to recall the past night, only to doze off again. The next shock came from being woken again. The brain flushed itself clean during the half hour of sleep, leaving Hank trying to recall his current situation all over again. He didn't completely wake up until Reese and Thomas lifted him into the shower as one of them pushed a toothbrush into his hand. The shower wasn't a strong enough cleansing before Reese's hand reached in and turned off the water. Thomas returned to the bathroom with a takeout cup of coffee and a half-eaten banana. Reese asked Thomas to find Hank some clothes as he helped Hank's towel-wrapped body lower onto the closed toilet seat. Being showered and sitting down brought Hank a feeling of peace until Reese tried to get him to eat some banana.

"You need food in your stomach," Reese said, as he wiped the remaining toothpaste off Hank's face.

The next minutes blurred as Hank drifted back to sleep on the toilet, only to be woken when his clothed body was picked up by both arms and led to the front door.

"Where are we going?" asked Hank.

"We're going to DRAB," Thomas replied. "We all need to get to DRAB."

Thomas maneuvered Hank's arm over his shoulder and grabbed him by the waist while casting a glare at Reese.

Reese grabbed the carrier filled with coffees and handed Hank his apartment keys and cell phone. Hank didn't want to go to the recovery center and didn't want to talk. He tried to get his unresponsive body to pull away toward his bedroom.

"That's a solid no," Thomas said as he tightened his grip. "You two have basically messed up this entire day, and who knows what else. I don't want to be here, and I know Reese doesn't want me to be here."

"Don't say that," Reese said. "It isn't helping. I want you here, especially now. We all need to be here."

"I'm not helping?" Thomas shouted. "You called. I'm here, and now I am not helping?" Thomas released his grip and felt Hank's rag doll of a body begin to fall. He tightened his grasp and pulled Hank more erect as he continued shouting at Reese. "Let's go. I can't wait to hear what happened."

"Neither can I," Hank said.

"Shut up!" Thomas replied.

Hank tried to convince them one last time to let him stay home. He promised to go to the recovery center the next day. He promised he wouldn't drink again. He wanted to crawl into bed and make yesterday go away.

"Hank, isn't it enough you decided to drink last night, that you lost respect for yourself and our friendship? Aren't things hard enough? We're friends. At least I thought we were. We're going to DRAB and we're going to talk it out."

Hank had no words. He felt Thomas's anger and had no idea what happened the night before beyond flashes of memory, so he resigned himself to go.

Thomas drove, Hank in front with the window open, the wind blowing on his face. Reese sat in back. No music played to break the mood, and Thomas did everything possible to avoid the rearview mirror so he wouldn't catch Reese's glance. Hank got the impression Thomas drove one of the most jarring car rides possible. They pulled into the parking lot of the recovery center at the side entrance with a direct route to the counseling rooms. They got out of the car, and the three of them started toward the entrance where Kate stood like a sentry guarding the door, her hair up in a ponytail and wearing dark sunglasses. She didn't move and didn't hug anyone as Hank sulked by her.

She muttered, "It happens. It happened. Let's go inside."

Reese handed Kate her coffee and opened the door, stepping aside to let Hank enter while the rest followed in a single line. The four of them looked like individuals dragging their feet on the way to their execution. Each in their own world and filled with questions. *Why did Hank drink again? Was this a one-time lapse or a relapse? Had they missed clues he'd been drinking for some time? Would this happen to any of them?* The walkers moved down the hallway toward a meeting room and the counselor. Kate slowed, wrapped her arm around Thomas's and put her head on his shoulder as they supported each other to get through the door and whatever waited on the other side.

27

The Ride Home

THE SESSION ENDED with Kate leaving first, headed toward the individual counselor offices, while Hank, Reese, and Thomas left for the exit. The three got in the car and headed back to Hank's apartment. Again, the drive contained no music, but this time Reese sat in front and Hank sprawled across the back with his eyes closed. None of them spoke.

During the meeting, all but Hank supplied information from texts, calls, and photos to reconstruct the previous night while he sat and stared at each speaker, hearing the story anew. The counselor pulled details from each of them. Kate described phone calls she'd gotten before she told Hank not to call anymore. Thomas blasted off a list of events at the speaking rate of an auctioneer. Reese sat silently as Thomas told the secondhand summary of Reese's decision to ride downtown and find Hank based on the frantic call he got from Kate. He biked the path from the restaurant to the taco bar where Hank sent his last text photo. Thomas told of how Reese spotted the group at Shanghai Red's but kept his distance. Thomas continued, saying how Reese freaked out being in a bar and seeing Hank drunk.

"You weren't even there." Hank tried to defend himself.

"I've got the receipts!" Thomas stood up and showed Reese's text photos of Hank holding a taco in one hand and doing a shot with the other. "I wasn't there, but what the hell were you doing there? You're lucky I was stuck at work and couldn't pick you up or you would have been in worse shape than you are. After seeing these pictures, I told Reese he had to get you out of there. I still don't understand what magic mushroom potion Reese took from his shaman to calm himself, but he said he finished off his entire bag of dust to get up the nerve to step in." Thomas turned his attention to Reese. "Can you tell me what an emergency dose is?"

"I needed to get centered, and the powder calms me. It chilled me out enough to get Hank back to his apartment," Reese answered.

"You got back because of the Uber I sent. Hank, you owe me for that and you're going to help Reese retrieve his bike from downtown."

Hank felt as if he were watching a horror movie, not knowing what would come next and fearing the ending.

The counselor let Thomas continue until he couldn't speak anymore. Then he asked Kate to share how she felt.

"I'm scared. I am so scared for you. This is the second time you've been drinking since we got out of here."

"I'm sorry," Hank responded.

"The second?" Thomas started to speak when the counselor held up his hand.

Reese looked in shock at Hank as he lowered his head.

"I know you said the first time didn't count," Kate said. "Hank, it all counts. Why? What's next?"

"Reese, you've said little." The counselor prodded. "We've mapped out quite a bit from the restaurant to the bar. We haven't heard anything about what happened after you two left."

Thomas turned his body away from the group to look out the window. Hank waited to hear so he could fill in the blanks. Kate stared at Reese.

"We got back to Hank's and got up the sidewalk before he barfed tacos and tequila all over a barrel cactus. I had to do everything I could to keep him from grabbing onto what he thought was a toilet. I dragged him inside and he drank some water but that almost immediately ended up in the toilet. I could barely convince him how soiled his clothes were and that they needed to come off. For some reason, he wanted to howl at the moon and tried to go outside in his underwear. I had to block the door to keep him in. He kept wanting to see the moon. I had to say the skies were too cloudy, and so he started howling at the bathroom lights, saying he was a werewolf. Hank, you wouldn't stop howling until I grabbed you and covered your mouth to keep you quiet. I spent all my energy on getting mouthwash in you a few times. You kept twisting to get away, so I finally picked you up and threw you into bed."

After a long silence, the counselor asked if there was anything else, at which point Thomas started to cry. Reese moved over to Thomas and crouched to speak directly to Thomas.

"I didn't want anything to happen. I didn't plan—"

Hank looked at his friends in shock.

"He started kissing me," Reese continued. Kate now turned her stare to Hank as she moved to get up and then returned to her chair at the direction of the counselor. Reese tried to share as much as he could, as all four of them were in tears. Reese looked right at Hank and continued with how he did his best to calm his friend.

"I had to keep holding you, hoping you would stay put and fall asleep."

Reese stopped talking. Kate looked at Hank and back at Reese. No one moved. The counselor was silent.

"But, did you fuck?" Thomas screamed into Reese's face.

Thomas had received a call from Reese that morning, filled with half sentences and an odd tone, saying they needed to talk. They didn't have enough time at Hank's for Thomas to hear the entire story before going to the recovery center.

"I know you're attracted to Hank. What happened with you two in bed?"

Reese grabbed both of Thomas's hands and met his eyes. "I

know he's straight. I care about you. About us. Yes, we kissed. We got a little physical, but nothing serious happened. Hey, no excuse, but I was still feeling the 'shroom dust. I'm sure he didn't know it was me. I don't think he knew who he was with, based on his blank stare. He felt empty and cold. He wanted sex or any form of affection. Thomas, why do you think I messaged and called you?"

Thomas pulled away and kept staring at Reese.

"I needed to talk to you as soon as possible," Reese continued. "Nothing happened to change *us*. We need to be here to take care of Hank."

Thomas remained quiet. Reese returned to his chair. Kate stayed silent, her sunglasses back on. Hank bowed. The counselor checked in with everyone one last time only to get no response. The session ended with nothing fixed. They left knowing they were all in recovery and had all survived the morning with the help of each other.

Thomas's car pulled up to the patio of Hank's apartment. Thomas and Reese took Hank inside and made him drink some Gatorade before putting him to bed. Thomas went outside and hosed off the barrel cactus and the trail of stink around it while Reese straightened things indoors. They cleaned up what they could while pondering the emotional clutter. Exhausted, they collapsed on Hank's couch. In the next room, Hank tossed and turned in bed, overcome with the thought of blacking out. *What happened to never again?* With that, he tucked into a ball to escape his shame surrounding the past twenty-four hours and hoped he could avoid the thoughts of his biggest blackout.

During the biggest blackout, the one he couldn't seem to break free from, Hank woke with an aching head along with every part of his body as he felt the cold, unforgiving cement floor. A stench of sweat and vomit came from his clothes, and the taste of blood filled his mouth. He tried to recall if he'd bitten his tongue or the inside of his mouth.

"You're in a heap load of trouble," said a nearby voice. Hank put his forearms over each ear to muffle the voice that amplified his headache.

"I'll be fine," Hank groaned, his go-to response on rough mornings, saying the words to the mystery person and to himself. "I'll be fine." He repeated in a whisper as he closed his eyes and tried to make the world go away. Hank had slept off hangovers in all sorts of places and didn't care about the location as long as the noise stopped. He had woken up in strangers' homes and in strangers' beds. Once he slept in the walled-off dumpster area outside a fast-food restaurant with bags of half-eaten food for a pillow.

The hangover persisted like a woodpecker at a maggot-filled tree trunk. His stomach calmed, but the pain in his head wouldn't stop. The severe lighting and cold made sleeping impossible, and a voice kept talking. *What was going on and who was the person screaming at him?*

"Shut up!" Hank's feeble voice tried to demand. The cut in his mouth broke open, and the person continued talking.

"You kept me up half the night with your moaning and puking. Jeeezus! What did you eat last night? You and everything that came out of you reeked! And I don't need to shut up. All your blabbering. I couldn't wait for you to finally pass out. You are going to get yours soon enough. They don't know if that girl is going to live."

A shock of reality coursed through his body. Handcuffs had pulled at his wrists in a squad car. His current bed was a cement floor in jail. Blood stained his clothes. The voice in his shared cell had said they didn't know if she was going to live. *Which she?*

Hank found out soon enough as he stood in front of a judge and heard the charges of vehicular manslaughter. The woman, Camila Flores, 23, rode away with Hank when he left the Tiki Inn hotel bar. She had died. His blackout memory recalled flash moments. Speeding down Vista Chino Drive. Screaming. Flashing squad car lights. His arraignment consisted of his lawyer and the judge talking back and forth. The prosecuting attorney succeeded in charging Hank with DUI vehicular manslaughter and released him to house arrest on $250,000 bail.

Adela's guest room served as his house arrest. At the start, the trial hit news sources. *Well-known Palm Springs family has grandson accused of manslaughter.* Over time, other headlines rose to the top, replacing coverage of the trial. Hank sat through several preparatory meetings leading up to the trial, but in the end, he was found guilty. Sentencing occurred with no screams for justice from the mourning family members of the woman who died. Ms. Flores was a loner from out of town with some past infractions. Willow and Adela were the only relatives in attendance and sat immediately behind Hank, even though he asked family to stay away. Lea sat watching from the back row. The other chairs were empty. The law firm hired by William consisted of experts in DUIs. The defense attorneys presented photos, testimony, and other evidence in an exacting process. The lineup of experts impressed the judge.

The law firm recreated the story of an admittedly drunk Hank, a known regular, sitting at the lounge bar with an equally drunk Ms. Flores doing shots with the bartender. The bar security video showed the bartender was aware of them leaving. Road construction signs on Vista Chino were not set up per the Caltran standards. A transportation expert testified that the noncompliant markers were covered with confusing graffiti over the sign's arrows. Cement fragments from the construction site littered the road. The law firm found two reports of flat tires from that stretch of road work similar to Hank's tire blown out. Experts couldn't say for sure whether construction debris or running into the curb caused the car to drive into the streetlight.

Camila, not wearing a seatbelt, went through the windshield. There were no witnesses to testify. The legal team covered every inch between the bar and the point of impact. They used the words *accident*, *unfortunate accident* and *faulty* often during the trial. They used *faulty* a lot. There were faulty construction signs, and even possible faulty car brakes. Counsel reminded the judge that faulty brakes cause 22% of car accidents. *If only* peppered the defense's closing argument. If only Camila had worn her seatbelt, if only the bartender had stopped them, if only the construction signs were compliant. The *if only* statements all wrapped up in a conclusion of: if only any one of these things hadn't happened, Camila Flores would be alive. The arguments resulted in a sentence for Hank to avoid prison time.

The judge reminded Hank of the gravity of the verdict and set $10,000 in penalties. Completing an addiction counseling program and meetings with a community-services officer were part of the six-month probation along with a driver's license. If any of these conditions were broken, Hank would serve six years in prison.

Being well coached on how to speak during the trial didn't matter, his sincerity and remorse were genuine. The entirety shook him like never before. He hit his low. All the *if only* scenarios left him with the reality of: *if only* he hadn't been drinking. The judge's sentencing stuck in his head. One mess up meant immediate lockup and anyone else without his legal team would have gone directly to prison.

Hank turned in his driver's license and headed to court-assigned treatment. The defense attorney requested Desert Recovery. Although assigned to a family-operated organization, there was no family at his admittance. Adela directed the staff to afford no special treatment during Hank's stay. In contrast to past visits when he arrived as an honored philanthropic guest, Hank was led to his dorm room and sat alone looking out the window. *Never, ever, again.*

141

28

Room Assignments

IT WAS THE START of Thanksgiving week and Lea stood in the laundry room of The Dwelling, restocking her cleaning supplies as her mother reviewed their cleaning tasks. Leandra came in to help on her daughter's busiest day of the year. They needed to prepare every sleeping quarter on that Monday to accommodate family members for the weekend. Robert asked the entire family to stay at The Dwelling for major holidays in the spirit of tradition and strengthening bonds. Lea checked her list and confirmed most of the family arrived Tuesday morning.

When Robert's grandchildren reached adulthood, they started vying for favorite rooms. This sparked his creation of a competition for room assignments based on the number of stock shares owned in Asuproz. He also gifted a distribution of stock to each grandchild and ended any bickering over rooms. The grandchildren tier of Spencer, Willow, Hank, and Steve could strive for better rooms by gaining more stock through involvement with the company or buying from one another.

In the beginning, room assignments started at the top with Robert, as the largest shareholder (and owner of the property), residing in the owner's suite. The rooms continued in order down to an Airstream RV alongside the pool. Robert purchased the RV many years ago when invited to an executive campout at the Albuquerque Balloon Festival. After the first trip, the shiny RV was parked at his home, never to be driven again. The vehicle got the most use back when Robert's grandchildren were teenagers and wanted to bring friends over to the pool. Robert obliged the sleepovers of the *hormone-dripping degenerates*, contingent on them staying in the RV.

During the early years, Robert gave the room assignment list to Leandra, and she set up each room, from outfitting the plushest casita with luxurious linens down to the simpler rooms. William maintained Robert's rules for assigning rooms and supplied Lea with the Thanksgiving room assignments for her to create her plan of attack. She and Leandra stocked amenities to match the needs or whims of the specific family member. Organization of linen and pillow preferences and avoiding any allergy causing soaps and shampoos filled Lea's morning tasks before she could begin any cleaning. Snacks that the parents were allowing for their children or themselves also needed to be in place. The countdown to arriving guests didn't stand a chance against Lea and Leandra as they prepared for the arrival of family. They darted from room to room assuring everything was in place. Lea smiled knowing Hank had accepted the invitation so she slipped some of her homemade ginger cookies into his room. They were from her recipe he had enjoyed since childhood.

29

The Calm Before the Storm

ADELA LEFT THE CAR DOOR open and rushed into the restaurant, handing her keys to the valet. She and Tiffany planned one last get together before Thanksgiving. The planned start time began fifteen minutes before she arrived. The hostess greeted Adela with a smile of recognition and didn't have a chance to leave her station before Adela scurried through waiting patrons and on toward the corner of the tree-canopied patio. Her pace relaxed as she neared the table, seeing Tiffany already seated. Adela's table request made for great people-watching and allowed privacy from the hive of eavesdroppers at the popular restaurant. Adela honed this skill by hosting numerous business and social dinners in LA and Palm Springs.

Rushing straight from her office, Adela had broken her personal rule on punctuality. A critical donor call ended poorly with an announcement to stop donations. Adela's attempt to persuade the donor to reduce rather than end the giving had failed with no way to change their mind.

Adela approached the table and started to apologize, but Tiffany pantomimed a shush motion while pointing to two iced teas and the phone in her hand. Tiffany had seen Adela's text about running late and placed the food order, so two chopped salads were on their way.

"That was my Hank," Tiffany giggled as she put her phone down. "He's enjoying his job at the tech center and keeps talking about the lunch you coordinated with Steve."

"Getting together was fun, and William tells me Hank is

making several contributions to the business. Everyone's impressed, and you should be proud."

Tiffany's smile grew as she straightened her place setting. "How could I not be proud?"

Adela hadn't heard if Hank told his mother about his drinking relapse so she decided to wait for Tiffany to mention it. The notification from Desert Recovery came to Adela's phone per Hank's in-case-of-emergency setup. There was no reason to think Tiffany had heard. The lunch progressed, and Tiffany didn't mention Hank for the rest of their time together.

The friendship of the two lunch companions had flourished since the first spa appointment. Texting, lunches, and overnights to Santa Barbara and other ocean towns became routine. They both agreed that a morning stroll along the beach was the perfect cure for life's challenges.

Two salads arrived as the discussion of local gossip transitioned to bigger topics. Adela enjoyed hearing updates about Tiffany's life. Tiffany, in turn, gobbled up how Adela managed her meetings, from medical boards to talks with the mayor. Adela discussed her tough business relationships, including those with her father and William while Tiffany shared stories of her private moments with William. She spoke about him clarifying how he wouldn't be escorting her on his arm to any public events.

"Tiffany, if that is what you want, I am happy for you both."

"It is easier than before, when I had to be his corporate wife and show up at all your family events. Oh, I didn't mean anything about your family."

"No, no. These required family holidays are a mixed blessing."

"Good. I love your family, but I have learned my limits."

Adela realized Tiffany had a complexity that went beyond her reputation. Layers of thoughtfulness shone through the emotive personality. Adela wondered if her life in the corporate world and as a part of her stoic family tapped down too her own outward expressiveness and could she learn more from her friend? The two women found each other's differences to be the perfect connection.

The tony and chic social circles in the small town of Palm Springs presupposed backstories for everyone in town. The lunch partners tried to figure out the reality of the person sitting across the table. Adela had heard talk of Tiffany's erratic mood swings but never experienced anything unusual during their lunches. Nor had she seen any moments off the rails during their overnight trips. Even their Rum Run escape in Malibu didn't amount to much more than a late-night karaoke bar performance and the need for large double dirty chai lattes and ibuprofen the next morning.

When they first met, Adela thought Tiffany a bit the simpleton without ambition, while Tiffany took Adela for a power-hungry executive with little interest in family. Tiffany got to know the caring side Adela had of family. She saw it in her love for Steve, his family, and for William's children.

During their first beach getaway, Tiffany showed her torso to Adela. She joked that at least it was spelled correctly, referring to a script font tattoo of her name. This led to discussing issues with pills for back pain caused by being on her feet all day at work. Her doctor diagnosed chronic pain instead of the chronic occupation of waitressing. Adela listened to her friend's story of getting caught in the oxycodone push by her clinic doctor. It was a familiar path moving from pharmacies to street supplies to relieve pain. Adela tried to understand when this occurred in Hank's life. Instead, she heard about the three different on-and-off treatment stays and a period in between when she got the tattoo below her navel.

Lunch didn't allow time for the depth of conversations they had at the beach. And yet for every question Adela had, Tiffany responded with one of equal magnitude. They finished their salads with Adela delving into Tiffany's feelings about not attending family events. She got a deeper perspective on how painful Spencer's verbal jabs felt. Tiffany countered with questions about the father of Steve. He was the person discussed even less than Tiffany at family gatherings. Adela gave some answers, leaning in so much that even Tiffany struggled to hear the responses. Those nearby in the restaurant couldn't make out any words coming from the two confidants. Tiffany realized there were many layers to Adela's romantic life, and she wanted to hear more.

Their last lunch before Thanksgiving ended. They faced reality: their two calendars had no free dates before the new year. So, they lifted their final sips of iced tea and toasted to 2019 and all it would bring. A cleared table and paid bill signaled the need to return to their separate worlds. Adela checked her phone calendar while waiting for the valet to bring their cars.

"January 1 is on a Tuesday; let's get together that next weekend. Time for a getaway? Laguna?"

"Perfect."

"I will see if the Surf and Sand has two rooms."

"It's a date!" Tiffany replied. With a final wave, they each got into their cars and drove away.

30

The First Call

SPENCER GLANCED BACK and forth between the two computer monitors on the desk where both his father and grandfather once sat as presidents of Asuproz. Months had passed since they visited and demanded new ideas. He scanned the screens again before finally giving up to scroll social media. Family shut down all his past ideas so the scrolling continued until his office phone rang. A glance out the door showed an empty assistant's desk. He answered on the second ring, a habit ingrained in him by his father, another required mannerism of someone sitting at that desk. *Never be too anxious and answer immediately or wait more than two rings and risk being rude.*

"This is Spencer."

"Good morning."

"May I ask who is calling?"

"This is Mr. Voile. I represent an Asian investor who is interested in buying your company."

"This is Spencer . . . I think you want to speak to my fath—"

"We want to speak to you."

"Mr. Voler? This is th—"

"It's Voile. I know who you are and I want to speak with you because you are the president."

"Which company did you say you were representing?"

"Are you free to talk? This is for the president."

"Yes, of course. What is this regarding?"

"What you need to understand is I'm the liaison for an Asian investor interested in the intellectual property and client lists of your company. We want to buy the company in its entirety. An offer will arrive via courier later today."

"You want to buy . . . How much is the offer? The company isn't for sale."

"Do you want to decline an offer you haven't seen? Look for a courier later today."

"I need more information!"

"You'll have it soon enough." The line went dead.

Spencer sat with the phone still to his ear, realizing he had lost his composure during the call. He felt a pang of regret not remaining calm in the moment of pressure, as his father had counselled.

There had been offers to acquire the company over the years, but not to him and not from outside the United States. Spencer heard stories from his father and grandfather after they had turned down opportunities to sell. He returned to his computer and searched for possible Asian companies in the same industry. Before finding any real candidates, he spotted a courier at his office door sidestepping the now-present administrative assistant. Bag over shoulder, fit and dressed in all black biking gear, carrying a legal-sized manila envelope, she placed the delivery on his desk, pulled out an e-tablet, took a photo, pushed a few on-screen buttons, and returned the device to her satchel. Spencer unsuccessfully attempted to get an invoice or anything with contact information as she turned and exited. There on his desk sat a completely blank envelope except for Spencer's name and title printed on an adhesive label.

Frustrated with his anxious handling of the conversation with Mr. Voile, Spencer decided to wait to open the envelope as his way of controlling the next steps. He left Pasadena for the drive to the Thanksgiving celebration in Palm Springs. Any delay in departure could turn the Tuesday two-hour ride into six hours of tortuous holiday stop-and-go traffic, especially in his new Maserati. Besides, Sybil and the children had gone out that morning to take advantage of pool time.

He hopped in his car, frustrated at not being able to convince his father of the value in hiring a jet service from the Burbank airport to Palm Springs. Spencer's mind raced with the value of having access to a jet. *People fly between LA and Palm Springs every day. My father has an antiquated mindset focusing on the number of phone rings before answering a landline versus grasping how private jets improve the image of companies.*

The Maserati zigzagged through traffic as he drove to the desert with the sealed envelope in the passenger seat. Curiosity, coupled with his desire to delay the start of holiday family time, prompted Spencer to pull off at the Tukwet public golf course. He knew the spot from a fundraiser his family attended and considered its décor and service suitable enough to get a drink and review the offer. The location, thirty minutes out of Palm Springs, offered a quiet sanctuary where no one would know him.

The bartender placed a bourbon old-fashioned in front of him, exactly as ordered, complete with muddled orange and four Luxardo cherries held together with a golf flagstick-shaped skewer as a garnish. His grandfather told stories of drinking Old Fashioneds when in New York, and the preference continued in California. Robert used to give the cherries to his grandsons when they were kids. The distinct aroma brought Spencer memories of childhood as he unknowingly rubbed his neck while picking up the glass filled with ice and the glistening dark liquor. The bourbon and orange fragrance caught his nose before he took a strong belt and turned his attention to the offer. Both the clasp and the glue strip were sealed on a paper envelope. Spencer chalked it up to another outdated business model and grabbed a knife off one of the table's place settings to slash open the envelope.

With the seal broken, he realized the weight wasn't from the contents but from the envelope itself. He pulled out a plain sheet of paper—no letterhead, address, or contact information. Spencer took another swig of his drink and pulled the cherries off the skewer with his teeth, sucking out the remaining bourbon before devouring them. The offer contained three lines of information.

Offer: $1.2 billion dollars

Stakeholders' Agreement to Sell: >70% of Shares

Agreement Deadline: February 28, 2019

He sat back on his barstool and finished off his drink while considering the words before him. None of the past offers had been as large. None had topped a billion dollars. Spencer had recently sold shares to his father for a down payment on his home in Pasadena, leaving him even less a majority holder. Therefore, he needed to influence several other shareholders in the family. He'd start with his father and a couple of others. The sale would mean a windfall for Spencer and probably include a plush transition salary for at least a year. The deal would mean a work-free future he deserved. His grandfather had already set up barriers to his real estate business idea, but this was different and he knew he could sway the family. Spencer hadn't kept track of the stock breakdown, so he requested a summary from Asuproz Corporate.

Spencer did a mental status report as he swirled the ice cube in his glass. An offer to buy the company had been made by an unknown source. He was the president of the company. His father had sway in the decision, but the offer came to him. He needed to figure out who supported selling the company, so Spencer dropped a twenty on the bar and headed for Palm Springs.

31

The RV

"I THOUGHT I'D FIND YOU IN HERE," Hank said to Willow and Uncle Otto as he entered the shiny silver RV off to the side of the pool at The Dwelling.

"Who else has arrived for turkey weekend?" asked Otto.

Hank shrugged off the question looking around the RV.

Willow hugged Hank, "How are you doing?"

He returned the hug without answering and grabbed a place on the couch.

"There are times I miss staying in here," he said to Otto and Willow, "except on the windy nights."

"Uncle O and your vow of poverty bumped us up to better lodging!" exclaimed Willow, and then reset her tone. "Or do you prefer Deacon now?"

"Uncle O still works fine for you two, although I may ask your brother Spencer to use Deacon Otto. He could use a reminder of piety from time to time. Besides, you've been more than patient when I slip up and call you Willy."

Willow waved off the comment, showing no foul.

"Enough of all this names-and-titles discussion. Remind me, I know the reason I'm in the RV, after selling my shares to your father. But, how did you two and your cousin end up changing lodging assignments so often over the last few years? Each visit you are in a different room."

Willow looked down at her chest and laughed, "Uncle O, I

didn't have these my whole life."

"True," Otto replied. "I am not that oblivious."

"Thanks to the extraordinary skills of surgeons in Colombia and Sweden, I got everything updated. That took time, surgical and hormonal help, a little therapy, and lots of money. I sold quite a few shares to Spencer and grandpa to reach my version of new and improved."

Hank added. "My shares went to paying lawyers, and even more lawyers after the DUI trial, to reach my version of not-so-new and hopefully improved."

"I am not oblivious to that either," Otto said, "and am thankful you are here."

Willow put her arm around her brother but Hank stiffened.

"The family got the best lawyers in California," Hank continued. "But I still had to pay for them. Thankfully, Steve wanted more interest in the company, so I sold shares to him. That's how he got more shares than Spencer. Which made for an extra bonus."

"I've never liked how my father pitted William, Adela, and me against each other in the business," Otto said, "and it's passed into the DNA of your generation. I'm frankly glad to be out of the fight for ownership of Asuproz. What's important to me is time with you kids and my congregation in LA."

Willow decided Uncle Otto might not have taken a vow of poverty as much as one of peace. The three were jarred by an unearthly growl like a tiger from outside the RV. Spencer arrived in his animalistic car.

As Willow, Hank, and Otto came out of the RV, Otto commented, "Another big car for a little man."

Willow and Hank smirked but made no comments. They were aware they got their height from their father as opposed to Spencer, who followed his mother's genes.

The clamor from Spencer's arrival brought everyone out to

the driveway. Steve and his wife came from the pool. William came out from the main house, followed by two skittish bulldogs trailing behind. Lea looked up from straightening cushions around the fire pit. The aide pulled the curtains to the side as Robert looked out from his casita to see his grandson's new car. Even the children playing in the pool looked up, finding the noise an interruption to their play time.

William greeted his son. "It's been great having your kids out here early to play with their cousins, but where's your wife?"

"Isn't she here? She's probably at our Palm Springs place," Spencer said. "I came directly from the Pasadena office."

"No sign of her yet; I guess she is the Ping for this visit," replied William.

Spencer rubbed his neck hearing the Ping comment, a reference to a children's book their mother used to read to them, *The Story About Ping*, where a family of ducks was let out from a boat for a swim. At the end of the day, the ducks got called back to the boat, and the last duck got a swat from the owner. Growing up, the Ping moniker went to the last child to any meal. No swat happened, but William didn't mind giving the Ping a smaller piece of dessert or assigning Ping an extra chore after the meal. Spencer recalled how he loved getting to yell out *Ping* at his half brother whenever Hank was late. Between room assignments and the calling out of Ping, the mood of the holidays had begun.

32

We're Gathered Together

EARLY THANKSGIVING MORNING, Otto set up the side kitchen countertop with fresh fruit, English muffins, and an assortment of jams, honey, and peanut butter as the coffee brewed. Lea left on Tuesday, not to return until all the weekend guests were gone. Adela appeared next in the kitchen and joined Otto at the island and prepared the turkey for its place in the pantry oven. Then she removed all things involving raw poultry, followed by two vigorous rounds of cleaning before her grandchildren explored the kitchen. Dinner typically began at 1:00 p.m. with Otto and Adela in charge.

The food traditions went back to their mother and her unchanging recipes and secret ingredients not shared beyond the family. The main dishes were turkey, buttery mashed potatoes, cranberries, sweet potatoes, a corn soufflé, and a specific stuffing she tried to teach to all three of the children: Adela's version was acceptable and Otto's being an exact match. William never took to learning the family recipes but valued the holiday and the time with family more in recent years than he ever did in the past. With the turkey preparation and sanitizing done, Otto brought out the second set of ingredients for potatoes and pies as Adela gathered rolling pins and other baking instruments untouched since last Thanksgiving. William entered the kitchen and put food out for the dogs before disappearing into the pantry to retrieve mixing bowls and a food processor. Years of muscle memory drove the siblings through their morning tasks.

William's first wife, Matilda, ran the Thanksgiving kitchen

during her time with the family and excelled at making pie crusts. With her passing, this transferred to the pie-making duo of Willow and Steve. They joined the morning group along with Hank, although they were not ready to start baking yet. The three found their way to the kitchen island after picking up coffee and plates from Otto's breakfast spread. Adela rounded the corner behind them, distributing hugs to each, with a bit tighter squeeze for Hank.

Robert entered the main house, followed by his aide.

"I'll be gone until Monday," the aide declared. "Robert's prescription schedule is on the counter by his pills in his casita, which he can manage himself. Everything will be fine."

Robert pulled his wheelchair away from the aide with a grunt.

"I am not an invalid and can still transfer from this contraption under my own power to take care of myself."

The aide responded without looking at Robert, "All this is true, but numbers for any backup support are on the side of his refrigerator. They can be here within an hour for non-emergencies, and his In Case Of Emergency info packet is on the side of the refrigerator if you call 911. I've left his shades open so you can see into his place."

Robert grunted again while the aide continued.

"Not that anything is going to happen because this stubborn cuss isn't ever going to die."

Robert grunted again, this time more approvingly. With that, the aide wished everyone a happy Thanksgiving and left. The influx of family members continued. Spencer's wife and children entered with the little ones running right to their grandfather. William became immobile with one grandchild hugging each leg. Sybil used the break to prepare a hot tea and to set out bowls of cereal for the children. She asked where Steve's wife and children were, then spotting them scurrying up from their casita so she got two more bowls. Willow and Steve started on the pie crusts while Hank made more coffee and turned on some music.

The song sparked William, Otto, and Adela to begin a good-natured argument about playing Christmas music on Thanksgiving Day. The debate centered on allowing holiday songs on Thanksgiving or waiting until Friday. Adela took the position of listening to Christmas music that evening while they washed dishes, and Otto insisted no Christmas music until Friday.

"After dinner," grumbled Robert, as Adela swatted Otto with a towel.

Food processor and mixer motors added to the clamor of conversations among various generations of the family. The home filled with a happy energy that even raised the spirits of the three most sullen household members: Robert and the two dogs, Oscar and Grammy. The fervor of activity reached a crescendo as Spencer entered the room and took visual attendance. Outside of his usual element of a meeting room at Asuproz, no one stopped or even looked up to give him recognition.

Spencer watched Robert drilling Hank with technical questions in the living room as they both scribbled on a piece of paper. William jostled with Steve's children, and Adela was engaged in a discussion with Otto. Spencer opted to join his children with their bowls of cereal. Willow, Steve, and Sybil were all covered in flour as they rolled out pie crusts. This part of the tradition had evolved into a baking food fight with plumes of flour being tossed between the three of them as a penalty for each missed family trivia question.

William broke free from his grandchildren and pulled Spencer to one side. Tomorrow would be the first board meeting with Spencer completely in charge.

"Spencer, this may all seem ceremonial to you, but there are required items we've discussed for the meeting. Do the lawyers have the information packets prepared?"

"It will all be done for the meeting. They sent me the presentation on Monday."

Robert maneuvered into their discussion. "I haven't seen the annual summary. When do I get my copy?" William's focus intensified on his son as Robert continued, "Son, you and I have worked too hard on building this company. We've created and recreated it. Where's my packet?"

Spencer looked at his grandfather and father, wondering how to present the purchase offer with the two of them focused on past financials and a slide presentation.

"Spencer," his father's tone brought him back into the conversation. "When are your grandfather and I, and frankly, the rest of the board, going to get the documents for tomorrow's meeting?"

"I'm trying a new approach."

Robert demanded, "I don't want to be in a room full of people reading required documents for the first time."

The tension broke with Spencer's children pulling at their father as his wife approached with her phone ready to take a photo. "Smiles, everyone!" Sybil commanded. "Let's get the four generations in one photo while we're all still free from the clouds of flour!"

33
Clean-Up Crew

THE EARLY THANKSGIVING FEAST and evening round of turkey sandwiches and extra pie, left everyone in a daze from tryptophan and sugar. Adela and Otto remained to clean the kitchen, empty the dishwashers, and put away any remaining cooking gear. William finished making his legendary turkey soup in preparation for the family lunch after the Friday board meeting, another tradition. The other generations went to their separate rooms, except for Spencer and Sybil, who took an evening stroll while their children played video games.

Otto turned to Adela and William to proclaim his thanks for the day and for the gathering. The siblings replied with an echo of their brother's gratitude. Otto took a sip of Cabernet Sauvignon, whose tannins completed a full rouge on his cheeks.

"I mean it. We're fortunate to still get together and enjoy each other's company. It's not a foregone conclusion anymore. Nowadays, families don't always get along."

"To be fair, not all families got along back then, and we didn't always," William quipped.

"True, but look at us today," Otto continued, as he dried some remaining drops off the bowl he took out of the rack. "We've been raised by a father who behaved like a lion trainer with his technique of throwing a single steak of recognition into the cage for us to fight over. Remember growing up back in LA? And somehow, we're still together. You even migrated out to Palm Springs together."

William responded, "Was it that bad? You two came first and must have had it worse. I guess he kept us all so busy that I didn't notice. And as for the move out here, that was Dad's idea. At least for me."

"Me too!" echoed Adela with a smile. "His remark about creating a better environment for his grandson was classic him. He never thought about me being Steve's mother and my part in the decision."

Otto concurred. "Even though I have my responsibilities in LA, he still has these required events, even if it means staying in that RV!" He motioned to his silver-clad home away from home in the courtyard.

William continued, "Well, I appreciated Dad's help back then. Matilda had been on bed rest early on when pregnant with . . . well, we thought the move would help, that it would be enough."

The two siblings looked over at William. He rarely spoke of Matilda's pregnancy or the baby in the many years since losing them both.

"The troubles she had during the pregnancy and the final months of bed rest and hospital visits . . . Dad was right about us moving to the desert and leaving the pace and the stress of LA. He orchestrated my house buy and arranged to have Leandra stop by on Fridays. None of our help could save Matilda. I guess it made sense that we stayed here after her . . . after she left us. I couldn't see uprooting the kids again."

Adela crossed the kitchen and gave William a hug. "And did any of us know he'd buy this place," she said. "And we'd all be hanging out for holidays at The Dwelling?"

"He probably did from the start. He always wanted to live here," Otto laughed.

William took the lid off the soup and offered Adela a taste. "That began the migration out here. My family moved into the house over by the Araby wash and then he bought this place. LA seems so long ago. You two were older. When I think back to growing up in LA, weren't we like all the other families?"

Adela laughed, "Well, we weren't. We got baptized into business life from the first day we were born. All those challenges to see how smart we were. And then comparisons began between me and the two of you. How about those birthday gifts?"

"The birthday gifts!" Otto set the dried bowl down during his laughter and steadied himself on the counter.

"The gifts could never be a bike or a game or even clothes, for goodness' sake! They needed to be a type of puzzle," William continued. "I never trusted my age. The puzzles were meant for someone older than my birthday."

"And the intensity increased with each year," Otto added. "The focus on grades and awards, plus the requirement to work in the business while we were in school, even those jobs were a test."

William started ladling the cooling soup into a container. "It didn't occur to me at the time that other people didn't start working in their family business at the age of fifteen."

"Or fourteen!" Adela chimed in. "Did we even get paid? I guess child labor laws weren't in place back then."

"Well, you were the miracle. A preemie baby then and continually ahead of the pack. Frankly, I don't remember getting paid for all those days during summer break. He called them family outings. I remember being glad when Mom came to collect us for lunch as our shift-break whistle."

"I know I didn't get paid when I worked there in high school," William said. "He told me I was part of the intern program. Addie, at least you got to escape to spend the summer with Aunt Emma and then went to Europe before starting college."

Otto glanced at his sister and took over the discussion. "Our sister spun some string of lies about needing to be around midwestern girls to learn how to catch a husband. I knew she only wanted to get away from the indentured servitude with her brothers. You even got to go to London. I think you may have invented the gap year."

Adela laughed and defended herself. "Trust me, I put in enough years of labor, and I deserved a break from you two! Those were some long summers working for Dad, and a break from you two to be with Aunt Emma taught me about life and even how to oil paint."

"It made us strong," replied William.

"That which does not kill us . . ." added Otto, trying to mimic the voice of their father.

"A teachable moment!" They all instantly jumped in, like contestants on a game show, with the winner serving up the best parody of their father.

"I guess," replied William, in a hushed tone.

"And we survived. I wanted to thank you both for everything along the journey," Otto said to his two siblings as he poured the remnants of the bottle into his wine glass. "The expectations have been set high for us and are still coming from that lit window across the pool." He motioned toward their father's casita. "You two continued to work for the family business."

"As long as they would have me," Adela smirked.

"But you took all those skills and grew the recovery center. You still amaze me with all you do while I stepped away from the professional world. I worried you thought less of me. I didn't hold up my end of the family agreement—"

"There are no agreements or expectations," William interrupted his older brother. "That guy in the casita would have been more disappointed if you tried to be someone you weren't. At times, I think you are the strongest one for truly being yourself."

Adela raised her wine glass, "Cheers to that!" The other two followed suit. "Here's to the clean-up crew! I am thankful to be part of this group."

As the last of the glasses and dishes were being put away inside, Spencer and his wife strolled through the neighborhood, illuminated by the bright moonlight. Spencer struggled to control his excitement.

"I have some news," he started.

"I want to talk to you as well."

"Is it important?"

"It is for me."

"You go first. Then we can talk about my surprise."

"I want a divorce."

"You . . . "

"I have been thinking about it for some time, and you know we haven't been good for a while."

"You want a divorce? Who have you been seeing?"

"Spence." Sybil stopped and shook her head. "Spencer, stop getting three steps down your rabbit-hole mind and listen to me. This hasn't been working and I can see the impact on our kids."

"So, it's because I am gone so much? We talked about this in counseling. I can be home more. In fact, that is about to change."

"You being home more would make it worse at this point. I've talked to my parents and they're going to help me and the kids for now."

"Your parents knew before me?"

"Spencer, I can't believe you're surprised by any of this, and it convinces me that I am making the right decision. We don't need to announce anything this weekend. I'm sorry to bring it up on Thanksgiving, but we haven't had any other time together. Every time I've tried, there has been an important business call or you aren't there at all. When you are here, it's like you've not considered any of the issues we've discussed. There's no spark, no love, no emotion left between us. It's over. We need to move on."

"I don't understand."

"Spencer. Really? That *is* the biggest issue. I agree you don't understand. You stopped putting any energy into this relationship years ago."

"Do you have any idea what this is going to do to the image of the company?"

"To the company or to you? Spencer, you pour time and money into your image, but it's never changed your self-absorbed, pretentious nature—something you could have fixed for free."

"And you're perfect?"

"Lower your voice. I'm finally realizing this is who you will always be. I'm done. Let's talk about this next week. We can figure out details when the kids are back in school. Now, what do you need to tell me?"

"Nothing. I don't remember. Let's go back."

"That's fine, but the kids and I are leaving first thing in the morning for Pasadena. You can let me know what you tell your family."

"Fine! I'm staying at the Palm Springs place tonight. I need to clear my head of all this for the board meeting. Did you consider I work tomorrow? You can let me know what you tell *our* kids."

34

Black Friday

SPENCER WOKE AT HIS HOME in the Araby neighborhood of Palm Springs. He was alone and still thinking about the night before as he lay in bed replaying his and Sybil's entire relationship. Had Sybil given him any sign things were that bad? Probably. Had he been completely faithful? No. Did he spend much time with the children? No. He justified his absence on fulfilling his role as provider. He also felt pressure from his father and from the entire family to keep the business successful as he fought for his own vision of its future.

There was still the offer. Thanksgiving had passed without him getting to share the news with anyone. They all were there, but he couldn't find time alone with any of them. Robert interrupted his only chance to speak with his father, and Sybil's surprise didn't help.

Spencer wanted to bring the proposal to the board meeting with a couple of family members ready to support him, but with no decision at Thanksgiving, he decided not to add the offer to the agenda and would take advantage of the months leading up to the February deadline to get everyone in agreement. He figured Sybil and the children had already left for Pasadena, ending any more conversation on that topic for the moment. Two items off his to-do list, at least for the moment. This meant he could go for a run and clear his head. He could map out future discussions with each family member during his cardio, so he laced up his running shoes and headed out the door.

Without presenting the offer, he had nothing else he needed to prepare for the board meeting. Once he finished his run, he'd meet the lawyers and finance officer, who were prepared with all the required paperwork. Spencer wasn't a fan of the annual meeting on the holiday weekend. But since the whole family was in town, they always held the official gathering at the tech center. From there, the family returned to The Dwelling. William's turkey soup and the remaining leftovers were mainstays. Spencer decided he should check in with his lawyer. He wanted to confirm that his prenuptial agreement kept any company stock out of his upcoming divorce. That would mean one less person he'd need to negotiate with on selling the company.

During his run, he resolved to begin the Asuproz buyout discussion with his father instead of other family members. He continued his trek toward The Dwelling, where he would draw his father away from the rest of the family. Spencer thought about his divorce and couldn't predict his father's reaction. Therefore, he chose not to share that news. He'd convince his father to sell the company and then they'd go to the casita to meet with Robert. That morning he would be able to get a promise to sell from the two most influential family members.

The crisp air kept Spencer's thoughts flowing, and with each step he reviewed his pitch. He looked up and found himself in front of Tiffany's yard. There he saw his father with a cup of coffee, reading from his tablet. Startled, Spencer stumbled—just as Tiffany stepped out the patio door holding two mimosas. She wore a robe so sheer that he could read her Tiffany tattoo. Next came a rapid-fire exchange of comments between the three of them.

"Dad, what's this?"

"Spence?"

"Spencer, oh my gawd. Why are you here?" The two champagne flutes shattered as they hit the patio.

"Tiffany?"

"Spencer? William, why is Spencer here?"

"Tif, I didn't invite ... Jeeez Spence, what *are* you doing here?"

"Tiffany? Dad? What are you doing with her?"

"Robert Spencer, be civil."

"Dad!"

"Spencer!"

"William, I'm going to go inside to get dressed."

"Dad! What's going on?"

Spencer became more accusatory as his comments continued. He claimed Tiffany trapped his father, saying she must have hooks for hands. William stood, to be eye-to-eye with his son, only to realize he was still in a robe as he cinched the loose tie.

"For gawd's sake, Dad, you're a mess." Spencer caught Tiffany peering out the window.

"Spencer, watch your tone."

"I can't even ... " as Spencer turned and headed back to his house. Spencer's entire morning plan dissolved. There would be no discussion of selling that morning and the three of them were never together again.

35

Executive Board Meeting

OTTO AND ROBERT ARRIVED at the tech center early. The company founder had no formal role yet insisted to be the first one present to welcome each attendee. Otto served both as Robert's personal aide and an unofficial facilitator to keep the agenda on track. Robert moved himself to the far end of the table with his wheelchair at its highest setting. Next came members of Asuproz's legal team—composed and silent. Their demeanor aligned with the professionalism established by Robert. The lawyer sat near Otto as the paralegal distributed agendas to each place. Corporate governance and protocol ruled the day.

Spencer and his assistant entered the room as his grandfather reviewed the agenda. Robert called out to Otto that his grandson sent more communication for the Walk of Fame event than for the board meeting. Spencer shuffled the papers in front of him; his silence filled the room.

"Will there be more than these meager topics?" Robert spoke directly to Spencer.

"We are sticking to fundamentals this year," Spencer replied, not looking up. There was no mention of the offer or any new business on the agenda.

Most of the remaining family members, minor shareholders, and corporate officers entered the utilitarian room; its design matching the mood of the attendees. Head nods and handshakes replaced the embraces seen yesterday. There were no assigned seats for the meeting. Still, each attendee went straight to their usual spots. Willow and Hank walked in quietly. The only sound came from Willow as she took Hank's phone from his scrolling hand and put it in her purse, always in older-sister mode. Adela passed by Spencer, headed directly to Hank, and whispered in his ear. He nodded, as she moved on and sat next to Steve. The two of them reviewed the agenda and scribbled notes. Most of the other chairs filled with required corporate officers.

Two chairs remained empty. One on the left end of the table by the door honored Matilda and her family's contributions to the business's success. Each family member automatically paused and touched the chair in reflex as they entered the room. The other empty chair belonged to William.

The top of the hour passed. The lawyer looked to Otto, who checked his phone and tried to get Spencer's attention for direction on how to proceed. William was never late. He normally accompanied Otto and Robert to the meeting, except not this time. Earlier that morning in Robert's casita, Otto got a call from his brother as he helped his father prepare. William said nothing to Otto about the morning outburst with Spencer and instead conveyed his desire to spend as little time in the meeting as possible. He told them to go ahead without him and that he would drive separately. Robert demanded Otto to use the speaker to his phone.

"Where in the hell are you? This is still your company."

"Dad, I'll be at the meeting."

"Your son's incompetence is bad enough, and now I've got to deal with your delinquency. What exactly do you think the title Chairman of the Board means?"

"Dad, I said I will be there."

"Are we going to get a formal agenda and financial report? What exactly are we approving at the meeting?"

"Dad let's see what—"

"This will be the last time our annual meeting is handled with such incompetence."

"Dad—"

"You need to replace Spencer." Robert pounded his fist on the table of the casita. "Did everybody get that?"

William's conversation with his father was more heated than the one earlier that morning with Spencer. Before saying goodbye, he told Otto to announce that the family lunch was canceled. He would see them at the board meeting.

In the meeting room, even more time passed. Spencer seemed frozen. Robert shouted across the table to Spencer, asking if William had decided to skip the meeting. Otto and Steve started conferring with the lawyer about contingencies. Spencer appeared to be in a daze. Willow elbowed Hank and pointed at the panicked face of their brother. Others in the room started checking their phones. Adela finally checked hers for messages and screamed out in pain, dropping her phone as Steve ran to her side. Before she could say anything, the door to the meeting room opened.

Tiffany entered and collapsed into Matilda's chair. "He's dead! William is dead."

36

Friday Night

HANK'S PHONE FLASHED and buzzed like a caution sign of his future. The phone sat on his glass-top coffee table, which amplified the vibration from each call and text. He didn't have any reason to read the messages because they posed questions he couldn't answer—how he was doing or if they could help. He had no answers. He had no idea what he needed or what to do with their prayers. Hank couldn't take any more of the noise and reached to turn off his phone. As he picked it up, the screen lit again and formed a glow in the darkness of his apartment. A message popped up on the screen.

Kate: I heard, are you OK?

Hank read the message and left his phone on. He still didn't know the answer to the question, even for Kate. He waited and then replied.

Hank: IDK

Kate: Need anything?

Hank: IDK

Kate watched her phone screen, waiting for more of a response. She started and stopped several messages and then deleted them. More time passed. Hank sat holding his phone, watching the bubbles of possible messages from Kate until they stopped, making his phone and the room go dark for minutes. All messages had stopped. Until finally the phone lit up again.

Kate: Srly Im worried

Hank: I'll be fine

Hank: I won't drink

Kate: Thats not what i meant

Kate: but good

Another twenty minutes passed in the dark with Hank staring at the words 'I won't drink' and trying to process their level of truth along with his feelings.

Hank: He and I started to reconnect

Kate: I know

Hank: Where r u

Kate: can I call

Hank didn't answer, unsure if he had a voice or if he could get words out. Texting was painful enough. More time passed.

Hank: Wish you were here

Kate: Whats going on

Hank couldn't put an answer into words but knew Kate would worry.

Hank: I wish I had more time w him

Kate: I get it

Hank: Im so sad

Hank: Hes gone

Hank's doorbell rang. He got up from the couch and opened the door to see Kate.

"I thought you were at your mom's."

"I was when I got the news. I hopped in my car and had to see if you were okay. I only planned to drive by your place . . . "

Kate stood in the entry as Hank dropped his head onto her shoulder and felt her support. She turned and kissed his cheek. None of the Hank-and-Kate rules of dating held that night. They made their way from the doorway to the bedroom, kissing. Their clumsy movements amplified the mixture of caution and passion as they explored each other's bodies: Hank's pants undone with one shoe still on, Kate's sweatshirt pushed up around her neck as Hank undid her bra. Somehow, in the tangle of sheets and misplaced pillows, the two completely undressed and finally got to experience what they had been imagining for months. The spontaneity overrode thoughts of being intimate with someone while sober. He cared for Kate and moved slowly, exploring her tight runner's body while watching for her responses, which echoed his movements.

The night continued with them intertwined and thrusting until Kate moved on top of Hank, pulsing to a point he couldn't control. During a final twitch of his body, she leaned down and kissed him, and then rolled over beside him. He lay there panting to recover and then, with a burst of energy, rolled on top of her. He kissed her as sweat from his hair dripping onto her body. His mouth traveled down her body to her breasts, moving from one to the other, measuring her reactions to discover his next focus. He continued down and kept exploring. He traced her torso with his tongue, then moved to her thighs. He went side to side until he paused between them, giving all his attention to her. His body echoed her movements. Her back arched, and his pace grew frantic to match her reactions. Her breaths became gasps until they both collapsed.

Kate woke the next morning and competed in the one-woman game of pre-morning scavenger hunt for her clothes. She rushed to gather everything with the goal of getting dressed and on the road to her mother's house in time to start Thanksgiving Saturday with her family. After the unforgettable night, she felt the pull to get back to Encinitas or the need to get away from facing what the night meant. She reached beneath a pillow, half-covering her bra, and kissed Hank on the forehead. Kate found the final item of the morning search and sped her pace. Circling in the air around her and the motionless Hank was their agreement to not get physical and to keep away from each other during the holidays. The plan failed in a wonderful way they'd never forget. Kate returned to the task at hand. If she left immediately, she could be back in time for her family's breakfast and the planned day of Christmas shopping.

Kate looked from Hank to the clock. She picked up a pen and paper off his desk only to set them back. She went to the bathroom mirror and pulled her hair back and paused in an attempt to read her own expression. The reflection did not have any answers. She returned to the bedroom, grabbed her keys, kissed Hank again, and headed to her car.

Hank attempted a feeble grab as he watched her leave. He still felt fragile, bombarded from every aspect of his life. The reality of his father's death returned to the forefront. He needed to check on Tiffany and Willow. He needed to call them and yet, not quite. He also needed a moment to hold off the impending world beyond and stay hidden in the protection of the bedsheet covering him. He rolled over to the other side of the bed. The linens were still filled with the remaining warmth from Kate's body and her entrancing scent. He breathed in the recent memories of them together as he hugged the pillow and closed his eyes. A few more moments. This new chapter in Hank's life meant a dream come true and the shadow of emptiness from a father he would never see again.

37

Toy Drive

"WE ARE FOCUSING on service to others," Thomas recited to himself as he looked in his bathroom mirror and applied a white base-layer of makeup to his face.

"What did you say?" Reese asked as he finished applying his own lipstick.

"I am dealing with all your good-deed-doing and its impact on me. Can we do some other of the events where I don't need to wear make up?"

"We can, but they aren't as fun."

It had been weeks since *Hank's reset*—Thomas's label for Hank's night of drinking. Reese refused to call it anything and focused on spending more time with Thomas. They went off the grid and spent Thanksgiving weekend camping in Joshua Tree National Park. During the time away, they discussed their relationship and reached an agreement on defining terms: important, couple, and together. The additional word *healing* emerged while they helped each other apply makeup from a countertop filled with cosmetics and glitter. The annual Christmas toy drive held by the Sisters of Perpetual Indulgence needed volunteers, and these two were applying final touches.

A sticker covered the side of Thomas's makeup kit.

The Sisters have devoted ourselves to community service, ministry, and outreach to those on the edges, and to promoting human rights, respect for diversity and spiritual enlightenment. We use humor and irreverent wit to expose the forces of bigotry, complacency and guilt that chain the human spirit.

Reese looked at the sticker and his nun costume laid out on the bed and laughed.

"The sticker should have added how we also go through a lot of foundation, eyebrow wax, false eyelashes, and pantyhose."

He helped Thomas put on his habit while protecting the makeup and continuing with his lecture.

"It's surprising how makeup from Rite Aid and a wrap of black fabric changes me. This morning, dog walkers avoided me out of fear. Now I am someone they bring their kids to for photos during the toy drive."

Reese shook his head and took a breath to steady his hand as he asked Thomas to close his eyes so he could work in the liquid eyeliner on Thomas's face.

"They are either scared of me or I am one of the invisible people, along with the gardeners, housekeepers, and pool cleaners. Add a little glitter and transform me into the sister that is handing out toys and I am more popular than a parade float throwing candy. Reese opened his backpack and pulled out two dolls for the toy drive.

"Do we wrap them?"

"No, they want the toys unwrapped so they know the age group," replied Thomas.

"Well, it's been a good few of weeks for collecting recyclables. Lots of holiday partiers filling the blue bins, so I could get these dolls and the accessories. You should've seen that lady at the store giving me the eye when I asked where all the brown dolls were. I went to a few different stores to find some Latinas."

They did one final check in the mirror. Thomas grabbed the donations, and the two nuns headed off to the event.

38

Regroup Group Session

THE DAY HAD COME. Hank plodded down the corridor of the recovery center to the meeting room. This was the first Musketeers session since his emergency meeting. Scheduled before William's death and Hank and Kate's midnight meetup, Hank anticipated an even longer session with the group. He arrived at the counselor's room a few minutes early and found the room already filled with Reese, Thomas, Kate, Adela, and Willow. The conversation stopped as Hank opened the door.

"Great, an intervention? Okay, you win! I. Will. Never. Drink. Again." Hank declared, placing his hand on his heart.

Kate looked away. "It's not a joke."

"Who's laughing?" he said as he flopped into the empty chair.

"We're worried," Kate continued. "About you. We want to make sure you're okay. You've had a lot happen in the last few days. We've all had a lot happen." The lack of response from Hank extended into a long silence.

Adela turned to Hank; her voice less steady than typical for her at the recovery center. "I want to let you know that I am here, not representing this establishment, but like Willow, representing support from your family. We are grateful you shared what has happened with us. Your friends came to Willow and me asking that we be here. This isn't an intervention. I miss my brother so much and . . . I can't imagine what you're going through with the loss of your father."

The counselor jumped in to reset the discussion, "Your

friends and your family want to show you support. We are here to talk. We want to discuss how you and your friends are doing today."

Hank looked out the window. Another moment of silence stretched on as the counselor waited for Hank to respond. No one in the room moved until Thomas sprang up, and in the process, he kicked over the coffee cup sitting at his feet.

"Ah crap, sorry about that spill, but this is bullshit! Complete and utter bullshit. Hank. Buddy. I'm so pissed at you." Thomas started pacing and realized he was trapped inside a chair circle of people, so he stopped right in front of Hank. "We are in this together and you go off the deep end. Don't you think I've wanted to have a drink?" He looked at Reese and Kate. "I know the rest of you are thinking the same thing."

Reese reached up to try to calm him but stopped when he saw Thomas's glare as he continued to rant.

"I'm jealous. Jealous as hell that you got to do the one thing that has been my favorite means of escape and I can't do it anymore. We can't do it anymore. You've brought it all back; the cravings, the uncertainty, having nightmares about drinking. What you do impacts all of us, maybe even more so. You have everything you could need and you still messed up. What am I supposed to do with that? What the hell am I supposed to do? I don't have your means or money or family or name. What does you breaking your sobriety mean for how I'm going to end up?" Thomas got right in Hank's line of sight. "And then you bring Reese into it!"

Reese interrupted, "It's cool, Thomas. He didn't know."

Thomas shot another look at Reese and continued. "No, I need to say this. Hank, you were completely selfish. Who knows what was going through your head after you blacked out? I doubt you knew. But you knew what was happening earlier. You knew to call one of us. You knew." Thomas returned to his seat. "Were you hoping Reese would start drinking or doing pills again? You have so many people in your life and even have family here today!

For Christ's sake, your family runs the joint! You've messed with us. Did you think about Reese or me? Have you seen how torn up Kate is? Look at your family!"

"Hank, man, you've got us all rattled." Reese put his arm around Thomas.

"Shit, Hank, you haven't been returning messages," Willow added. "We care about you. We love you."

Kate looked up. "This isn't how we wanted this to go today. We didn't plan to start with a battle."

Adela looked at Kate and replied, "Never fear quarrels."

" . . . but seek hazardous adventures." Reese finished the quote together.

"Alexandre Dumas," Adela replied.

"From The Three Musketeers," Reese added. "Except now there are four of us. All for one."

"And one for all." The other three said in quiet unison.

The conversation went on until everyone had time to express their feelings. Before Hank arrived at the meeting, they agreed to let Hank know they were there for him and to let Hank talk through anything he wanted. Kate explained the happenings on the night of William's death and thought they should discuss it. The calmer plan didn't materialize, although Thomas's outburst got them to the same endpoint, with Kate and Reese echoing Thomas's fear of uncertainty for their future sobriety. The session ended with Hank reiterating what they all knew: he took nothing for granted and was going to live day by day.

39

The Funeral

WILLIAM'S RENOWN STRETCHED from the desert community to Hollywood. He sat on numerous corporate boards and was a major donor to many nonprofits. His memorial commanded attention. Spencer planned both the public event and private funeral. Otto, Adela, and Willow were in a haze, and Robert wouldn't leave his casita. Spencer managed requests from a range of organizations all wanting representation at the memorial. He issued a corporate press release and sent emails to key customers. The notice contained a list of William's accomplishments, the family preceding him in death, and the ones left in mourning. Spencer also felt the need to define a cause of death:

William suffered a massive heart attack while driving to the annual corporate board meeting of the company he helped create. The cause of death was attributed to a combination of heart failure and a subsequent collision. He died instantly.

Absent were the details from earlier in the morning when William, body soaked in sweat, collapsed into the patio chair after Spencer left. The obituary didn't discuss how angry William became at Tiffany's urgings to go to the hospital. Yet another person in his life tried to tell him what to do. The memorial notice didn't state how he considered her home a sanctuary. There was an omission of him resting outside before going into Tiffany's house to get dressed in clothes he kept there. Absent was reference to him parking his car out of sight in the second garage bay. Other missing information, that Tiffany would never forget, was it being the first time William asked her to be more public and suggested they share the morning together on the patio.

He drove away that morning as Tiffany stepped into the street with her arms wrapped around her body. No tributes spoke of William making it a block before swerving to the left, straightening the car's path, and then running the stoplight—where a delivery truck t-boned his car. Such details didn't evoke angels carrying him to the afterlife and were omitted.

Tiffany witnessed the crash and ran to the scene. Squad cars, an ambulance, and a firetruck followed. Tiffany immediately texted Hank and then tried calling and texting the only member of William's family she could. The message to Adela said: "Terrible car crash. I think William is dead." One of the officers tried to calm her. The EMTs found no signs of life in the motionless body covered in blood. After several futile attempts, they placed the body on the gurney and drove away. A second squad car took Tiffany to the Asuproz tech center. She ran ahead of the officer to the door of the conference room and broke in with the news.

It seemed as if everyone attended the public memorial. Hank accompanied Tiffany. Even the on-scene police officers and EMTs were present. The three-hour visitation crept to five as the long line moved past the closed casket. Groups of the Palm Springs moneyed set, colleagues, family, and friends attended what became the largest social gathering of the year. There were times when the noise reached a party level, and two mournful-toned violin players raised their volume to remind attendees to return to respectful whispers. Anyone of significance in Southern California, known or unknown to William, was at the memorial. The pastor at Our Lady of Guadalupe led a closing prayer in front of the hundreds of attendees. He took a moment to remind those in attendance of William's dedication to the church and then ended with a solemn Amen.

The public memorial ended, and the attendees went their separate ways. The immediate family appreciated the community support while at the same time were completely drained. Only to have to take part in the family's private memorial the next day.

Spencer requested an immediate date for the funeral, a relief for the priest as he wrapped up Thanksgiving services and prepared for the first week of Advent and the four weeks leading up to Christmas. The morning of the funeral, the pastor stood with Spencer at the altar of the intimate church, making final decisions on the scriptural readings. William's casket sat near the altar as the organist played "Here I am Lord," and the statue of Our Lady of Guadalupe watched over him. Robert and Otto entered and took their places at the front. Leandra, Lea, and her family sat halfway back, all wearing black, rosaries in hand.

A car service dropped off Adela, Steve, and his family at the front doors of the church. They were about to go in when Adela spotted Hank wandering a block away. She and Steve chased after him as Steve's wife brought their children inside. Hank stopped when he heard them call his name. He struggled to steady his breath as Adela and Steve reached him.

"It's my mom . . . It's—she's out of control. I swear we only wanted to be near the funeral."

Adela put her hand on his cheek. "What do you mean, *only* near the funeral?"

Hank explained that Spencer had made it clear—at the public memorial—that Hank wasn't welcome at the private funeral and that his mother should stay away, too.

"This morning my mom called, said she needed to say goodbye to my dad. She asked me to meet her at Baristo Park so we could go together to the church. She wanted to sit outside and be able to say her prayers during the service. She promised not to interfere."

Hank blurted out everything, his body shaking with his erratic breaths. He said Tiffany looked too haggard to attend a funeral or be in public.

"She screamed about being completely alone. She blamed me for ignoring her and for spending more time with my other family. She said that without William she didn't have any family."

Hank shook his head and looked away, trying to find a way to continue. "She didn't make any sense and had such rage. That's when Spencer drove by and stopped. He rolled down his window and started berating her appearance and behavior. Spencer told us both to leave. He turned to his children, schooling them to not end up like my mom, and then drove on to the church."

Hank said Tiffany yanked her arm away and yelled for him to leave her alone. Then she ran down the block and disappeared.

"She was inconsolable, and chasing after her would have made things worse. I didn't know what to do, but I felt drawn toward the church, wanting to be there out of respect for my dad. I thought I could pull myself together enough to sit in the back, but then I chickened out and decided to go home."

Adela and Steve were stunned by Spencer's decision and tried to convince Hank that no one else in the family knew. Their reaction was nothing compared to the shock on Spencer's face as he stood at the front of the church. Spencer heard the rear doors open and watched as Hank walked down the aisle with Adela on one arm and Steve on the other. Adela's defiant stare shut down Spencer. The three of them preceded down the aisle and moved into the front row, opposite Willow, Otto, and Robert. The final remembrance for William began.

40

Fire Pit and Takeout

AFTER THE FUNERAL, Otto invited Hank to The Dwelling for dinner—on condition that he bring takeout Thai. Hank looked forward to spending time alone with his Uncle Otto after attending an AA meeting. The plan changed when he ran into Reese who promptly invited himself to dinner. Hank suspected his friends were taking shifts to keep watch on him, and for the moment he didn't mind. The evening dining of spring rolls, Pad Thai, and yellow curry with Otto and Reese at the fire pit helped Hank on an unbelievable day. The spice of the curry heated the insides as the fire pit took care of the rest.

Dinner ended as a chilly evening breeze filled the desert valley. Otto's body slouched deeper in the chaise lounge. Finished with food and conversation, he pulled up one of the tartan print blankets as his floppy hat tipped low on his face. He looked like a Scottish shepherd napping as his dog tended to the sheep. Otto drifted off, so Hank motioned to Reese to lower his voice.

"Oh, shush yourself. All I'm asking is where you two stand. I know you spend time together and you certainly accessed the benefits part of the friends-with-benefits, but what are you thinking for you and Kate?"

Hank continued a gesture for Reese to turn down the volume and wished it would go all the way to zero. They both had been in this situation before. Reese's nocturnal mind tended to ramp up as everyone else wanted to drop off to sleep. This time, instead of Reese's usual diatribe on a book he had read, the talk consisted of a Q&A session where Reese posed personal questions more appropriate for the person in the relationship than in his role as a third wheel. This went on with the same question asked several ways, with limited responses from Hank, who had collapsed from mental fatigue. The motionless Otto didn't contribute to the discussion or help dilute the interrogation.

Finally, Reese stood, signaling the end of his questions and the start of his televangelist-styled lecture. Hank couldn't think of a way to avoid the performance.

"It's all about energy. This fire is energy! What are your feelings for Kate?"

Hank responded with a shrug. "I think she likes me. I don't know." Then he pulled his blanket closer to his face.

"The knitting mill put energy into that blanket and you are warm. The moon up there? It's not shining on its own. It's because of the sun. The sun is all the way over on the other side of the earth and shining on the moon. Energy is reflecting to us. Energy comes and goes, and life comes and goes."

Hank felt a tear run down his face, remembering the last time he'd seen his father.

"Too much energy will kill us and not enough will leave us to die," Reese continued. "I see it all the time with the lizards by the creek. During the hottest times of summer, the sun parches everything. Some of those four-legged reptiles can't find water and die. Too much energy. Then, on winter nights when the temperature drops much colder than tonight, the lizards get all motionless. They can't move and fall from tree branches. It's not long before a screech owl makes the lizard a snack. Not enough energy! That's like you and Kate."

Hank looked up with a baffled expression. Did he get called a lizard or a screech owl in the scenario? Reese got frustrated by his friend's expression.

"I'm not talking about the animals. I'm talking about entropy and energy. The sun is energy. This fire is energy. The meals I help distribute. Energy! Love, love is energy. The chaplain at the lunch program says God is love. Well, love is energy and critical to life. You can't expect to say you are in love with Kate if you don't put any energy into the relationship. The moon up there isn't going to shine all by itself without the sun. No one is writing any songs about a big dark rock in the sky because no one is going to see the moon without the sun shining on it. You need to decide whether you're going to put some real energy into your time with Kate or if you're going to let it get cold and drop from a tree and die."

"Can't you just tell me what I should do?"

"Alexandre Dumas said, 'In general, people only ask for advice that they may not follow, or if they should follow it, that they may have somebody to blame for having given it.' Hank, you are going to have to figure out what to do with your energy."

Hank sat dumbfounded as Reese returned to his seat. The sermon ended. Everything went quiet until the hat fell off Otto's head as he bellowed out a loud "Amen," stood, grabbed his hat, and shuffled over to Hank.

"You should listen to your friend." And then he wandered off to the RV.

Things went dark in the RV soon after Otto's departure. Hank stayed silent in an attempt to avoid another lesson from Reese. The light still glowed in his grandfather's casita; Hank wondered how his grandfather was doing with the death of a son. The thought of knocking on the door of the casita vanished when the lights went dark. Even Hank's grandfather was done with the emotion filled day. Hank turned off the fire pit, and he and Reese left The Dwelling to go their separate ways.

41

"We're All Misfits"

As HANK APPROACHED Kate's place, he saw the blinking red and green lights in the window and the glow from a Christmas tree. Hank appreciated his friends keeping his time full since the funeral; including a movie night. The temperatures in the '70s for the last few days made the 10-foot Santa yard inflatables and holiday lights on palm trees seem even more amiss than most years. Kate greeted Hank at the door with a hug and a kiss on the cheek.

"Merry Christmas—are you set for this?"

Reese and Thomas were in the living room making a commotion, pouring Chex Mix and Bugles chips into bowls. Reese declared the four Musketeers deserved a holiday gathering free from counselors and open-ended questions about how they were doing. Reese had the perfect option. His favorite holiday television special was *Rudolph, the Red-Nosed Reindeer*, and he wanted to share the magical show with his friends, especially if one of them had a decent flatscreen TV. Kate did, and owned an old VCR tape player.

"We are watching the tape recording!" Reese exclaimed as he produced it from one of the compartments of his backpack.

A declaration from Reese couldn't be ignored. After all, he named them the four Musketeers when they first met in rehab. Kate, Thomas, and Hank were on the back patio of the recovery center during one of the breaks when an orderly escorted Reese to the detox rooms on the first night of his stay. He greeted the group with, "Ah, my companions, Porthos and Aramis, and you must be D'Artagnan," as he spun around, swinging an imaginary sword. They were known as the four Musketeers from that day forward. Kate suspected that Reese enjoyed the group moniker and the naming of the others so he could be Athos, the self-declared leader of the group. They were all surprised he could remember assigning their names when they were together later that week. Hank's first night with Reese out of detox consisted of him tossing and turning, completely restless, and reciting something to himself. He finally curled up in a chair, clinging to the armrest. The admissions staff eventually returned Reese's backpack, and he slept better from then on. Reese's introduction to the group was an odd beginning, but it worked, and they formed a bond to be there for each other, all for one . . .

In good times and in bad, the Musketeers gathered to confront the world. They had survived the Hank reset and were moving forward. Holidays were an extra important time to connect, and the movie night at Kate's peppermint-candle-scented home was the perfect setting. Soon, everyone settled around the television. The show started with the opening scene of the talking snowman who helped introduce all the characters: Santa, Mrs. Claus, all the elves and reindeer, and Rudolph. The four of them attempted to put Bugles chips on their fingers and compared stories of toys they wanted as children. Reese was the champion of Bugles fingernails. He claimed this as childhood foreshadowing of his future talents in the nail department.

The show continued, leaving the group silent during the scene with Rudolph on the island of misfit toys as each toy showed its defect and why no one would want them. None of the Musketeers made a sound until Reese broke the mood and yelled out along with the dialogue, "We're all misfits!" Everyone laughed as Thomas repeated a character saying, "I'm a choo-choo train with square wheels."

By the end of the night, Reese decided he wanted a Christmas gift from the Land of Misfit Toys and began mimicking a cowboy with a squirt gun that shot jelly. Thomas took on the role of Mrs. Claus and ordered the cowboy and elf Hank to help clean up everything on the coffee table.

As the rest of them brought the dirty plates and glasses back to the kitchen, Kate slipped sandwiches and a banana into Reese's backpack along with a few dollars, deciding that some people deserved a Secret Santa.

42

Marbles

MARGARET MCGREGOR, the fourth of seven children, was born in 1950 as part of the family of Patrick Michael and Mary Catherine McGregor. The parents met at their childhood Boston parish. The two could have walked out of a Norman Rockwell painting, the classic American freckle-faced couple, filled with hope and innocence. Part of the Greatest Generation, Patrick went off in duty to fight the Nazis. Mary Catherine waited, volunteered, and planted a victory garden.

Time made Mary Catherine stronger. She grew to love Patrick even more through each letter received. They kept her heart going all the way to the end of the war. He returned to Boston and kept the wedding promise made before deploying to Europe. That promise filled her with joy and became his one last grasp of hope.

The label of "liberator" was bestowed with great fanfare—unless you were one of the US troops liberating captives from concentration camps. Patrick was not in Paris, where women and children greeted the US soldiers with kisses and wine, but instead he was at Buchenwald. Patrick and others in his company faced the horror of emaciated bodies stacked like kindling, waiting for the ovens. He gathered a small child into his arms and watched helplessly as the remaining soul left its body. The image burned into every future thought. His screams couldn't purge abhorrence from his mind. Days passed before he could hold down food, one of many liberators trying not to fall apart.

Thankfully, the war ended, and he returned to the United

States to marry his sweetheart. The wedding took place in the same church they both attended in their youth and where they baptized their children, born almost every year.

Mary Catherine thought the children would help Patrick heal and overcome the emptiness she saw in her husband. *Time heals all wounds* counseled her parents, and became Mary Catherine's prayer. There were moments when Patrick would be holding one of their children and he'd break into tears, screaming as he ran to cower in their bedroom or the garage.

The birth of their seventh child, Ian Mark McGregor, broke him. In one of Patrick's fits, he dropped the newborn baby into a chair and ran off to the garage, followed in pursuit by his daughter, Margaret. Only five years old, she couldn't catch up to her father to tell him everything would be fine; the way her mom had told him so many times before. She opened the garage with the hopeful message at the same moment Patrick pulled the trigger. Her father's blood wet her face and dress as his body fell to the ground. The bullet shattered his skull and splintered her personality into as many pieces.

For Margaret, the impact was immediately apparent in her outbursts. She went from moody to disruptive in seconds. Teachers mistook her mumbling for backtalk. She didn't finish the ninth grade before being institutionalized by her single-parent mother, struggling to handle a troubled daughter while raising the other six children. One of the chicks had to be pushed out of the nest to save the family. Margaret stood at the front door of the dilapidated government building, left with two changes of clothes and seven hugs, never to see her family again.

Over the years, Margaret endured a pattern of mistreatment across various institutions, until she was ultimately released when her facility lost funding. Her discharge had nothing to do with her capabilities, leaving her to care for herself alone in Riverside, California—only herself and the voices in her head.

One morning, some concerned community parents chipped in for train tickets to remove Margaret from their neighborhood and stop her sleeping in the elementary school playground. They placed her on the Amtrak train accompanied by two community escorts. With $16 one-way tickets, the two escorts took Margaret to Palm Springs. Margaret was left at the train station while the men were picked up by their wives. The two couples drove back to their homes in Riverside, celebrating the investment of less than $50 to improve their neighborhood.

In Palm Springs, the years passed without birthday celebrations or other milestones. Margaret wandered the city streets, invisible, like another grain of sand blowing through the desert. Her skin surrendered to the sun, baked to a neglected dry leather. The lines covering her face were embedded with dirt and sand from wherever she managed to sleep. Mats of gray straw-dry hair tried to escape from a faded tie-dye scarf left from a past music festival. It served as her crown of homeless royalty. Her last shower and testing of vitals came from a charity med-a-van two years prior. It also was when a volunteer dentist extracted her four remaining teeth—a preventive measure against infection. The procedure removed her ability to say her name, which from her lips became a gummy saliva-distorted Mar-et or Mahrah. The closest any listener could understand; her name was Marbles. Perhaps the nickname came from her sounding like she had a mouthful of marbles or that she had lost her proverbial marbles.

The December night air chilled Margaret, driving her deep into one of the under-road ravines for the night, dragging a dilapidated baby stroller containing her possessions, including a trash-stained doll. She laid the stroller on its side to use as a footstool, sitting with her back against a cement beam and softened by a discarded patio cushion. Sleeping while sitting up wasn't her preference but a learned survival position. Too many men had gotten their advantage over her in her early days after leaving the institution. They rarely stole anything but tried to leave a deposit along with bruises from holding her down. Lying down to sleep left her too vulnerable to those on the prowl.

She began to drift off while clinging to her doll when she heard a voice.

"Marbles, is that you?"

She looked up, startled. A flash of light broke through the darkness. She fumbled for the knife tucked inside the doll.

"I've got something for you," the voice continued, as a hand reached out with a few dollars, a banana, and two sandwiches wrapped in Christmas-printed Saran wrap.

"Anng uu, ans," she said, as Cans, or Reese, nodded, placed a gentle hand on her head, and walked away.

43

Christmas Presents!

NONE OF THE MUSKETEERS were late for the breakfast gift exchange; even the two perpetually tardy members arrived early. Reese led the line entering the diner and claimed the round booth in the corner. Along with his backpack, he carried a red bag tied with a ribbon, and wore a Santa hat. The morning dog walkers got an extra eyeful spotting Santa Cans. Close behind were Hank and Kate, followed by Thomas in a bright green Grinch shirt. Festive music played over the speakers announcing "It's Christmas time in the city."

Sparked from deep childhood reflexes, the Musketeers struggled with anticipation of opening gifts. They had wanted to do a gift exchange ever since watching the Rudolph Christmas show together. Kate thought a White Elephant exchange would be fun, where each person brought one gift, someone opened the first gift, and then it could be stolen by the next person instead of opening the one they were given. Other rules for trading before the next person's turn were confusing to Reese, and Thomas didn't like the thought of getting a gift and then having someone steal it. They finally decided to go with a Kris Kringle approach and drew names for an exchange of one gift each.

They placed the gifts in the center of the table but needed to decide the order of opening. Thomas pushed for a youngest-to-oldest. Hank thought everyone opening their gifts at once would be best. Reese bellowed that Santa got to decide, pointing to his hat, and declared ladies go first. Kate approved and asked who had her gift. Thomas reached into the pile and pulled out a present wrapped in snowman paper with snowflake ornaments. She carefully removed the wrappings to reveal a book from the local thrift store: Things I Know for Sure by Oprah Winfrey. Kate smirked and hugged her diner-booth neighbor.

Thomas immediately created his own set of rules. He decided the person who gave the last present got to open the next one. The rest of the Musketeers succumbed to his wishes, if only to avoid one more speech. Hank handed Thomas his gift, which he tore open to reveal gift cards to several favorite fast-food places in town. He raised the gift above his head and announced he was the winner of Christmas.

Hank took the comment as a thank you and picked up the red gift bag with a tag bearing his name. He untied the ribbon and pulled out a large candy dish. Several Three Musketeers bars and one Snickers candy bar filled the bowl. Hank examined the gift with a questioning look.

"It's like the four Musketeers except they don't make a Four Musketeers bar. And one of us is a little bit nuts!" Reese said.

Before anyone could decide who represented the nut bar, Reese reached his hands out to the remaining wrapped gift, which consisted of a larger package with a smaller one on top, held together by a red ribbon. Kate pushed the package across the table. "Open the larger one first." Reese pushed the ribbon off the gifts and ripped open the wrappings. He broke into laughter at a bright neon pink gun that shot jelly cartridges.

"It's like the cowboy gun from the Rudolph the Red-Nosed Reindeer show!" Reese said as he opened the smaller package, revealing boxes of jelly cartridges. He stood holding both gifts high and made a new ruling: *he* was the official winner of Christmas.

44

The Shaman

THE GUSTS AND RAIN had mostly subsided before daybreak, leaving the streets of the Deepwell neighborhood filled with scattered palm fronds and splotches of puddles for Reese's nocturnal recycling adventure. He gracefully balanced several lawn bags of cans on his bike, avoiding interaction with zealous neighbors protecting their real estate. He never understood the self-appointed law enforcement neighbor shouting, "Those aren't yours. Leave our recycle alone." Reese realized in the world of haves and have-nots, both groups were sources of irony or genius on any given day.

Thirty aluminum cans weighed a pound, and the rate of about a dollar a pound distracted Reese in calculations as he determined how many bags of cans created a comfortable weekend. He knew which homes were vacation rentals, an important fact because they hosted more pool parties and produced a bigger yield. Reese completed two bag drops on Hank's patio, where they would sit for his retrieval once the recycling center opened. Holiday celebrations created a year-end windfall.

Reese finished filling another set of garbage bags as he traveled the pre-morning streets. The wind bursts increased and caught the bags like they were sails on a schooner, jerking the bike back and forth. Reese wove between the downed branches but was helpless against the car. The driver could have been coming home from a late-night party or rushing for an early flight. It didn't matter. The speeding car clipped the bags and sent Reese flying as it sped off.

Everything hurt. He cautiously tested his limbs to self-diagnose any sign of broken bones. The mangled bike sat next to Reese, making him feel worse. He needed to get out of there before the morning power walkers started their day and their likely calls to the police. One of the full bags miraculously cushioned his head while his phone took the blow of his hip hitting the pavement. The screen showed signs of functioning through the shattered display as he navigated the sharp edges to call Thomas. No answer. He tried again and left a message. The mix of pain and shock compounded the need to get help, so he called Hank. The next minutes vanished as he collapsed onto the bags on the predawn morning.

Hank found Reese and loaded him, the bike, and, at Reese's insistence, most of the bags into his car. Reese demanded Hank forgo the hospital and take him to a house at the edge of the mountains belonging to an old tribal Cahuilla healer.

As Hank helped Reese up the sidewalk to the stone-structured house, the door opened and there stood a middle-aged woman, in a long skirt, who reached out and placed her hand on Reese's chest. He let out a big gasp and steadied himself on Hank's arm. She invited them around the back of the house and into a kish. The branch-framed structure covered with dried palm fronds appeared to outdate the establishment of Palm Springs. Its domed roof enclosed a dark interior except for a shaft of moonlight shining through a vent at the top. This barely illuminated the dirt floor and a sunken water trough in its center.

Hank couldn't discern the source of the hazy air filling the hut. Did it come from the dried palms or burning incense? All his senses were confounded by his surroundings. The area within the hut didn't seem of this world or at least not of his typical world. A fragrance mixed with a mild sulfur smell. The combination conjured up thoughts of a past religious sacrifice.

The shaman led Reese to a stool and undressed him. She signaled Hank to help guide Reese's injured body into the hot springs filled trough. Reese rested in the steaming water as she reached to a small table for a palm-sized wooden dish filled with a hummus looking paste. She fed a spoonful to Reese and then one to Hank, who swallowed the room-temperature mixture with its neutral flavor. Next, she reached for a copper pitcher and filled a cup for Reese and refilled it for Hank. Its sweet agave and citrus flavor sent a rush of hydration through his body. Hank tried handing the cup back to their host, but she had already moved next to Reese, placing one hand on various parts of his body and using a brown-glazed pottery dish to catch water from the trough as a rinse. Her chanting continued, seemingly without any breaks to inhale as she tended to his head, shoulders, and any other parts, with a blessing of water and her healing touch. There were moments when her hand hovered over an area for longer durations while she kept her eyes closed. She grasped at the surrounding layer of air over the body, pulling the energy away from Reese. The hymn-like blessings lulled Hank into a bit of a hypnotic state as all Reese's injured areas received attention. Then the host abruptly stopped, saying "Done."

She motioned for Hank to help Reese out of the water and back to the stool. Reese moved more adeptly and didn't need any help as he dressed. The source of the water bath must have been a thermal spring. Hank's mind raced trying to decide whether the hut sat on a spring or if the water came from another source. He also wondered how the food and juice were ready or who notified the shaman. It didn't matter. His friend seemed better and he needed to get home.

Then a grunt came from the dark edge of the hut, not a dog or another animal. A man, who looked as old as the kish, slowly approached. The elder continued toward the group. Hank wondered if this person brought additional healing to the ceremony. The elder's smooth movement continued as if he were floating. Hank had reached complete exhaustion and yet tried to focus on this latest development. The older shaman's path stopped in front of Hank, meeting his eyes without blinking or changing gaze. Hank stared back and took in the energy coming from the silver eyes mirroring his. The silence broke as the healer took a deep breath in and put his hand on Hank's chest. The energy between the hand and his chest warmed to a point of being hot. Hank wanted to pull away but didn't feel he could. Then he heard a raspy voice come from the old man, "Awaken." The elder then placed the same hand on Hank's throat, which filled his neck with the same heat. The elder healer repeated, "Awaken." Energy surged through Hank's body. He found himself mirroring the deep breathing of the healer. The elder closed his eyes, and Hank followed the action. With Hank's eyes closed, a feeling of weightlessness and a glow of calm filled his body and mind.

The next thing he knew, sunlight came into the hut from the now-opened entrance flap. Hank's eyes squinted as he adjusted to the brightness of the morning sun. A completely dressed Reese and their host started to leave. The elder shaman could not be seen, but the warmth and openness in Hank's heart and throat remained.

45

The Third Date

THE SUN'S LIGHT dried the streets by the time Hank got Reese to Thomas's apartment. There, Thomas went into full Mother Bear mode. He welcomed his boyfriend, the broken bike, and three bags of recycling into his apartment. Thomas's final words to Hank were that he had things covered and would reconnect after the holidays. Hank left Thomas's apartment feeling a buzz of energy and wanting to share the shaman experience with Kate.

He and Kate still had their rule about not being alone together on holidays. The calendar showed December 21, not a holiday. Hank and Kate went through their first two non-dates without any physical contact. Then, they broke all the rules for their night together. Since then, Hank pulled his energy away from everything except his sobriety.

The experience with Reese left Hank with too many thoughts, most being about Kate. He called her, saying he needed to see her immediately and asked if she could drive. His car held the scent of empty beer and soda cans from conveying Reese. Kate met Hank at his apartment where he told her about Reese being hit and how Thomas was probably washing and crushing each can from the bags filling his kitchen floor. They both agreed Reese and the cans were well cared for.

They decided to drive to the Thousand Palms trail again. It was the destination they never reached on the first non-date. He waited until they got there to share the entire story. The sunny morning and nature trail provided a quiet location for talking about what happened with Reese. They started down the path to the first oasis. Towering palm trees canopied a wooden walkway traversing the oasis ponds. The untrimmed trees with their dried palm skirts reached from the desert floor to the thirty-foot-high canopy, creating a cool and humid microclimate in the middle of the desert. The oasis sat above the San Andreas fault line, a fracture in the earth that allowed water to rise to the surface from the aquifers and brought life the roots of hundreds of palm trees.

They continued along the trail as Hank explained how the hut from the previous night felt as ancient as the oasis where they stood.

"The experience was creepy—well, it wasn't so much creepy as it was from another dimension."

"What happened?"

Kate looked at him, trying to decide whether Hank was exaggerating, but he looked so solemn. She received the early morning texts from Hank, and wanted to hear more. He described as much as he could remember up to the point when the shaman laid his hands on Hank's heart and throat. He stopped walking and turned to Kate; his voice steadied. He told her that Reese and he left the hut as different people.

"Different how?"

"I am so lucky that the Musketeers are in my life. Your support is everything."

"Hank."

"Let me finish. I know how hard my drinking must've been—for you, Reese, and Thomas.

She looked at him and shook her head.

"Hank, that is what we do. We're here for each other. Why did you go to help Reese?"

Hank felt his heart and his throat getting warm as he searched for an answer.

"You didn't ignore the call from him," she continued, "and

you didn't question it. You went to help, and we are here to help you. We aren't here to just drink coffee together or exchange dumb gifts. We care about each other."

"Despite my recent behavior, my sobriety is the most important thing to me, and the Musketeers are a close second. You all have made life manageable and even enjoyable. I guess I'm starting to realize that now."

Kate smiled. "I'm glad."

"And I don't know what you see in me," Hank continued, "but I need to tell you that I think the world of you and feel so lucky we met. I . . . you are . . . I am so grateful we know each other."

"Well, you're not exactly perfect," Kate replied. "And that's fine with me." She wrapped her arms around him.

As they hugged, he leaned in and kissed her.

"This might qualify as a date."

46

Pick a Color!

ADELA SPOTTED TIFFANY standing in front of the bakery and felt an unusual nervousness. It was the first time seeing each other since William's passing and her encounter with Spencer at the funeral. Adela didn't want to wait until the new year to check in on her friend. The text invite she sent started with an apology for being caught up in her own grief. Tiffany replied by pushing it all aside, and agreed to meet under the condition that she would be the organizer.

As Adela parked, she realized she'd never noticed the bakery tucked away in the corner of the strip mall. She often drove by the adobe-style retail space without paying attention to the storefronts. The 1980s sun-bleached salmon stucco exoskeleton contained a series of independent businesses and the donut shop. None of the signage had been updated in years. Even the faded lines on the parking lot were so neglected that they served as subtle hints rather than visible markers of where to park.

Tiffany waved in a slightly frantic motion, relaxing after seeing Adela's recognition. When they hugged, Tiffany held on longer and tighter than Adela had expected.

"Well! Here we are," Adela said.

"I hate to put a condition on our day," Tiffany said. "You were so nice to connect, but I can't talk about William today." Tiffany reached out and grasped Adela's hand. "I know you lost your brother and you know what he meant to me, but I'm exhausted. I've cried so much over the past month and will keep crying, but I need a break from talking and thinking about him— about us, for a moment, for this morning. Okay?"

"I'll try if you do, but no promises." Adela touched her hand to her eye in the hope of not breaking their agreement in the first minute.

"Agreed, we can have a good long cry the next time we meet."

"Again, I appreciate your invitation to meet. Today's going to be hysterically fun. I know everyone has their own criteria for donuts, but this is the best in town."

"If the line is any indication, the entire town agrees with you. How did you find this place?"

They both had their coffee tumblers because of Tiffany's advice: while the baked goods were magical, the coffee could be hit-or-miss.

"The dentist's office used to be a video rental store back when Hank, Willow, and Spencer were kids. It was when I attempted to be their mom. One of the few times they would all calm down was on outings for donuts and picking movies for the weekend. That's a lifetime ago. Remember renting movies? Anyway, I am glad you haven't been here before. You've planned great times for us and I want to share my favorite places. My treat!"

They reached the front of the line and picked pastries from the display case. Adela selected a classic glazed old-fashioned donut and Tiffany chose a custard-filled Bismarck with a glossy chocolate-dipped topping. They found two empty chairs at a white metal patio table; its layers of paint chipped from years of use. Childhood memories stirred in Adela as she opened the pastry bag. An aroma of warm fried dough, chocolate, and sugar swirled up to meet her nose.

"I'm going to need coffee to digest the smell of these," Adela said. "And what's this? Did you order more?"

"No. Those are the donut holes. You get one with each purchase. They are light as air and melt in your mouth. Try one!"

Adela pulled one of the extra treats from the bag as the donut hole nearly collapsed under her touch. Tiffany motioned for her to pop the entire morsel into her mouth. Adela obliged and slowly closed her eyes as she entered a flavor filled dream state. The bakery nibble completely collapsed with less resistance than a cloud of cotton candy. The moisture from her mouth completely melted the contents, leaving the warm taste of cinnamon sugar.

"Wow, that alone may be the highlight of my entire day."

"That's hysterical." Tiffany giggled. "I'm glad you like it. Now try the donut. Hand me the bag and a napkin. Our nail appointment is in twenty minutes, and it's a few doors down."

"I may regret my choice after seeing your Bismarck."

Tiffany giggled again as she held up a plastic knife and cut their choices in two. The taste testing began.

"Tell me about this salon."

"I hope you aren't put off by the outdated appearance. Everything is sanitary. Oh, and the crowd can be a lot. The chatter, and the . . . I hope you'll like it. We'll have fun. Hysterical. Everyone talks at once. It's the best way to get updates on pop culture and the buzz here in town while being pampered. We're set up for mani-pedis, sitting next to each other so we can talk or sit back and listen to the scoop."

Adela examined her fingers and toes, happy to have a moment to give them some care.

"If this salon is half as good as the bakery, then my nails will get their needed attention before Christmas and a great escape from . . . " Adela paused and looked away.

"Hey now, you promised . . . no crying over donuts." Tiffany held up her half of Bismarck.

The pastries were devoured with no decisive winner emerging from their sampling. They both committed to a return to judge the other offerings.

The energy blast entering the gauntlet of the neighborhood salon overpowered any residual somber mood from the bakery patio. Adela signaled to Tiffany that the place was everything she had described. Someone at the counter demanded their names. Another handed them smocks. A third stylist held up a tray of color options while squawking at them to pick a color. Adela didn't notice a pause between the first, second, and third requests for a color choice. In the excitement and sugar rush, she said she would take the same as Tiffany.

A beautician escorted them to chairs where their feet were submerged in a warm, sudsy bath and their hands received skilled attention. An assistant lifted a bottle of water with a straw to Adela's lips while another scratched Tiffany's back. Across the room, someone sneezed into the tissue-lined hand of a manicurist. All needs, large and small, were addressed.

The room piqued all Adela's senses. There were overlapping conversations—Beyoncé's latest appearance, a chef poached from LA, the newest customer being asked to pick a color. Fragrances mixed in the air with acrylic fumes while dryers hummed and salsa music played in the background.

Adela could barely keep her thoughts in order. All the chatter quieted when Mimi, the queen bee of the swarm, started talking about an episode of a National Geographic show.

"So here we are cleaning feet and hands and trimming nails, and did you know that nails replace themselves completely twice a year and skin about once a month?"

The salon audience all listened intently.

"That's what they said on the Nat Geo show on TV last night. About a hundred hairs fall out every day, and the length grows six inches in a year."

The woman scratching Tiffany's back stopped and lifted a lock of her hair, trying to guess an age. Mimi took Adela's hand from the soaking bowl and wrapped it in a warm towel. She slowly massaged and dried each finger while continuing her synopsis of the show.

"The body is fascinating in how it replaces so much of itself during life. Guess which parts don't change?"

"Muscles?" came a shout from a chair.

"No"

"Bones!"

"Nope"

"Teeth?" Tiffany guessed.

"Great guess, but your baby teeth are replaced by adult ones."

"Well, Kim has had several of her parts replaced over the years!" one of the nail technicians shouted while hunched over and scrubbing a pair of feet.

The entire room erupted as Kim took the cue to do a runway catwalk and show off the latest version of her body. The applause and cheers died down with the next guess.

"Brain, the brain doesn't change."

"Bingo! Your brain and about half of your heart stay the same. Do you know what other part doesn't change?"

Most of the room went quiet again. Quizzical faces did self-audits of their bodies.

"The lenses in your eyes." Mimi gave the answer. "About half your heart, brain, and the core of your eye lenses are the same from birth or before. Which made me think—"

"Here she goes, Sister Mimi is going to testify again," Kim said, with both hands raised up in the air.

"Oh hush. I'm saying it's fascinating what is replaced over time and what is with us forever." She took Adela's hand to assess where to begin the manicure. "So many people are holding on to anger or regret in their brains or trauma from images that passed through the permanent lenses of their eyes. They have a broken heart or undying love."

"Amen!" Kim said.

"These body parts make us who we are and may dictate how

we behave. Some parts don't last longer than these sad, ignored, overgrown cuticles—corrected in seconds." She raised Adela's hand. "Others are deep inside us and may never change, there for life. How we handle them is what must change." Mimi raised her pitch.

"New cells in our body aren't going to flush out what's deep in our heart or mind. We must make that change in our attitude." She put Adela's hand back into the soaking bowl and laughed, "And sometimes, if we give them enough care, even sad and ignored cuticles have a chance to improve."

The room broke out in laughter, with the biggest chuckle coming from Adela as she responded with her own "Amen."

Adela and Tiffany ended their time with a hug in the parking lot. Adela declared the morning of pastries and salon life coaching exceeded her expectations.

"Less than two weeks until our Laguna weekend. We can have a long cry at the beach," said Tiffany, wiping her eyes.

As she drove away, Adela reflected on memories long buried—ones deserving her attention. She wondered if parts of her upbringing—or even DNA—set an unchangeable path. Did she have the power to change? Her first thoughts went to the impact of being raised by Robert. She decided life experiences left lasting marks—etched into her deepest parts—and they needed attention. The experience set Adela reflecting on her life. With both hands firmly on the steering wheel, she finally focused on the neon chartreuse-colored nail polish adorning her fingers and decided they would be one of the first changes for the new year.

47

Tombstones

SPENCER BEGAN CHRISTMAS MORNING at the cemetery, maintaining the yearly holiday tradition since his mother died. It felt far removed from his childhood visits when his father led him and Willy to the graves of his mother and baby sister. Instead, Spencer arrived alone, having no one else he felt would join him. Robert canceled the family Christmas party. His father was gone. Sybil and their children were in Hawaii. Willow hadn't communicated with him since Hank's disruption at the funeral. As he drove up to the graves, Spencer realized this was his only Christmas family gathering that year.

But to his surprise, he spotted an unfamiliar car as he reached the headstone. Had Otto come to pay his respects to his brother? Spencer welcomed the company and hoped to hear some sage words on the first Christmas without his father. He parked the car behind Otto's and walked around to join him. Spencer froze. The flowers dropped from his hand. Not his uncle, but Tiffany.

"What are you doing at my family's grave? Why are you here?"

Tiffany looked up. She stayed kneeling and turned away to complete her task of wiping off the headstone with a towel. She poured some water from a bottle onto a rag and rubbed dirt off the brass memorial plaque, cleaning its raised name and date, a month old. Tiffany had spent the morning cleaning the headstones of William, Matilda, and their baby.

"You don't belong here. Get out and leave me with my mom and sister . . . and dad!"

Tiffany dropped the rag and stood to meet the eyes of her stepson. Her voice cracked as she struggled for words. She straightened her body and pressed her shaking hands against the sides of her body.

"I have every right to be here. As much or even more than you. We loved each other."

"Love?" Spencer cackled. "You trapped him once by getting pregnant, and you somehow clawed your way into his life again. You've always found a way to trap him. My father never had feelings for you."

Tiffany recoiled, stepping back onto Matilda's grave. "Spencer. You don't know. You only care about yourself."

"If you weren't around, our entire family would be better," Spencer said as he grabbed Tiffany's arm, trying to yank her away from his mother's headstone. She pulled away and fell backward onto Matilda's grave.

"If you weren't around, your father would still be alive," Tiffany screamed as she stood up and gathered her things. "You killed him. You made him have a heart attack. You killed him! You destroyed him and sent him to his grave. You took him from me and you probably caused your mother's death too! We all know she was a drunk, and you drove her to her death."

48

New Year's Eve

THE FOUR MUSKETEERS went their separate ways after a New Year's Eve breakfast. Kate decided to remove any holiday dating pressures by returning to Encinitas to be with her mom. They'd ring in the new year with pizza and ice cream sandwiches like in her childhood. Reese and Thomas had tickets to Judy's Sober Send-Off to 2018. The party at the community center featured dancing and intermittent Judy Garland song breaks as a variety of drag performers did tribute performances throughout the night. The countdowns started at 9 p.m. with the live feed of the Times Square ball drop, repeating each hour until midnight on the West Coast. Hank opted out of an event where he'd be playing midnight-kiss dodgeball over four countdowns. Emotionally exhausted from the passing of his father and stressed about his mom's mindset, Hank decided to stay home after getting permission from Thomas, Reese, and Kate to be alone.

His last phone call with Tiffany consisted of her mood set to giggly. "Hysterical, that's simply hysterical," was her go-to response—always followed by a forced laugh. Over the years, Hank understood these behavioral tells as a lead-in to a meltdown followed by an inconsolably dark mood. Childhood memories reminded him how his mother's exaggerated laughter shifted to tears as she spiraled into an emotional storm.

They had Christmas dinner together, where she broke into tears over the Spencer confrontation and in the days following, she only listed excuses not to meet. Everything after his father's funeral made them both feel disconnected because being together forced a reminder of William's death. Hank called again with the hope that he could see her on New Year's Eve.

"Mom, I was thinking we should get together today."

"What did you have in mind, sweetie?"

"I was thinking of someplace fun for dinner before the crowds show up or having takeout at your place and a movie night to close out the year."

"Stay home for New Year's?"

"Like old times when we lived together. I could pick up dinner from wherever you want. It will be fun."

"I've talked to some of the girls from the country club, and we're thinking of going out. I need to start my next chapter as soon as possible. I'm not getting any younger."

"Going out?"

"A few of the hotels are having parties in their ballrooms, and then we've got tickets to the block party at the casino with music and fireworks. It's going to be so much fun tonight, hysterical."

"Mom. What if we skip the party this year?"

"Marlene's already got us tickets. I'd invite you, but a sober son as a wingman isn't going to help, and Marlene is counting on me."

Hank abandoned any hope of seeing his mother that night, worried because she usually pushed him away when needing him most. He took her advice and focused on his own new chapter, which meant staying home. The Musketeers exchanged early evening New Year's messages. Hank thanked them for asking, but refused Reese's and Thomas's offer to forgo their party and spend the night with him. Hank let them know he had pulled out some hamburger and turned on the grill, all set for a quiet welcome to the new year.

49

Happy New Year

OFFICERS LOPEZ AND JONES rounded out the year with the most insufferable shift—overnight squad car duty on New Year's Eve. The officers knew their night paled in comparison to larger cities and yet, the shift brought its own share of drunk and disorderly. The two officers, along with the other assigned squads, covered the downtown and surrounding areas. They were also on call as reinforcements for the block party. They took solace in not being on foot patrol duty outside the event and instead drove up and down the two main streets of the city until 1 a.m., when they widened their scope.

After bar-close, the two patrolled the city parks to check for possible late-night revelers congregating after leaving downtown. Jones pulled out the floodlight, directing the beam out the squad car window as Lopez slowly drove their route. For the most part, things remained quiet. There were random sightings of couples getting caught in one act or another. A slow panning spotlight caused the revelers to hurry away into the dark. Neither officer wanted a pursuit, or even to use a megaphone. The officers decided the first hours of New Year's Day didn't need sirens or other noise from the squad car.

The mild overnight temperatures meant many partiers walked the short distances from the downtown fireworks celebration to their homes or nearby hotels. The waning moon made for a particularly dark night as the officers focused on their task of patrolling. The instructions from the police chief specifically demanded citizens not find condoms, needles, or other adult paraphernalia around town on New Year's Day. Complaint calls meant a chance of an all-squad meeting later that week to discuss the degradation of the city. No one wanted a gathering with city council members asking why the police force couldn't protect the children. That phrase made Lopez smirk. Most of the city didn't have children. The vacationing grandchildren made up the real reason to be thorough. Thanksgiving, Christmas, and Easter weekends were the grandchildren-holidays. To avoid another teachable moment from the city council, all officers working the holiday were asked to do everything they could to keep the city safe and clean. The sergeant had mocking undertones but a serious message. He didn't want any incoming complaint calls.

Jones and Lopez investigated the typical spots. They started in the parks adjacent to the more affluent neighborhoods, the ones most likely to complain. As the night continued, they moved south. The officers checked the parking lots of now closed restaurants where couples may have decided to act on the throes of passion in their cars. The officers continued driving.

"Saving the best for last?" asked Jones.

Lopez nodded, "It's for the children."

The best meant Baristo Park, a small nondescript little park filled with a swing set and other playground structures. The park supported the apartment buildings housing families on the south side of downtown. It was a block from the Palm Springs Cooling Station, a nonprofit facility supplying basics to the less well off: a place to shower, cool off from the heat, wash clothes, and get some fundamental support. The donors thought excluding overnight lodging would keep the surrounding businesses and homes from complaining. Instead, the lack of lodging became the problem. After the guests of the Cooling Station left for the day, they'd go to Baristo Park and spend the evening. The overnight resting spot turned into a site for dealers to peddle their goods, a constant source of 911 calls any night of the year. On New Year's Eve, the officers made it their last stop with the hope that at the late hour, anyone they encouraged to leave would stay away through morning.

The officer turned on the floodlight showing an unoccupied park until the light beam illuminated a bench. Jones motioned her partner to pull over. The officers got out and moved toward the vagrant, their flashlight beams leading the way. The sun would be up in a few hours and the residents didn't need to start their new year with someone passed out in the children's park. The agreement between law enforcement and the homeless community was well known on both sides—children's parks and school yards were off limits. Jones got out her baton.

"Hey, you need to get up."

They moved closer. A small woman in a party dress lay motionless.

"Ma'am, you're going to have to leave."

They reached the bench and stopped. The body's skin shown pale and waxy in the flashlight beam. Lopez looked at Jones as he reached for his radio.

"Lopez here, we have a deceased at Baristo Park, needing assistance. Yep . . . Yep, okay . . . yea–notify the coroner."

Jones headed back to the car to get the police tape. They weren't clocking out quite yet.

50

NOK

A FIRM KNOCKING jarred Hank from sleep. He muttered, "I'm coming," while grabbing a baseball cap and stepping into some shorts. His morning brain fog didn't clear as he made his way to open the door. Instead of seeing any-time-of-day-visitor Reese, he discovered two police officers asking him to identify himself. They invited him to take a seat at one of his patio chairs and a series of questions followed. His answers came out before his brain could catch up with the situation. Yes, he was Hank. He confirmed Tiffany was his mother.

What did they say about a park?

Did she have any other children? No. *Some paperwork was being put together?* Yes, he was alone at the apartment. *Was there anything they could do for him?* Hank missed a beat and didn't understand why they were sorry. The second officer repeated the information to Hank. Hank still didn't comprehend their words.

Next of kin?

"Two of our colleagues found her last night at Baristo Park. Initial signs are an overdose, but final lab work will take time. There were no signs of foul play, and she still had her jewelry. Her purse and phone were underneath the bench where we found her. You can claim them at the station." The officer repeated, looking down at a note pad.

"These deaths happen all too often here in the valley," the officer said. "Fentanyl is a powerful drug."

The other officer jumped in. "Can we do anything for you?"

Hank stayed silent. The first officer repeated himself.

"Do you have any questions?"

The world around Hank crumbled. He couldn't make out the faces of the officers and didn't comprehend their words as he sat slumped in the chair. He and his mother were together for Christmas dinner. He wished he had pushed harder for them to spend New Year's Eve together, recalling his mother's words from their conversation.

"Hysterical, the fireworks will be so much fun! It will be hysterical!"

She waved verbal emergency flares in his face. With the almost daily ebb and flow of Tiffany's emotions, he wondered if he could have known she was at her limit.

Hank sat staring out beyond the two officers as they continued talking. His mother's delirious voice echoed in his head from a recent phone call in which she described time with William on the morning after Thanksgiving. She said he was so happy about the time with his siblings and that he wanted more time with her. Hank recalled his mother's joy in hearing William wanted to sit outside together to enjoy the morning. She said he wanted to do more together in public. Then her mood took a dark turn with talk of Spencer's arrival and William's heart attack. His father was gone. She was gone. Hank tried to replay yesterday in his head.

The police officers stood in silence waiting for Hank to respond.

She wasn't invited to Thanksgiving. Spencer made a point of keeping her from his father's funeral. She spent Christmas talking about the fight with Spencer at the cemetery and how much his words hurt.

A cough from the officers brought Hank back to the current situation. One of the officers pressed a business card into his hand before leaving him on his patio. His father and mother were gone without warning. Hank stayed in the chair until the sun's heat drove him inside to the couch where he decided to call the helpline. To his relief, the automated clicks ended with a connection to his regular counselor.

"Hank, is that you? How are you this New Year's Day?"

Silence.

"Hank, what's wrong? Are you there? Where are you?"

The silence continued.

"I'm home. I . . . It's . . . I'm home."

"What happened, Hank? Did something happen on New Year's Eve?"

Another long silence.

"It's my mom," Hank struggled to find words.

"What about your mom? Did you talk to her? Did you see her last night? Hank, we've talked about your mother's expectations and tone and how they impact you—"

"She's—she. She's dead."

His mouth went to a choking dryness as he tried to comprehend his own words. There was a commotion from the other end of the call, followed by silence. Hank thought that he might have been disconnected. More time passed, and then a response.

"I am so sorry, Hank. Are you sure?"

"The police were here."

"Hank, I don't think you should be alone. You should be with family . . . can you be with your friends?"

"It's New Year's Day."

"Go to Desert Recovery. You should go to the Center. I will call and they will be expecting you. Take a taxi or car service. Tell me you'll go to the Center. Hank?"

"I'll try." Hank ended the call. He sat on the couch, still stunned. Kate was with her family and who knew where Reese and Thomas ended up. They wouldn't be the right company this morning. He scanned the room for an answer and looked down at the floor where he had dropped the crumpled business card of the police officer. Proof that his mother was dead. He buried his head in the couch pillow. The cold, hollow feeling of being an orphan entered his thoughts. Both parents were gone. The pain pierced him as he curled up in a ball on the couch with images of both his parents flashing through his thoughts. A half hour passed and he thought he could control himself enough to call Kate, but no. He couldn't say the words aloud a second time— declaring his mother dead. He couldn't call Kate or talk to anyone. He needed to block all his thoughts. Nothing worked as images and memories bombarded his mind until finally interrupted by another knock on the door, followed by someone turning the knob. Had the police returned?

"Hank, Happy New Year! Oh my gosh, help me out. Thank goodness the door's unlocked. You need to give me a hand. Would you look at me? I decided I had to start the year with someone, and your cousin Steve is nowhere to be found. He is probably out to breakfast with that lovely wife and my grandchildren. Did they consider asking their Nana to join them?"

In scurried Adela with her hands filled with two coffees on a tray and a pink bakery box. She made a point of looking at anything but her nephew as she carried the box into the kitchen.

"I know I should have called, but does anyone answer the phone anymore? Especially on New Year's Day? I brought us two coffees and some donuts from that Swiss donut shop. I hear the coffee can be iffy, but it's better than nothing." Her voice continued from the kitchen. "Oh look, you have a coffee maker. If you don't like the taste of this, you can throw it out and make some fresh. I got us pastries. Let me put them on a plate for you. Wait there . . . I've got it. Do you mind if I—where are the— what if I use paper towels for plates? Do you like yeast or old-fashioned donuts? Have you ever had these donut holes? Did I say Happy New Year? Well, Happy New Year, Hank. Here I come with some treats for the new year."

Adela reentered the room.

"You get the chocolate donut." Adela stopped to catch her breath as she reentered the living room and set the items on the coffee table. She continued to avoid eye contact and prattled on in a way she never had in her life.

She rarely was contacted from Desert Recovery on a holiday, which already had Adela in an alarmed state. The urgency raised several levels when the caller confirmed her as an emergency family contact for Hank during a crisis call to the helpline. She flew out the door of her home and was halfway to the donut shop before the call from the recovery center ended. She got two pieces of information: Tiffany died and Hank needed help. She created an excuse to see her nephew not knowing what emotional state she'd find him. The donuts justified a visit with an extended stay. Entering Hank's apartment made her realize she didn't know her own emotional state so she focused on being there for her nephew. The reality of the situation forced her to fill the silence with an erratic circle of topics reminiscent of her dead friend.

"Did you know they are open today? Swiss Donut, this cute place over on Sunrise Way. Open on New Year's Day and a line formed behind me. What time does a baker have to start work to be ready with a full display of donuts? And there are donut holes. You are in for a surprise." Adela grabbed one in a paper towel and turned away from her nephew to return to the kitchen.

"I left the coffee in here." Adela took another deep breath and worked the paper coffee cups from the cardboard formed holder. "Hold on. I've got them." She brought the cups into the living room. "Here. Careful, this is hot. Or it used to be. No cream or sugar, right? There's an apple bear claw in the box if you don't like the donut." She set the coffee in front of him and opened the pink box of pastries. Adela kept going for the next ten minutes with a monologue about any topic but Tiffany.

Hank didn't have the strength to take part and couldn't form words. He sat staring at the donut in his hand while Adela tapped into all her strength to keep any conversation going. The room thickened with grief. A mother gone. A friend lost. Death filled the air.

Adela exhausted all streams of consciousness and finally gained some composure. She paused and thoughtlessly looked at her hand that held a donut. Neon chartreuse-painted fingernails surrounded the baked good, the color Tiffany picked. Adela dropped the pastry and fell into the chair.

"Hank, I've heard. I've heard the news about your mom."

51

The Second Call

"PLEASE ACCEPT OUR CONDOLENCES on the recent passing of your father and mother," said the voice from the other end of the phone. Spencer sat on the edge of the bed in his Palm Springs home.

"She wasn't my mother; my mother died years ago . . ." Spencer's voice trailed off.

"Well, please accept our condolences on the deaths in your family. We hope this doesn't hinder your ability to move forward with the acquisition."

The voice went from sympathetic to calculated crispness, which threw Spencer and made him wonder if they wanted to ruffle him, except why should they know his mother? The recent news articles weren't even clear about Tiffany's relationship to the family. The caller spoke of Tiffany's death, and yet the conversation took Spencer back to thoughts of his own mother's death.

"Again, we understand you're dealing with a loss in your family, yet you made an agreement to sell the company."

The voice brought Spencer back into the conversation and he replied, "We have an agreement! My father is gone, and with the transition of the estate, there will be no problems moving forward. Thank you for your call." Spencer pushed the call-end button and returned to his childhood thoughts in a world of his princess mother and her two boy princes.

Spencer grew up with sweet stories about his mother that

continued long after her death. He faintly recalled birthdays filled with constructing homemade crowns from colored paper, aluminum foil, and stickers. He loved those birthdays. Actual memories blended with reimagined and embellished recollections from childhood photos. Spencer recalled Leandra being at their Araby home during Matilda's hospital time—and that she stayed on after their mother returned. Matilda, pale and withdrawn, spent much of her time in bed after returning from the hospital. Spencer didn't understand what a Cesarean delivery was. He remembered Leandra explaining how doctors cut into his mother and it filled him with pain as if they were cutting into him.

His new baby sister lived for three days. Neither Spencer nor Willy got to see her. Matilda would have fired Leandra immediately if she had known Leandra shared the C-section news with her children. In the days before the delivery, Spencer and Willy listened to their mother's instructions on how to be good big brothers to a baby sister. They practiced all sorts of tasks, like holding a doll while supporting its head. They were experts at being gentle. Both princes were ready for everything except the heartbreaking news that she wouldn't come home.

Adela and Otto stripped the home of all baby evidence: clothes, diapers, baby furniture—even the little doll. They removed everything from the nursery before William came home with Matilda and even had the room painted beige. The two brothers never watched their baby sister lie in the crib or got to hold her while being careful to support her head.

The day Spencer remembered most vividly occurred on his mother's first morning back from the hospital. He lay beside her in her bed as she tried to comfort him before he left for the bus. She told him that even though he didn't have a little sister, they would always have each other. With that, she kissed him, and he left for school.

That afternoon, Leandra took Willy to the park to help give Matilda some rest time. They stopped by the school to pick up Spencer to give him a ride home. Both children cheered with anticipation for Leandra to drive faster so they could be home.

She had reached their street when their world changed again. An ambulance pulled away with sirens blaring. Leandra could barely get the car pulled over as the ambulance passed by. Spencer bolted from the car and ran to the house. He got inside before anyone could stop him, running from room to room trying to figure out what had happened. Blood covered his parents' bathroom floor and trailed into their bedroom to the edge of the bed. He dropped down and touched the red pool of liquid half-covered by a wet bath towel.

Spencer thought back to that day and looked at his fingers. His mother died years ago. That other woman who died on New Year's Eve was Hank's mother and not his. He bought his childhood home as his way to stay closer to his mother. They were like the royal family. She was Princess Di, also gone too soon. He recalled the months and years after his mother's death, trying to be a prince without his queen. The challenges increased as his father found Tiffany as a replacement for his mother.

William never truly understood the use of royal titles between Matilda and their boys. He simply knew they liked calling each other princess and prince. He suffered the fatal flaw of hearing something important from someone he loved and then unintentionally ruining the moment. In the situation following the death of Matilda, William knew his children likened their mother to Princess Diana. He responded by naming his new son Harry, after Princess Diana's second son. William self-assessed a perfect handling of the situation, giving his sons a brother named after a royal family member. He failed to understand that if two of the children were named William and Harry, it pushed Spencer out of the royal story. Tiffany didn't like any of the reasons for the name, but felt forced to agree, although she refused to call him Harry and chose Hank.

These memories muddled Spencer's plan regarding the sale of Asuproz. With no father to mentor him, he needed to gather his thoughts and decide on his own how to get the family aligned to sell the company. Spencer didn't need everyone, but the offer required 70 percent. Bringing everyone together was too risky.

Any one of them could decide to make a power play, be in a contrarian mood, or be too despondent from the deaths. With so many strong-willed people, he chose not to have them together without knowing what they were thinking in advance.

Spencer rarely talked to his grandfather and didn't want to start now. His grandfather tended to like Willow the best. They had a special bond. When Willy announced to the family he was transitioning to Willow, Grandpa Robert was surprisingly supportive, and their relationship grew even stronger. He chastised Spencer over a joke about removing a Willy to become Willow. Spencer never understood why people didn't appreciate his humor. He missed his mother and being one of the two princes. Enough! He needed to figure out the share distribution after the closing of his father's estate and to tie up any loose ends. He needed to sell the company, get divorced and start his new life.

52

House Cleaning

HANK STOOD ON THE DOORSTEP fumbling with his keys to find the one to his mother's home. He moved from key to key as if they were prayer beads to instill calm before entering. The door stood between him and his childhood home, where he and Tiffany lived when the rest of the family moved into The Dwelling. He ran the keys through his fingers again as he tried to recall the last time he'd been inside—months, more than a year? In recent get-togethers, Tiffany insisted on meeting at restaurants, saying she'd been a waitress her entire life and didn't intend to have her son visit so she could serve him. Hank's hands stopped. He grabbed the key and put it in the lock.

The Musketeers offered to join Hank and sent reminders they were a phone call away. He convinced them he was fine. Still, he half expected to spot Kate faking a morning run, Thomas sitting at the end of the block in his car, or Reese already inside, having found an unlocked window. Hank turned the key and felt the sliding of the bolt. Click. He touched the doorknob cautiously, as if testing the temperature on the handle of a sizzling cast-iron pan. Then, with a firm grasp, he opened the door.

Hank scanned the living room with a hesitation to enter. Familiar Terrazzo floors stretched throughout, and the same sofa sat with throw pillows still covering a faint wine stain. A new recliner sat in a prime location opposite the television. The forgotten reality presented itself. He was in his mother's home and in the part-time getaway for his father. His mind battled emotions of happiness for them reconnecting and emptiness from their deaths. He tried to focus on why he was there: a simple walk-through to throw out perishables, a task that should have been done days ago.

He closed the front door and walked through the living room into what used to be his bedroom. A mirrored vanity cluttered with makeup and hair products stood where his bed once was. Two portable clothes racks lined the wall. They held a mix of extravagant outfits and two faded, brown waitress uniforms. Below them were a pair of support shoes, stained with grease and ketchup. Faint perfumes clung to the walls and garments as an aromatic talisman that never fulfilled its promise of good luck.

He noticed the bedroom closet, containing a limited assortment of men's golf clothes, office attire, and casual wear— all unmistakably belonging to his father. Any doubts he or his siblings had about the relationship between William and Tiffany were banished by the mingling of lives on display. Hank glanced from closet to clothes racks, recalling times he saw his father and mother wearing the array of outfits. He went to his mother's favorite dress and ran his hand along the silky fabric, not letting go, holding on as long as he could, picturing her in her elegance, preparing to go out for the night.

Hank finally shook free of the moment and moved on to the kitchen where the required tasks were located. The smell of rotting food overwhelmed the bedroom's fragrant mix of Elizabeth Taylor's White Diamonds and Estée Lauder's Pleasures. The kitchen countertop next to the refrigerator contained mixings for Bloody Marys, Old Fashioneds, and Manhattans. The always-ready bar also displayed his father's favorite Baccarat. William had been gone for nearly two months, and yet the crystal tumbler remained with a bourbon stain inside, unwashed from its final use.

Hank moved past the bar and started pitching rotting fruit and bakery goods into the trash. Next, he opened the refrigerator and found a limited number of perishables beyond restaurant leftover containers and cocktail garnishes. Having addressed the source of the odors, he opened the jars of assorted olives and cherries, draining the liquids into the sink before disposing of the remains. While there, he felt the need to wash his father's crystal drinking glass. The hot water hit its bottom and brought out a vapor of bourbon and bitters, along with memories from his childhood. Without much effort, he scrubbed away any signs of a final cocktail his father had with his mother. The Baccarat sparkled in his hand and stood apart from the dozen or so dusty bottles on the countertop.

He set the glass beside the sink and began opening bottles and emptying them down the drain, starting with the liqueurs. Crème de menthe and crème de cacao went first, followed by Cointreau, cognac, and Drambuie. The aroma dizzied Hank's mind and numbed the pain of missing his parents. The hard liquors were next. Hank opened the bourbon and, in memorial or out of reflex, poured some into his father's glass. He held the newly cleaned tumbler up to the sunlight and watched the tannin-colored liquid swirl around. Hank recalled a tasting class where the expert demonstrated the appearance of 'legs' or 'tears' of the bourbon as the curtain of liquid slid down the sides of the glass. The stronger the tears, the heavier the liquor.

Hank dropped the glass, creating a clanging around the base of the stainless-steel sink, an alarm to his reality. He realized the long-past tasting session had the order wrong as he looked down at his father's glass, draining of its intoxicant. For him, the reverse held true: the heavier the liquor, the stronger the tears. The old mantra of "never again, never ever again" rang through his thoughts, although this time it seemed irrelevant. He picked up the glass and said, "I forgive you," to his father. He looked around his childhood kitchen and said, "I forgive you," to his mother. Hank then looked at the chair where he sat alone, twenty years ago, eating cold take-out from the container, and he said, "I forgive you" to that child and to the current Hank. He washed the glass again. Then, he poured the rest of the bottles down the drain while the faucet ran wide open. He brought the bag of rotting food and the empty bottles outside to the bins, following Reese's instructions on trash-sorting etiquette. Hank took a final look back at his childhood home with the feeling of both his parents' presence as he stepped into a new chapter of adulthood, without them and without alcohol. The raspy shaman's voice filled him as he realized it was his responsibility to "awaken."

53

Otto by the Firepit

WILLOW STOPPED BY her grandfather's casita to deliver his requested library books. She didn't understand why he wouldn't buy them. Why not order the books from online stores or read them on an electronic device? She still remembered the birthday, years ago, when she got him an e-reader.

"You might as well take that back to wherever it came from," Robert said as his form of gratitude to Willow.

Ironically, Robert lived for technology, but he made it quite clear he didn't enjoy the electronic medium when it came to books. In place of the e-tablet, she agreed to pick up any requests from the library. He regularly added one from the stack as her reading assignment. Their tie grew even stronger over the years, as did her appreciation of the book exchange moments. The death of William filled recent visits with awkward pauses and fumbling words between them. The addition of Tiffany's passing brought the two to near silence during their visit. Regardless, she felt a sense of relief to courier books as part of some normalcy and enjoyed the affection she got from Oscar and Grammy sniffing at her feet when they met her at the door of the casita.

That night, Robert broke their silence with one of the repetitive stories a family member endures from their grandfather. The bravado-filled part autobiography included the reminder that the Astors and Andrew Carnegie funded several libraries in New York and across the country. He recounted his New York City days surviving on little money and spending hours in those libraries. The buildings supplied shelter as well as something to do when alone. He reminisced about finding comfort there. In the end, she respected how this transferred into his love of books and his being a major donor to the local library. He spoke of how he missed the scent of a building filled with books and the unique aroma when first entering the stacks area. He likened it to breathing in knowledge. The sermon ended with him saying, "Reading those books helped elevate me to the success I am now." The phrase left a deeper imprint with each time Willow heard it. She gave her grandfather a hug and packed up his book returns.

The sun finished its evening task of sinking behind the mountains as Willow left her grandfather's casita. She closed the door and headed toward the driveway, only to see Otto in the dark by the unlit fire pit facing the western mountains.

"Uncle O! I didn't expect to see you."

"Willow? You startled me. Come join me, but first, could you turn on the gas to the fire pit? And you're going to want to grab yourself a blanket. Mother Nature is showing her more frigid side tonight."

"Sure. Do you need anything else?"

"I'm good. Lea brought me some hot tea as she headed out. Come sit with me."

"What are you doing out here in the cold?" Willow said as she ignited the fire pit and sat on the sectional next to her uncle.

"Damn, it is cold." Willow wrapped the blanket around herself.

The heat from the flames wasn't nearly enough to keep her back warm. She snuggled into the corner of the sectional, knees tucked in close to her chest, and the blanket completely engulfing her. She had spent the last hour talking with her grandfather about the value of books and happily settled in for even more enlightenment from her uncle. The recent death of two family members had sent everyone into a reflective mood. She wanted to hold on to any moments with the remaining family.

"What brought you out here tonight, Uncle O?"

"I had to clarify some things with your father's lawyers. We were over by the gazebo and must have missed you. Everything was warmer when we started. I wanted to meet out here instead of in your father's house or in the RV." Otto inhaled deeply as he gazed up at the remaining glow of a cobalt and indigo ombre silhouetting the mountain. He took a sip of tea, but the cold liquid sent an unexpected chill to his lips jarring him back to Willow's question.

"So, the meeting wrapped up and I decided to stay out here to watch the colors change with the sunset. The clouds created a burst of pink and orange tones earlier. Did you see the entire canyon engulfed in peaceful hues?"

Willow nodded, more to avoid interrupting Otto's thoughts than to agree.

"The lawyers left and I needed a moment of calm. Some of my favorite times are sunrise and sunset in the desert. The world becomes serene as if it slows. Even the birds take a moment to rest." Otto took another pause before continuing. "This family has done some amazing things. My father and brother created a company that neither of them envisioned forty years ago. Addie has done the same with the recovery center. We all find a sense of ourselves in different ways. Sometimes—especially when the world presents jarring moments—I need to sit in silence."

"I don't think I've had a moment to pause," Willow said.

"Willow, it is good to spend time and reflect. Especially now. Even amid the shock, I am trying to find gratitude for the time I had with my brother." Otto's eyes were closed and his words slowed. "I hope William had chances to do that. He was full-on business for so many years. Every minute caught up in growing sales or helping Dad find the next new thing. Trying so hard to impress our father. My brother followed our father's footsteps in the company and tried in his way to exceed your grandfather. Willow, I was glad to see my brother focusing more on himself recently. He seemed to not want to put the pressures on Spencer that he felt running the company. Anyway, it was his journey. We all have our own."

The evening darkness covered all of Palm Springs in its moonless sky, and the mountain range stood completely invisible except for a distant flashing light at the top from the tram station, sending its own Morse Code message to the town below. An icy breeze came down from the snowcapped mountains, causing Otto to cough on the chilled air.

"You are an example to us all—following your true journey." Willow nodded a thank you as Otto continued. "I certainly am going to miss my brother." A tear ran down his face during a failed attempt to smile. "Now get over here and help me up. I'm sure both my legs have fallen asleep, and I need to get to the RV before I succumb to the elements. Tomorrow is going to be a full day; maybe I should say goodbye now in case the chance escapes me tomorrow."

"Say goodbye?"

"You know my visits are typically only for holidays, except this year has been so different. I never imagined I would be here for two months. Even a lowly deacon on leave needs to return to his parish."

"I think we all got spoiled with you being here since Thanksgiving. You could move to Palm Springs."

"Stranger things have happened, but I'm happy with my visits. I hope to keep my spot in the RV if one of you doesn't claim it."

They both smiled.

"Remember, I do have a life in LA and it's time for me to head back. This may not make sense, but I need a vacation from this vacation town."

54

The Last Will

LEA AND LEANDRA FOCUSED their cleaning on the great room of The Dwelling. Everything needed to be ready. The owner of the home could no longer give them directions, but they knew their assignment. Leandra turned to Lea.

"All those years of getting a cleaning list," she said with a chuckle. "As if we didn't know what to do."

Both went silent as Willow and Hank entered the room. Lea offered them coffee and pointed to trays of food on the dining room table. Others filed in from the crisp morning air, hugging themselves for warmth. The family gathered in the main room, looking out at the pool and the snow-covered mountains beyond. The rain on Sunday morning left the skies a brilliant blue as sunlight created sparkles on the heaps of snow atop the mountains.

Hank sat beside Willow on one of the couches while Steve and his wife joined Adela on the other. Otto and two attorneys sat in three chairs at the front of the room. A projection screen lowered from the ceiling. On it appeared Spencer and his wife in two separate chairs, staring into a camera from their Pasadena home. Lea left the main room and headed out past the pool. The family's attention turned as they watched her help Robert make his way to the main house, followed by the two dogs. The morning chill swirled into the living room as an additional jolt of reality when the sliding glass doors opened. Robert and Lea entered, along with Oscar and Grammy, who took attendance by sniffing each of the humans in the room before settling at Otto's feet.

Robert waved off Lea's fussing over him as he positioned himself next to a table where Otto and the attorneys sat with identical bound documents. Otto put his hand on his father's shoulder, and Robert covered Otto's hand with his own. Robert's face was unreadable, matching the solemnity of the other attendees. The group remained quiet until Spencer's voice came over the speaker system in a shout like someone ordering food at a drive thru.

"Granddad. It's good you're here. This is an important time. I am happy you can join us. We've had some time to mourn. I've got everything covered moving forward, so you can relax."

Robert lowered his head and stayed silent as everyone else turned to the screen where Sybil shook her head in dismay toward Spencer. Otto tapped some files to bring the attention back to the front. The two attorneys signaled they were ready to proceed. Jess Taillefer was Robert and William's attorney and financial adviser. He handled William's personal matters, while the other attorney was from Los Angeles. The difference between the two was a study in contrast. Jess wore his best Tommy Bahama shirt, a comfortable pair of shorts, and hadn't encountered a razor in years. His exceptional skills in law and finance conflicted with the appearance of someone heading to an all-you-can-eat buffet at the casino. The other attorney had a large latte at the ready and wore a crisp suit with shoes shined enough to produce a glimmering reflection from the sun.

Otto started. "William named me the executor of his assets. I didn't ask for this or want to do it. He approached me some time ago and I agreed, but I brought in the experts in case there are any questions. I don't know why he picked me except he kept referring to me as Switzerland when we discussed his will. So, let's get to the details."

Jess Taillefer handed Otto a piece of paper on a clipboard. "Thanks, yes—okay, thank you, Jess." Otto adjusted his glasses. "Jess put together an outline for me. A bit of a cheat sheet to help with the process. Thank you all for being here today. Like I said, this shouldn't take much time, but I wanted you to be together for the reading." Otto paused and scanned the paper in front of him. Robert looked at Otto, then Jess, and back to Otto, and cleared his throat.

Otto steadied himself and began reading from the document, "Part One: I, blah blah blah, living in Palm Springs, California, ok . . . sound mind and body, and so on, over the age of 18, declare this as my last will and testament. I revoke all previous documents . . . blah blah blah. Part Two, I hereby nominate, constitute, and appoint my brother . . . there's a lot of legal description. In the event that Otto shall predecease me or choose not to act for any reason, I nominate and appoint Jess Taillefer, my attorney, to act in his place."

Otto picked up a pen and put a check next to the first two bullet points on his list.

"I am going to stop naming the parts to speed things up. William has a no-contest clause. If any beneficiary contests the will or any of its provisions, the share or interest in the estate given to the contesting beneficiary is revoked and shall be disposed of as if that contesting beneficiary had not survived him."

A third checkmark was made on the list.

"All debts and taxes must be paid in full before any disbursement of my estate." Otto put another check mark on the list as Jess broke in and explained there were no unusual debts, and the taxes were typically reconciled by the end of March. The other attorney followed along on his e-tablet.

A noise came through the TV speaker from Spencer. "Otto, are we coming up to the distribution soon?" His voice bellowed through the surround-sound speakers.

Otto looked down at his list to the next bullet point. The corporate lawyer took a long drink of latte, and Jess turned to look at Robert. Otto started again.

"I give all my tangible personal property and all policies and proceeds of insurance covering such property to my wife, Tiffany Ramirez, of Palm Springs, California, whose Social Security number ends in 2401."

The room erupted.

"Tiffany?" came a shout from both Spencer and Sybil through in THX Dolby sound from the speakers.

Leandra started laughing much too loudly and turned to Lea, "It's time to change the room assignments again! Spencer goes in the RV, and Hank is in the big suite!"

Steve turned to Adela and asked if Tiffany and William were still married. Hank put his head in his hands as Willow shouted, "Holy crap," and put her arm around him. Spencer started shouting questions through the TV about a prenup, as Otto checked the last item on his list.

Lea tried to quiet her mother's laughter but instead knocked over the entire tray of coffee cups, sending them crashing to the floor. The commotion triggered the dogs to rise to attention with their full barking volume typically reserved for an unknown guest. Only Jess noticed the smile come across Robert's face as he looked at Spencer on the projection screen. None of them saw the LA attorney put down his latte to pull a file out of his briefcase. The mayhem was stopped by Jess Taillefer, banging his heavily jeweled gold rings on the table and calling for quiet.

Although Jess handled William's last will and testament, the LA attorney, not one of Asuproz's lawyers, instead represented the deceased and held the last will and testament of Tiffany Ramirez. The room went silent again. Spencer muted the audio feed from his end, and the video portion went black. The LA attorney held up the papers and began reading.

55

The Other Side of the Camera

SPENCER AND SYBIL REMAINED in their separate chairs, flanked by their divorce lawyers sitting off-camera. The live streaming of the family in Palm Springs continued as the soon-to-be-divorced couple tried to understand what they heard. In all the excitement, no one shut off the camera at The Dwelling. Sybil turned to her lawyer and asked what it all meant. Spencer scribbled a note on the paper in front of his lawyer, who was messaging on his phone.

Sybil questioned to her lawyer. "Why did I have to sign a prenup when Tiffany didn't? How is this fair? How do we know if William and Tiffany's marriage is valid?"

She looked up at the screen. "Who owns The Dwelling?"

Sybil's lawyer stopped typing, closed her computer and said it was time to return to the law firm.

Spencer sat watching the screen to log everyone's actions. Willow hugging Hank made him regret not speaking with Willow about the buyout at Thanksgiving or at their father's funeral. Spencer realized Otto knew the will's contents in advance but he couldn't figure out the timing. He and Otto could have investigated the status of the marriage certificate or done a search on its legality or verified the will. But Spencer knew Otto's focus on detail, and it became clear why Otto kept pushing off the reading of the will. The delays had nothing to do with his excuses of the holidays, probate court, or getting an open time on the calendar for the lawyers and family. Otto was being his methodical self. Spencer got angrier thinking Otto should have come to him. As the president of the company, Otto owed him that level of respect.

The feed from The Dwelling showed Lea and Leandra cleaning up the spilled tray and broken cups. It looked as if they were smiling. When the time was right, Spencer would fire them both due to their lack of respect. All these changes disrupted his plan for the Asuproz buyout. He didn't know what to do with Adela and Steve. Adela stayed busy with Desert Recovery. Steve was a threat and knew all the contracts. Although neither of them had caused him any problems in the past, they tended to vote as one and could be a barrier. Robert drove his wheelchair past the camera and out the door toward his casita.

The terms of his father's will made Spencer consider Robert's legal documents. Could they be as convoluted? Previous sessions with his own lawyer covered the different options for setting up assets for children. Per stirpes versus per capita inheritance methods impacted children differently upon death. Spencer didn't remember what the Latin phrases meant, but he knew if his grandfather set up a certain version of per capita, assets were only for the living chain of his grandfather's descendants. The death of his father broke his descendant link, potentially leaving him and Willow out of luck and not getting anything from their grandfather when he died. This would mean all his grandfather's assets would go to Adela and Otto.

This was a total mess for Spencer. He wondered why he hadn't asked his father for clarity on the will. After all, it was important for the company's future. As for his grandfather, their spotty relationship didn't currently support an estate discussion. Robert might even change his beneficiaries out of spite. Being the namesake grandson didn't have a payout. Spencer needed to rely on other assets. He kept tabs on family and coworkers his entire life, recording information in his self-named dirt file for when leverage was needed. The notes helped him understand how their lives were going and how to sway them when needed. He used the information to persuade those around him. His mind raced through the catalog of dirt: Jess Taillifer, Sybil, Adela, Steve, Willow, Robert, Otto, Hank . . . Hank! Of course! The tapes.

Sybil and her lawyer had left the Pasadena home. Spencer turned off the video feed to The Dwelling, gathered some things and hopped in his car. He sped past Sybil on his way to Palm Springs while placing a call.

"This is Spencer; meet me at the employee entrance. I will be there in two hours, and I need you to get me into the data-storage room. If you want to keep your job that Asuproz is currently funding, you'll get me in and keep it quiet. Pull out all the training videotapes you have from the counseling sessions with my half brother. I want to be able to view them as soon as I arrive. Have the tapes ready, or I am prepared to share that information about you with Adela, and she will fire you by tomorrow. Frankly, you won't be able to find a job in the entire valley."

Spencer flew through traffic toward Palm Springs, replaying the reading of the will. The live feed images of his family members brought clarity to his biggest threat. He needed Hank to have a reason to decline his new fortune. Spencer needed a way to convince him that he didn't want the shares of the company. Spencer's lawyer was already getting a copy of the will from Otto and would confirm what would happen if Hank declined.

He ordered his lawyer to investigate the validity of his father's marriage and will. Spencer knew how to get Hank to renounce any interest in the stock or any leadership in the company. Spencer had the kind of dirt on Hank to force him to decline his inheritance. Spencer would make him say it was for the strength of the company and to follow his father's true wishes. Spencer mentally composed Hank's rejection letter as he continued toward the desert. His lawyer would find way to make it legal, but first, Spencer needed to confirm the contents of the tapes.

56

What Happened?

"WHAT HAPPENED? You've gotta tell us!" said Thomas.

Reese and Thomas were almost bouncing in front of the coffee shop as Kate and Hank walked up. The four got their beverages and headed to the back courtyard for privacy. Hank had their undivided attention. Instead of his father's shares being split between Hank and his siblings or going to his grandfather, the entire portion transferred to Hank via his mother. William's will and his marriage to Tiffany were valid at the time of his death. William's lack of clarity around their relationship may have been confusing, however, he was married, which both lawyers confirmed. Also, Jess vouched for William's personal reconnection with Tiffany.

"But your mother died before they read the will," Thomas said.

"She did," Hank said, "but her passing was after my father. We heard lots of explanations of how wills and marriages work in California. Frankly, I don't know what it all means except both lawyers declared everything valid. The constant reminders, legal or not, that they are dead made the entire process unbearable."

None of them, not even Thomas, pushed Hank to say more. But he looked up at their expressions and continued with the story.

"Therefore, all my father's interest in the company and all his assets passed from him to me through my mother's estate. As much as my grandfather demanded prenuptial agreements for the family, there wasn't one for my mom and dad. There were other details about The Dwelling, and a portion of the assets is split between the treatment center and a fund for the library."

Thomas interpreted, "Hank owns a new crib! Is that what I heard? When do we get to move in?"

Hank took a break to sip his coffee and tried half-heartedly to match Thomas's excitement.

"The lawyer answered all the questions from the family, and in the end, I am the largest shareholder in Asuproz. Thomas is right; I am the future owner of a kick-ass compound."

With that, Reese stood up and declared he was going back into the coffee shop to get everyone muffins. He held his hand out for money from Hank, who obliged while at the same time saw his phone ringing from Spencer. Hank let the call go through to voicemail as the cash from his wallet disappeared into Reese's hands. During Spencer's second unanswered call, Hank turned off his phone and focused on his friend's celebration. Hank let them have their moment, even though none of this news would bring back his parents.

57

Phone Calls

HANK PUT OFF RESPONDING to Spencer's texts and calls until he couldn't handle the constant buzzing any longer. Although the reading of the will changed both their financial realities, Hank's parents were dead, and he missed them, regardless of the complex relationships.

Spencer called again and Hank forced an upbeat answer.

"Hello, Spencer. Is that you?"

Spencer's attempt at civility rang insincere. A clumsy discussion of nothingness continued until Spencer couldn't compose himself.

"Hank, we need to talk. Did you get my emails? There is real business to discuss."

Hank had received emails along with text and voice messages outlining the buyout of Asuproz. They were filled with urgency although lacking detail. Spencer also demanded confidentiality, even with family members. Hank stayed true to the confidentiality, not knowing what agreements Spencer may have signed as part of the offer and didn't want the company to be in legal trouble. Even more reason to get the topic addressed.

Spencer demanded to speak in person and claimed business discussions needed to be face-to-face and away from company offices for confidentiality. He offered to meet at his Palm Springs home because he didn't want their grandfather or Otto involved. None of Spencer's excuses made sense to Hank, and he didn't want to meet at Spencer's home, but in the end agreed. He mostly wanted to be done with the topic. Spencer stumbled through a statement about their past and wanting to start anew. The awkward phrases made Hank imagine Spencer rehearsing a few times. Hank had never heard the word "anew" come out of his brother's mouth. The comment and the location were irrelevant. To Hank, their discussion wouldn't matter either. He could tell his brother had another scheme in mind, and based on the quality of other plans, Hank wasn't interested and only wanted to get the messages to stop. He ended the call with an agreement to the meeting in Palm Springs. At least he didn't have to go to Pasadena.

Spencer's phone vibrated: *Unknown Caller* appeared on the display. Over the past week, Spencer had let a couple of the calls go unanswered—his deliberate negotiation tactic. The caller left voicemail messages asking for a status on the offer. Not wanting to overuse his stalling, Spencer answered, knowing Hank would be showing up later that afternoon.

"Spencer, I am so happy to have reached you," the now-familiar voice said. "We seem to have missed each other these last few times, and I wondered if you had any updates for us. Has your company lost interest? Are you telling us to go elsewhere?"

"It's not that . . . my family is still in mourning."

"Yes, of course. So, you are saying there are no more details? Has something changed?"

Spencer rubbed his neck wondering if he actually missed his father or if this was the freedom he deserved. "Everything is under my control, and I will meet the deadline."

"Good. So Asuproz is set to sell?"

"I said by the agreement date. And when are we meeting? I want a contract in advance and have a face-to-face."

"You confirm you have a majority, and we'll send it."

58

The Threat

HANK RODE HIS BIKE to the open security gate of his first home. Any feelings of nostalgia vanished upon seeing Spencer with all the seriousness of a prison. The yard, originally open to the street, now hid behind walls and hedges. The entry area was unrecognizable from where he first lived with his half family. The remodeling of the house and new landscaping erased any resemblance its past.

Spencer acknowledged Hank and escorted him into the house.

"Welcome. It's been forever since you've been here. What do you think of the updates since you were living with us?"

Hank tried to take in all the changes. Every surface shone brand new. Carrara marble floors, crisp white walls, and matching furniture conveyed an ice castle in the desert. Spencer had completely removed any signs from their youth. Hank hadn't felt like he belonged in the house as a child and even less welcome now. The polished floors shone with a slick-wet appearance, instilling unease for anyone traversing the surface. Hank wondered if Spencer enjoyed the unrest he created for his guests.

Once in the great room, Hank scanned for a place to sit. Uncomfortable with the first three options: a white leather Eames lounger, a clear acrylic armchair with a white faux-fur accent pillow, and a white baseball catcher's glove-shaped loveseat, Hank settled into one of the hanging white rattan swing chairs to the right side of the fireplace. As soon as he sat, his body momentum created a slow twisting movement. Spencer took the opposing twin to Hank's chair, keeping both feet firmly on the ground. Sybil and the kids were gone. Spencer didn't offer a beverage or anything but instead got right to his objective.

"What's your decision on selling the business?" he asked. Spencer tried to make eye contact as Hank kept swaying. "We are coming up on the deadline, so it's imperative to know where you stand."

Hank unintentionally continued to twist in the spinning chair. He couldn't figure out why they needed to meet at Spencer's. Hank didn't so much ignore the question as his mind was preoccupied with the dramatic changes to the house and why everything needed to be changed. Spencer pressed for an answer with raised frustration.

"You need to remember that I am the president of Asuproz."

"And?"

"I know what's best for the company and for the entire family. It's time to sell, and the price is a good one."

"Spence, how do we know the value of the company versus the offer? We've had evaluations, but are they current with the latest technologies being launched?"

Spencer started to turn red. "Hank, I am sure you are excited about the new product as a technical employee of a company I run, but I don't appreciate your questions."

"What's the reason for the deadline? I am not sure I accept the premise of making such a critical decision before getting new financials or considering other bids."

Hank stood up from the swinging chair and continued. "An exploration team could put together an updated valuation with the new tech and all our corporate real estate. And I need to ask, did you designate your Maserati as a company car?"

Spencer grasped the chair ropes more tightly as Hank continued his train of thought.

"I could lead the team as part of my transition into a

leadership role."

Spencer jumped from his chair.

"Listen, half brother," Spencer shouted. "I've been the one who has carried the company for the past few years and even more so these past months. I've created the growth and value while you were off recovering yourself, or from what people say, failing at your attempts. I should be making the decision to sell. The technicalities of your mom's questionable marriage are elements I can rectify to save the deal."

Hank snapped back.

"I'm no legal expert, but I know enough about things to know I have the majority share in this company."

Spencer reached for a remote and pushed a button, causing a TV screen to emerge from the ceiling.

"I didn't want things to go this far. I didn't want to use this, but a good businessman is ready for any situation, something my father taught me," Spencer said.

"What are you talking about?"

"Sit there without swinging and watch!"

Hank looked up at the screen to see his own image sitting at a table at the recovery center. A time/date stamp advanced across the bottom of the videotape display. A camera filmed Hank talking to a counselor about how he had been drinking and driving since the DUI arrest. He confessed how he drove his mother home after drinking with her. The counselor's off-screen voice led the discussion and asked why Hank did not consider other options. A series of statements from Hank confessing to drinking and driving continued on the video.

"Where did that come from? What are you doing with this?" Hank shouted and stared down at his brother. "Those recordings are confidential. They were supposed to have been destroyed. Do you have any idea what that tape will do to me?"

Spencer tapped the remote again and the screen slowly

vanished into the ceiling. "I'm no legal expert, but I know enough about things to know when the judge sees this tape you will be going to prison for at least six years, and that counselor will get fired. I will be happy to make sure this recording gets into the hands of your judge. It's amazing how evidence can find its way to the press. Especially considering you killed that innocent young woman."

Hank fell back into the chair as his brother's smile grew.

"Hank, you don't want to go to prison. I can't imagine you'd survive. But this company doesn't belong to you and certainly didn't belong to Tiffany. You're going to refuse the will. You're going to make a statement that you don't want the pressure of the company and it doesn't match your father's wishes. Your wish is for the company leadership to stay with me."

Spencer stood over his brother. "Are you getting this? You will be making a statement. You can write a letter to refuse any equity in the company." Spencer paused, looked around his home. "In fact, that goes for ownership of The Dwelling too; you will refuse it along with the company stock. Therefore, those shares will split between Willow and me, along with the house. Turn a letter over to the attorneys immediately. I am heading back to Pasadena and expect to receive your signed letter this week. Now, get the hell out of my home. I'll return on Friday. It's your choice if those recordings find their way to the judge."

59

The Break-in

REESE AND HANK STOOD IN THE SHADOWS outside Spencer's dark house as Hank checked his watch. Midnight. Reese tried to convince Hank to wait a week for a new moon if they were going to break into a house. Hank couldn't wait another day. After his meeting with Spencer, he called the Musketeers together and told them about the tape and being blackmailed. He had to break in and steal the tape if it was still there. Thomas and Kate tried to stop the plan, but Reese countered by describing how easily they could be in and out of any home. All Hank knew was he needed to try immediately. He described Spencer's home and surrounding grounds to Reese before they headed out. The alarm system was the same as The Dwelling except without security cameras. Reese wanted to go alone but Hank wouldn't let him. He needed to confirm they got the correct tape or tapes.

They arrived on bikes to eliminate any noise and to avoid a car or license plate appearing on neighborhood security cameras. Reese led Hank behind a wall of bushes lining the street and hid their bikes. Hank felt nauseous as he stood staring at his brother's house. He zipped up his black sweatshirt and pulled the hood over his head.

"No one should be inside," he said, as Reese got ready to climb the wall surrounding the home. Hank waved him off and they went to the side gate used by gardeners and pool maintenance people.

"We don't need the code to get into the yard. That's the lazy man's way." Reese tried to get Hank away from the gate.

Hank turned and prepared to try the lock code, knowing it was the same as at The Dwelling. His brother used all the same support staff. The code had to be the same. He hesitated and then typed on the keypad. It responded with beep sounds: 2–0-1–9. No movement of the bolt. Had Spencer used a different code for his locks and the house alarm? Hank tried to think through the options: his birthdate, some other favorite number. If Hank didn't have the gate code, he wouldn't have the house code, foiling the makeshift break-in plan. It was falling apart before they even got into the yard.

Hank had one more idea before giving up. He put his finger up to the keypad again and typed. Beep, beep, beep, beep. A confirming double beep came from the keypad as the cylinder turned. Spencer had not updated the gate code at the start of the year. 2–0-1–8 was the code. He hoped the same worked for the house and alarm. The apprehension of robbing his brother became more real as the service gate shockingly opened on its own. Hank jumped back to see Reese waiting on the other side of the door.

"I got frustrated with all your tries and decided to open the gate," Reese smiled.

His gymnast body made easy work of the wall in a stealth climb before opening the gate from the inside. Hank shook his head. They still needed to get into the house as Reese pointed to an area where he could climb up onto the roof.

"Let's go for the skylights."

During their planning, Thomas spotted the home's skylights using an online satellite photo.

"Hank, buddy, I've done this so many times. Skylights are easy to pry open, and then you drop in."

Earlier in the day, Reese had told the group he used to break into empty homes during the summer to get out of the heat for a good night's sleep. His monitoring of recycle bins let him know which homes were vacant of their winter owners. On cooler nights he'd stay outside on hammocks or chaise lounges of the homes and use the exterior pool shower to clean up. He told Hank the trick of having backyard campouts meant leaving before the lawn maintenance and pool people arrived at dawn.

Hank listened to his friend and wondered how it ever came to him preparing to rob his brother. Hank and Reese made their way along the side of the property and followed the path to the backyard. Like during his childhood, the kidney-shaped pool sat adjacent to a pergola seating area with an outdoor shower for swimmers to wash off any chlorine before bathing in the sun. When Spencer, Willy, and Hank lived there, Leandra made the children use the outdoor shower before they were allowed inside, especially if they had been in the muddy river wash behind the house. A fun place to play in the summer, although the small stream grew to a creek in spring when the snow began melting off the mountain. The children weren't allowed near it when the snowmelt started. Hank could hear the gurgling water from the wash as he approached the back door to the house. He hoped the sounds of the currents muffled Reese's late-night chatter.

Hank used last year's code on the back door, and the bolt turned. He opened the door, and they both entered. An alarm system started a countdown. "30 . . . 29 . . . 28." The entrance led into a hallway with a bathroom on one side and a built-in cabinet filled with beach towels and a shelf of sunscreen tubes. "27 . . . 26 . . . 25." Hank traversed the hallway to the alarm panel. "24 . . . 23 . . . 22." He entered the same code as the door and heard a loud double beep. The countdown stopped. "Disarmed."

They made their way through the house, first checking the room where he met Spencer. There were no electronics there, only a screen and projector. They canvassed each room in the house, opening cabinets and closets. Hank investigated the primary suite and the closet but didn't find the videotapes. They kept looking until they reached the study. Another door with another keypad. Beep beep beep beep, as Hank entered 2–0-1–8. The door unlocked and they entered the study. Across the room was another door and another keypad. This had to be it. Beep beep beep beep. Then the security alarm started ringing. Hank froze, trying to figure out what triggered the alarm. He couldn't think clearly. Reese grabbed his arm to get him moving and they ran through the house and out of the door toward the side gate. Hank panicked when he saw the squad car coming up the street. Reese pushed him toward a dark corner of the yard and slipped back into the house. Hank stood motionless while two officers walked up the path to the pool area where they spotted Reese fully naked under the outdoor shower.

"Cans?" called one of the officers as he directed his flashlight. "Cans, is that you again? What are you doing on this side of town?"

Reese reached for a towel and wrapped it around himself. "How about some privacy? I'm bathing here."

"Okay, okay, but Cans, you can't keep breaking into people's homes. It's bad enough that you use their showers."

Reese looked up with a dumbfounded expression. "I didn't break anything. The gate was open and the towels were here." Reese casually dried his body while talking to the officers to keep their attention. He inquired how they were doing and apologized for bothering them. The officers had encountered Reese more than once on someone else's property. One officer made a perfunctory survey of the area while calling the security company to report a false alarm. The other officer escorted Reese out, where he waved goodbye as the squad car drove away. When the taillights were out of sight he circled back to meet.

"What now?" Reese asked.

Hank had no idea and was out of time. He wondered if there would be a police report to Spencer about the alarm. They retrieved the bikes and rode away.

60

Bingo!

FOR ONCE, a threat of heavy precipitation came true as the skies delivered two consecutive days of showers. Drenched from the rain, Reese and Thomas entered the community center to start the setup for the evening's Valentine's Day bingo fundraiser. Thomas's wet shoes squeaked as they headed to the volunteer check-in table. His quickened pace gave an air of anxiousness.

"You have to tell him," Thomas said.

"He doesn't need any more bad news. We'll keep it to ourselves for now." Reese reached for the sign-in clipboard. "And this is wrong. It says I am doing the ticket stand. I need to be on the floor during bingo to check winning cards. I am bringing my Christmas present from Kate. Any wrong answers get shot with blobs of jelly."

"Hank needs to know. You need to tell him—and give me that clipboard. You're signed up for organizing the ticket stand over there. This is the afternoon check-in sheet. The second sheet is for evening assignments, and that's when you're a bingo card checker, see! Go open those boxes and set up the table. Hank said he'd come here from work and you must tell him today. Even more reason we need to stay with him all day. Kate's at her mom's, so we are on watch duty. I told him we'd be getting in costume at his place, then he's coming back here with us. Thankfully, Willow is hosting pizza for us after bingo. His brother is dangerous. We need to keep them apart."

"Can we tell him together?"

"No. The other volunteers are coming in now. I've got to get this place set up."

The Sisters of Perpetual Indulgence sponsored the fundraiser and Thomas needed to assure everything was in place. This also meant Reese and Thomas were obliged to recreate their sister roles last seen at the Christmas toy drive. The bingo proceeds went to a local safe house for children, and a celebrity drag star planned to call the numbers. This would bring in a large crowd, which made Thomas a bit frantic.

Less than two days had passed since the attempted break-in, and Hank's thoughts weren't on the fundraiser, but the Musketeers asked for his help, so he went to the community center. Hank didn't have time to shake off the rain before Thomas pointed him to the ticket stand and Reese.

Most of the ticket area was organized, leaving Reese and Hank to put out neon-haired good-luck trolls for sale. Reese remained quiet as they set up the station and Hank took the silence as a nice break, typical of his friend's daytime lower energy. They opened a big box of trolls and started setting them out by the sign declaring Lucky Bingo Trolls along with price tags. Hank learned Reese's technique for hand-shaping the neon hair straight up before placing them on the tiered display. He marveled at the variety of sizes and hair colors and admitted the troll faces and their molded smiles did cheer him up and were truly magical. Hank needed some magic but instead he got Reese grabbing him. It was time to talk.

"I've got to tell you something," he started.

Hank looked at his friend and braced himself for another rollercoaster ride. What was he about to hear? Whatever it was had kept Reese quiet the entire time and Thomas at a distance. Hank nodded and waited to hear the news about his friends.

"This is about your mom."

Hank tried to connect what Reese knew about his mother.

"She didn't die. I mean she didn't OD. I mean she wasn't the cause of the OD."

Hank sat in the chair.

Reese looked over to Thomas and then back to Hank. "I was crashing for the night in one of the dried-out drainage pipes under Belardo Road. I wanted to check in on a friend and needed to get away from being indoors. I couldn't find my friend but found a good spot and was about to crash for the night when some guys showed up at the end of the pipe looking for customers. These were two of the serious dealers in town, so I stayed quiet and they either didn't see me or thought I was asleep. They obviously didn't understand how the end of the five-foot diameter cement tube turned into an amplifier for anyone listening inside. The main dealer, Nick, bragged about his big win."

"What does this have to do with my mom?"

"Hold on. This is where it gets freaky. The dealer says a rich dude, one of his coke clients, wanted to know what else he could get. The dealer ran through a list of the usuals for polo shirt dudes. It was Christmas Day and Nick figured the guy wanted to have his own holiday party. The dude smirked and said he wanted some Big8. He wanted octo-dose fentanyl pills. The other guy asked why and how he even knew what they were."

Hank's heartbeat shook his chest. He couldn't get Reese to speak fast enough, and yet he didn't want to hear any of it.

"This Nick guy said the buyer asked about a waitress, a former client named Tiffany. Nick said he knew her and her bad debt. Hank, I am telling you, I didn't know what to do. Nick said the polo shirt guy would cover what she owed and an extra 20K, but Nick had to do more than produce the pills. He said Nick needed to get a few into Tiffany."

Hank's body shook as he tried to control his breath.

"Nick proposed a price, and the guy reached in his pocket and held out a stack of cash with the promise to supply the second half when the job was done."

Reese spoke faster to get the rest of the story out.

"The Nick guy said it was the easiest money he'd ever made and cleaned up a past account. One of his dealers got assigned to trail Tiffany until they could accidentally bump into each other in public. Being the holiday season made it easy. Reese continued to tell how Nick's dealer confirmed the job was done and Nick got the second payout."

Reese wrapped up the story as Thomas approached.

"How'd it go?" Thomas asked and then saw Hank's face. "Hank, I didn't want to believe it but I put my feelers out and there's a buzz in the shadows. Someone even said he drove a Maserati." Thomas and Reese looked at Hank and decided they needed to leave the building. As they got in the car, Hank's phone rang. It was Spencer. Thomas grabbed the phone and pushed the cancel button.

61

Nun Sense

WITH KATE IN ENCINITAS, it was up to Reese and Thomas to keep Hank occupied at his apartment. They filled time watching old sitcoms on TV, accompanied by Thomas's running commentary. Thomas kept in contact with Kate, letting her know the entire story. They needed her back in Palm Springs for support. She asked them to stay with Hank as long as they could, and she would relieve them. Hank stayed silent, alternating between staring at the TV and sitting with his arms crossed and eyes closed.

The storm intensified as Kate continued toward Palm Springs. Reese and Thomas became restless about getting to the bingo fundraiser. Thomas brought their costumes in from the car. His last trip for his makeup kits left him drenched and standing in the entryway of Hank's apartment.

"Could one of you lend a sister a hand?" he asked as he tried shaking his body dry. "It's a mess out there." Thomas decided it was time for Reese and him to prepare for the fundraiser, and he tried to change the mood to one of costume and glitter energy. Reese helped Thomas pull on a body wrap with various foam inserts to add curves only the spiciest nun would have. Hank started pacing the living room, which made Thomas turn off the television and turn up some dance music as Reese and Thomas's transformation continued.

"I think he's going to explode." Thomas updated Kate while in Hank's bathroom, hoping the music would muffle their voices.

"Can you take him to bingo?"

"He's not in a state to go anywhere, and his shithead brother keeps messaging."

"Let me try calling his aunt."

"Okay, but he's getting worse. When can you be here?"

"No idea. The rain has gotten heavier, and my phone keeps changing the ETA. That is, when I can get a signal. Let me call you back."

Reese went into the living room to calm Hank.

"There's nothing we can do. We don't have evidence. There's no proof that Spencer was responsible, and no one is going to confess."

"The dealer isn't going to risk anything," Thomas yelled from the bathroom.

Hank retrieved his phone from the charger to see a string of messages from Spencer. The two nuns convinced him not to read any more of them, Thomas continued to ask Hank to join them at the fundraiser rather than stay home alone. They asked him to call Willow and have her come to his apartment. She could make pizzas at Hank's for the post-bingo dinner instead of at her place.

Hank's phone rang again, and he let the call from Spencer go to voicemail.

Reese grabbed the phone and tucked it in his bra so Hank wouldn't dare take it from an irate nun. They all jumped when Thomas's phone rang.

"It's someone from the fundraiser checking on our status. I'll take it in the bathroom." He left and closed the door. "Where are you?"

"Somewhere on the 215 in stopped traffic," Kate said.

"What are we going to do?"

"I got in touch with Hank's aunt—"

"You didn't tell her!"

"No, I said we wondered if any family was around to spend

time with Hank tonight."

"How did that go?"

"She freaked out, thinking there was something wrong."

"There actually is."

"There isn't yet. But she said she was in LA with her son and brother. Willow is the only family member in town."

"We are working on that, but she wasn't supposed to meet us until after the fundraiser. We can't find her."

"Well, I couldn't tell his aunt anything else and I didn't even know what to say. I told her we would handle it."

"Reese and I need to leave. Maybe Reese can stay, or we can get him to come with us."

Thomas hung up and returned to the living room to see Hank had gotten Reese into a frantic mood. Thomas reassured Reese that telling Hank was right, especially with Spencer's blackmail threats. Hank needed to know Spencer's mindset, and Hank agreed. All three of them bounced around the apartment as the nuns finished their final touches. Thomas could not convince Hank to join them and they were not sure what to do next until they finally heard from Willow. Her cell service kept dropping off in the storm. She made it to her apartment and was ready for Hank to join her. Having a solution, Thomas texted Kate, and the two nuns gathered up all their things, and did a final check in the mirror.

Reese reached into Thomas's bag and pulled out the final accessory, his Christmas gift. The jelly-gun had been accessorized. Painted black and covered in press-on jewels to match Reese's earrings and nun garb. He tried cheering up Hank by showing off his gift but got no response. Even seeing them in full nun garb didn't help and it was time to leave. Thomas made Hank promise to head directly to Willow's and to wait until they were together to tell Willow about Spencer.

The second consecutive day of rain in Palm Springs came down harder than the first. Thomas and Reese's makeup-covered faces, surrounded by their black clothes, were bound for disaster if sheets of rain washed their faces off onto their costumes. Thomas grabbed two umbrellas and his car keys. The rest of their belongings had to stay behind. They prepared to make a dash to the car, but Hank called them back.

"You needed to tell me. I needed to know about Spencer. Thank you, and thanks for being here. I wish I had the strength to help at the event. I promise to pull myself together for dinner at Willow's tonight. So, get your sister-asses over to her place as soon as you're done." With that, he hugged Thomas, and in a sleight of hand, Hank reached under Reese's wimple and grabbed his phone.

"For when Kate calls," Hank declared. "If she's driving back in this mess, I want to be near my phone in case she gets stuck in the rain."

"You better not have messed up my face doing that," Reese said and then asked, "Are you sure that's what you want? Thomas needs to run the event, but I can stay with you."

"I don't need a nun to babysit me. Go do your good-deed stuff and meet us later." Hank tried to channel the bingo troll's molded smile. "Willow and I, and hopefully Kate, will be waiting for you."

The nuns left, and Hank returned to the couch. The calls and messages continued from Spencer with greater frequency. Hank kept his commitment to his friends and didn't answer as his anger grew. The continued calls made him wonder, had Spencer found out they knew? He couldn't know. The calls had to be all about selling the company and the blackmail tape. The rain hit harder against the apartment windows. The full storm came after all. Hank decided to get to Willow's before the streets got worse. During the drive, he could decide whether to tell her about their brother. He grabbed his keys and opened the door, seeing yet another text from Spencer.

Spencer: *Pick up, or I will come to your place or Kate's and find you. I need that letter today.*

With that, Hank called his brother, reaching deep inside himself to remain calm. Here he was trying to compose himself while talking to the killer of his mother. Spencer screamed during the entire conversation. Hank didn't know what to do, but he knew he needed to confront his brother. He told Spencer he'd meet him at his house, but he wanted the tape. Spencer told him the papers would be ready to sign.

As he got in the car, Kate called. She had barely gotten to the Palm Springs highway exit through all the rain. They had closed several of the main roads from the highway. Hank asked her to meet the guys at bingo. He told her he would join them but needed to see his brother first. It was the last she heard before his phone cut out. Struggling to see the road with her windshield wipers on high, she rushed to the community center.

Hank made his way to Spencer's house through flooded streets and neighborhoods blacked out from power loss. He reached his brother's place and pulled up through the open gate to the driveway where he saw Spencer standing outside in his raincoat, soaking wet. Hank pulled further up the side driveway to the edge of the property. As Hank got out of the car, he could hear his brother yelling.

"You're not my brother. You are no part of this family! You're not taking away everything I've worked for!"

Hank could barely hear over the pouring rain. Spencer's left hand dug into his neck as the rain poured down his face. He maneuvered to his perceived alpha position and stood on the retaining wall of the wash.

"You're going to sign the paper!" Spencer demanded.

"Where's the tape?" Hank replied.

"You're never getting the tape. I need some insurance."

"Spencer, I don't even care about the tape anymore. Do what you need to do, but I am not signing any papers or turning anything over to you."

"The shares shouldn't have gone to a fake son and his whore

waitress mom! She deserved what she got, and you're going to prison."

Hank clenched his fists and moved toward Spencer. "Why did you have to kill her? Why did you murder my mother?"

Spencer stood in shock. He couldn't imagine how Hank or anybody knew. Spencer expected the night to go differently, but it didn't matter because he had a backup plan and wasn't going to allow Hank to defy him. Spencer pulled out a gun.

"This ends right now!" Spencer declared.

Hank automatically responded by raising his hands in the pouring rain and watching Spencer reel out of control as his brow furrowed and jaw tightened. Spencer's entire arm shook, so he placed both hands on the gun to steady his aim. At that moment, a figure broke through the sheets of pouring rain. Both brothers turned, dazed, from a voice coming from the silhouette of a nun shouting at them to stop.

Spencer started laughing.

"Stop right there!" Reese ran toward the two brothers.

"Oh my God! Is that your freaky friend, the can man?" Spencer said while keeping the gun pointed at Hank.

Reese kept moving toward the two brothers, attempting to get between Spencer and Hank.

"Great. This gun has more than one bullet, and now I have a better alibi. Defending myself against homeless intruders."

"Not today, Satan!" Thomas appeared from the dark with a flash of metal in his hands.

Even in the rain, Spencer could see Thomas held a gun, although he didn't know it only shot jelly pellets. He turned his aim from Hank to Thomas. Shots rang out. Spencer grabbed his abdomen and felt the ooze and pain in his gut. A big flash of lightning crackled across the sky as Spencer's body turned and fell into the ravine, the rapid waters pulling him away.

Kate ran past Thomas to Hank and embraced him as he

stared at the spot on the embankment where Spencer once stood. An echo of thunder shook the ground as Reese yelled that they needed to get out of there.

62

Another Call

THE MUSKETEERS ARRIVED at Willow's and shared the shocking story with her. The rain and power outages continued, forcing them to spend the night, although no one could sleep. Hank remained at Willow's that morning while everyone else left to go home or to work. Reese and Thomas returned Hank's car to his apartment garage so it would not be out on the streets for Spencer to spot. Hank called in sick to work and watched the local news for any possible updates. He couldn't calm his mind and wished his overly present friends were still with him instead of off processing their own reactions to the past twenty-four hours.

"One moment, I'll connect," the helpline receptionist replied to Hank.

"How are you doing, Hank?" the voice answered the call.

Hank's emotions were on overload. The video recordings came from Desert Recovery, so Spencer must have known someone at the recovery center with access to the confidential tapes. He decided the need to talk was more important than trying to figure out Spencer's accomplice. Hank listened to the voice from the helpline and tried to decide what to say. He couldn't comprehend that he could've been killed by his brother who had a tape that could put him in prison. The Musketeers and Willow had vowed their silence and to stop Spencer. He sat holding his phone and started talking about the sadness surrounding the death of his mother and continued about her flaws and their erratic relationship before mentioning he found peace with who she was. He started talking about the guilt of failing to help her deal with her challenges of depression and drinking. Hank got more frantic discussing the loss of his father and how they never quite got to a relationship that either one of them wanted. Hank's comments flowed without interruption except for his own tears. He bounced back and forth describing the relationship with both parents and with his siblings.

The counselor tried to interrupt Hank, but he continued with his ramblings until they escalated to mention of Spencer pointing a gun at him.

The counselor went silent.

Hank revealed the blackmail, the videotape, and the threat of prison. Everything came out about Spencer, although Hank didn't say anything about the other Musketeers. Instead, he said his brother slipped and fell into the rushing water, and for all he knew, had crawled out and was back home. In telling the story, Hank realized the tape was probably still at Spencer's house. He knew once Spencer got back home, he would share the tape with the police. Hank kept thinking out loud and didn't know what to do. He told his counselor the tape was still at Spencer's house, and when it went public, he would go to prison. Hank started hyperventilating and kept repeating "tape" and "jail." He tried to continue.

"The tape was out of context. I didn't say what I meant!" Hank pleaded with the counselor like he was talking to a judge at a trial. "I drove and had part of a drink. I wasn't drunk. My mother was drunk. I tried to save her. I needed to save her."

There was commotion coming through the phone and then the counselor told Hank to calm himself and that their time was up. The counselor recommended he call back later leaving Hank distraught. Was the call being recorded or had the counselor decided to call the police? Hank needed to break into his brother's house again and get the tape. He went to grab his keys and realized his car was gone.

On the other end of the helpline was Robert. The ongoing

mystery helpline counselor to Hank was his grandfather. Lea startled Robert when she came up behind him in the casita. She had spent the night of the storm in the servant quarters of The Dwelling and stayed there to help Robert because the regular aide couldn't get out of their home due to closed roads. It also wasn't safe for Lea to leave and someone needed to care for Robert.

With Lea in the doorway, he turned off the speakerphone and voice modulator.

"Are you free now?" She asked.

Robert closed his notebook as she motioned to the tray of food. Robert asked her to enter, and he pointed toward his table. Lea stepped through the open door. Robert nodded and mumbled a thank you as she set the meal down and picked up the dirty dinner tray before leaving the casita. Robert watched as Lea hurry back to the main house and rush out of the compound.

Hank needed his friends and texted the Musketeers to come back. Willow got back to her apartment where she met Reese and Thomas coming up her entrance. Once they all were there, Hank tried to explain about how the tape still had to be at Spencer's and they needed to retrieve it, if Spencer hadn't already returned home. The three convinced Hank he needed to stay away from Spencer's or anywhere his brother may be. He still had a gun. None of them should go near the place. Thomas and Willow got Hank to sit down as Reese burst out the door followed by Thomas chasing after him.

"You can't go. He's dangerous."

"I am going to get my eyes on the situation," said Reese. "I can handle myself. Stay put and keep Hank and Willow here. Don't answer any calls from Spencer."

The other two watched out the window as Reese pedaled down the street in a blur.

63

Clean Up

LEA RAN FROM ROBERT'S CASITA into the main house. She let the tray crash into the sink as she continued, grabbing her purse and racing for her car. She heard everything Hank said to Robert and knew the treacheries of Spencer. She also knew every inch of Spencer's home, including the media closet. Her drive consisted of a maze of road closures to get to Spencer's home. Some routes were flooded, and others were completely washed away.

After navigating the streets, she used her remote to open the gate and pulled into the driveway of the house, ignoring the service door. She pulled out her keys and opened the front entrance. Inside, she noticed the alarm wasn't set and the sound system was playing "The Best Is Yet to Come". She yelled out in as calm a voice as she could.

"Hello, Mr. Spencer. Are you here?"

She went from room to room, hearing music playing everywhere.

"Mr. Spencer, I am here for cleaning day. I got here early today."

She checked his bedroom, his bath, the guest rooms, and the living room.

"Mr. Spencer. Such a crazy rain last night."

She walked into the garage and touched the hood of his car. It was cold.

"Mr. Spencer, let me know if you need anything special

cleaned today."

She went to the kitchen where the door stood open to the pool area. She looked outside and didn't see any signs of Spencer. She couldn't tell if anyone was there. She closed the back door, grabbed her cleaning bucket from the pantry, and headed to the office with its closed door. She knocked and went in.

"Mr. Spencer?"

Another empty room. She ran to the electronics closet, entered the code into the keypad, and opened the door. The room's automatic lights turned on and surprised Lea. She calmed herself and spotted the VCR player. Lea opened it and found an old tape with writing on the label with Hank's name and a date. She put it in the VCR player and hit the start button. Lea watched it for seconds, hit eject, and dropped the tape into her bucket. She closed the door to the equipment closet and ran to the front entrance where she opened the door and found herself face-to-face with a man. Lea let out a short scream and dropped the bucket. The tape fell out onto the front entry. They both looked down and saw Hank's name on the label.

"I'll take that." The voice said, as Reese reached down and snatched up the tape. "There isn't time," he said, as he put the tape in his backpack and rode off.

Lea stood there in shock watching Reese pedal off and disappear at the end of the street. The police car didn't even slow as it passed by him and drove toward Spencer's house, sirens blaring. Lea continued to stare as the squad car arrived and pulled into the driveway alongside her car. The officers greeted her at the door as one of them helped her pick up her cleaning supplies and the other officer looked into her car windows.

"You scared me with the sirens," she said.

"What are you doing here?"

She looked down at her bucket. "It's Friday. Cleaning day."

64

The News

THE TV GLOWED as Hank, Kate, Reese, and Thomas sat in Willow's living room and watched intently.

"Jon Whit, Channel 3 News. It's been an unbelievable couple of days in Southern California. Three people are known to be dead due to the storm. Tram Road and other streets have been washed away. There is damage everywhere. As for fatalities, a rescued woman later died from a heart attack and a man seen paddleboarding in Escondido got swept away. Names are being withheld until family is notified. And right here in Palm Springs, we are sorry to report a death in one of our most philanthropic families."

The reality penetrated everyone in the room as the photo of Spencer appeared over the shoulder of the news anchor. It was a publicity shot of Spencer leaning on his car in front of the house. They all sat paralyzed, Willow in disbelief, Hank still in rage. It took Thomas jumping to his feet and cheering to break the mood. The victory moment was short lived as the others stayed seated and Thomas retreated to the kitchen.

" . . . his body was found on February 15 along the river wash, quite a distance from his home in the Araby Cove area abutting the same wash. There is no evidence of foul play. This storm dropped four inches of rain at Palm Springs International Airport, making it the wettest day ever recorded. Stay tuned here for . . . "

Reese turned off the TV.

Before anyone could say a word, Thomas entered from the kitchen with a tray of mugs. "Anyone thirsty?"

Willow sat silently next to Hank as he gave her a hug. "How are you doing? How did it . . . are you okay?"

She turned to her brother and buried her head in his shoulder. Willow represented the family to identify the body. Sybil remained in Hawaii with their children and wasn't talking to the family. Robert, Adela, Otto, and Steve got word when Willow left the coroner, but this was the first time it was in the news. Willow recounted visiting with police and hearing the report of significant water in the lungs and a massive bump on his head indicating signs of a concussion. They couldn't tell which of the traumas caused Spencer's ultimate death. The body sustained abrasions and cuts traveling down the wash, but it was Spencer's body. The police officer shared how Spencer probably went out to see the rushing water like so many people that night, slipped, and got caught in the current. The investigators found nothing suspicious at Spencer's home.

Willow and Hank looked at each other with the relief of surviving it all, as their eyes welled.

"I'm probably in shock," Willow said. "That asshole is gone. He was still my brother, and I'm not sure how I feel."

"I am so angry, but I know what you mean," Hank replied.

Reese made his way back into the kitchen and brought out the coffee pot.

"Darn good coffee maker. It's like yours, Hank. People have no sense of what's good and bad anymore. They don't know what they're throwing away."

Thomas raised his mug for a refill. "Give me some more of that."

Willow gave the group a moment to settle in before she reminded them of her statements to the police.

"The police know you all ended up here for pizza and spent the night due to the storm closing so many roads, and we didn't talk to anyone else after bingo because phone service was down."

She told the truth with one omission. That night, Kate

270

showed up as the volunteers closed bingo early due to the storm. She let Thomas know Hank had gone to his brother's. A sense of panic set them off to Spencer's home. After the encounter, Thomas and Reese arrived at Willow's wearing soaking wet nun garb, followed by a shaken Hank and Kate.

Although Spencer had fallen and disappeared into the dark rapids, none of them knew his fate for the rest of the night. The next afternoon, the police called Willow to identify the body. By then, Reese had already gone to Spencer's and returned to Willow's with the VCR tape.

"Let's be grateful this is over." Willow looked at each of them.

No one responded until Hank stood and proclaimed, "To our Queen, the Musketeers shall always be loyal."

The other three stood, raising their coffee mugs like swords as Hank led their cheer.

"All for one and one for all; united we stand, divided we fall."

Willow stood and joined them. Their attempted cheer produced faint smiles. The storm came to the desert with power and force like had never been seen before. The flood swept away so much and changed many lives, but probably none more than those around the coffee table that morning.

Willow's guests started to leave. Reese grabbed his backpack containing the old videotape of Hank before heading out the door with Thomas. Reese had many skills, like finding treasure in others' trash and making things that once were someone's treasure completely disappear, which is exactly what happened to the videotape.

65

The Two Musketeers

THE FOUR MUSKETEERS left Willow's home. Reese and Thomas drove off, leaving Hank and Kate standing outside. Hank turned to Kate with a sudden sense of relief. He took her hand and pulled her in for an embrace. A full year had passed since leaving treatment. Hank experienced setbacks to his sobriety, family loss, and the rollercoaster of all things Spencer. He attempted new ways to handle life and had spent the last six weeks filling journals. He started the practice when entering treatment. The counselor recommended he capture his feelings. In the beginning there was not much success. The routine evolved recently into a daily practice of writing and sketching as a way to reminded himself, he couldn't change history and didn't need to do everything on his own. He was done with drinking, exhausted from drinking, and placed it in the past. He stopped writing "never ever again" and started focusing on the future. He gave Kate another hug.

Kate looked at Hank and started to speak. "I know you've been through so much, but I have to say this. I worry I tried to force a relationship for us. Maybe it's time for me to make a change and move back to Encinitas so you have time to process all that's happened since Thanksgiving."

"I was wondering if—" Hank started.

"Hank, I've pushed you too much."

"I was wondering if we could have a second date. I don't need a break from you. We are here for each other. Didn't you tell me that before? We need to be there for the important people in our lives."

"Are you sure?"

"Certain of anything? No. But I know I want to put energy into us and see where that'll lead. Apparently, I also need to learn a lot more about a certain company and decide on my role, so I want to make sure I am not pushing you either. And I need to deal with handling Spencer, my dad, my mom."

They hugged again and walked toward Kate's car. Hank squeezed Kate's hand.

"The last few months have made me think of the critical people in my life. You are at the top of my list, even though it's taken me a while to get here. Reese and Thomas are too. And there's someone who shouldn't be alone right now.

He spun Kate around so she faced back toward Willow's door. "There is someone we need to support."

Kate smiled. They returned to Willow's place and found her still sitting on the couch. Kate sat Hank next to his sister.

"I'm going to take these dirty mugs into the kitchen, and then you both are going to fill me in on everything about you two growing up. And Willow, so you know, Hank and I are officially dating. I'll get these dishes cleaned up, and then I want to hear your stories about my guy and more about you. He loves you to pieces, and I am kind of fond of him and you, so get ready to start talking."

Epilogue

LEA LEFT THE LUNCH TRAY NEXT TO ROBERT as he sat at his desk reading the morning paper. He waited until she left his casita and completely closed the door before reaching in a lower file-drawer for the folder labeled Marge. The information came from the technical director of Asuproz. The folder had technical status reports, financials, electrical schematics, and patent submissions. Those files were all pushed to the side as Robert found what he needed: Beta Tester Contacts.

Robert scanned the names stopping at the third row: Calvin Moore - Actor, Producer, Helpline volunteer, Contact Information. He turned on the metal box connected to his phone. He waited for the light to turn green.

"Hi, who's calling?"

"Calvin Moore?"

"Excuse me. Who am I speaking with?"

"Calvin. This is Mr. Voile. I represent some Asian investors interested in an alliance to buy out Asuproz."

"How did you get this number?"

"We're calling about business. You are a wildly successful businessman. Some might say it's in your DNA."

"What are you talking about? And Asuproz is a family-owned company."

"Ah, so you are familiar with the company. Good. It's a family company and will stay one. I have some important information you'll want to see."

Calvin paused before responding. "What information?"

"Expect a file later today. You will want to pay particular attention to the genetic testing results and look for a call to follow."

Characters

The Family

Robert, 92, patriarch and founder of Asuproz, lives at the family compound with his son, William.

> **Adela,** 69, Robert's daughter and default matriarch, divorced, president of Desert Recovery, a national addiction center.
> o **Steve,** 44, married with two children, works for Asuproz in contract negotiation.

> **Otto,** 67, Robert's son, deacon at a Los Angeles-area parish.

> **William**, 65, Robert's son, current Asuproz CEO & past president. Married twice.

> First wife: Matilda (dec'd).
> o **Robert Spencer,** 36, new Asuproz president, married to Sybil with two children.
> o **Willow,** 34, former employee in Asuproz finance.
> Estranged wife: **Tiffany**, 47.
> o **Hank**, 26, Asuproz tech center engineer.

The Four Musketeers - a friend group, including **Hank**, who met in recovery and remain supportive.

> **Kate,** 27, Hank's romantic interest.
> **Reese**, 31, a drifter in Palm Springs.
> **Thomas,** 23, uninhibited conversationalist.

Additional Characters
> **Lea**, 46, family housekeeper and her mother; **Leandra**, 69, former housekeeper.
> **Jess Taileffer,** personal lawyer to Robert and William.
> **Calvin Moore,** 33, single, former TV child star, current movie star and successful producer with holiday home in Palm Springs
> **Robert's healthcare worker**, 45, providing care for many years.

Tony V. George, a native of Minnesota, now calls Palm Springs, California, home. He bought a place there shortly after his first visit to the desert. He enjoys exploring the town to see the many characters who inspired this book. He has also run over twenty marathons and enjoys traveling the world observing cultures to find what makes us different and what connects us. He is working on the next *Mid-Century* book to figure out what happens next (and before) to the characters from *Mid-Century Melee*.

The author would like to thank friends and family for their support throughout the entire process, especially the following beta readers: Barbara Snow, Lou Bender, Daylan Jellinick, Rhonda Habel, Donna, Lisa W., and Rebecca Carlson. And thanks to his kid sister, Mittens, for listening to all his gripes and questions.

Please share this book with friends. Leaving a review at your point of purchase and other gathering sites of readers would be appreciated. The author can be reached at www.tonyvgeorge.com.